Keeper of Souls

The Fates will not be ignored

Raven M. Stevens

This is a work of fiction. Names, characters, places and incidents are either the product of the author's imagination or are used fictitiously. Any resemblances to actual persons, living or dead, is entirely coincidental.

Copyright © 2021 Raven M. Stevens

Cover design by: Sadie Schinke

All rights reserved. No part of this publication may be reproduced, stored in or introduced into a retrieval system, or transmitted, in any form, or by any means (electronic, mechanical, photocopying, recording, or otherwise) without the prior written permission of the author.

To my love, who has been by my side every step of the way

Forever and always

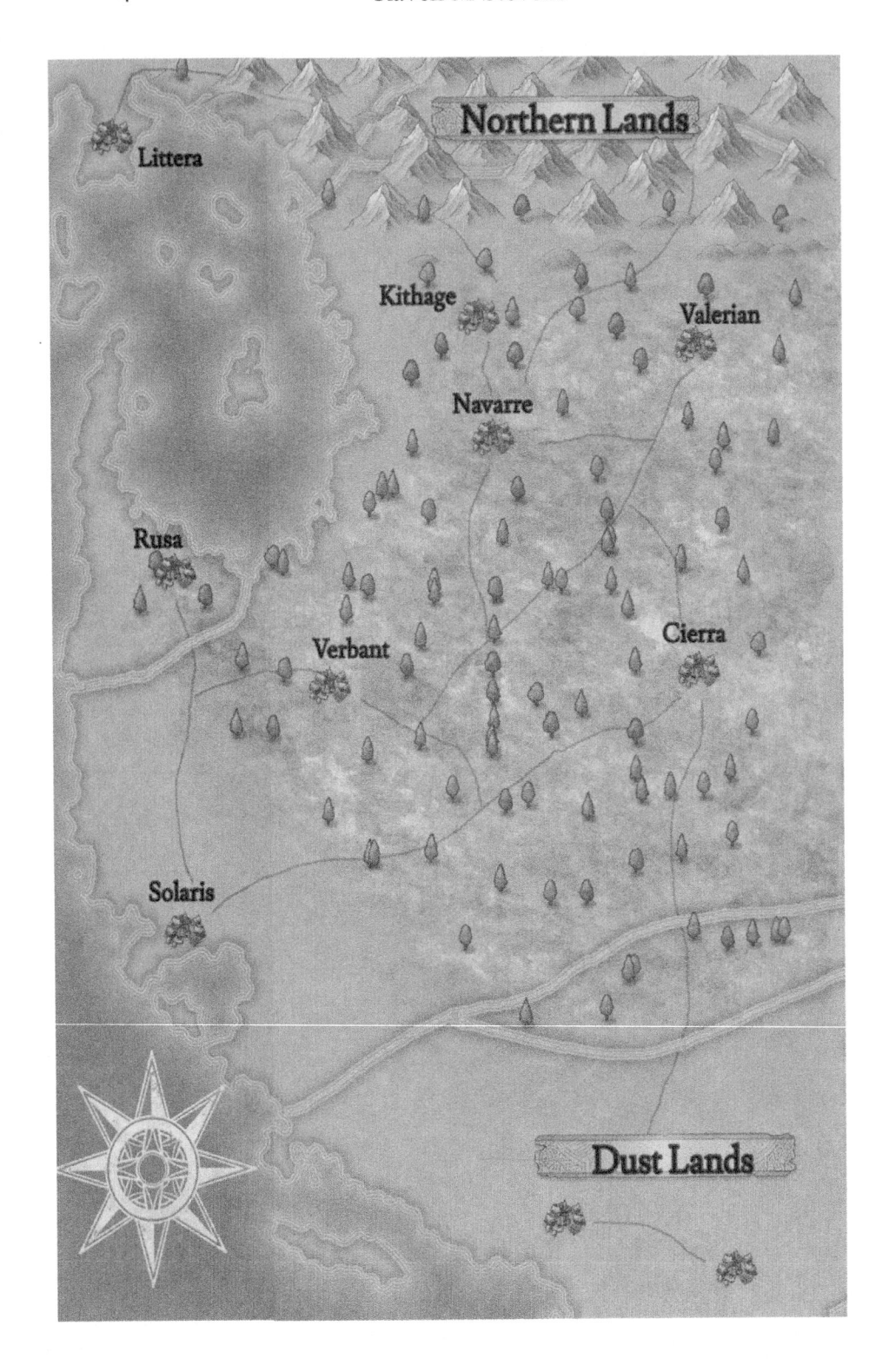

Chapter One
Terra

The Fates were not pleased with Terra and not even the pomegranate trees that towered above her could protect her from the shrill voice calling for her.

She closed her eyes and prayed to the gods that it was merely a figment of her imagination. *You have got to be kidding me.*

"Your Highness!"

It was not her imagination after all. Maybe if she remained silent, she wouldn't be discovered and then the person would be on their merry way.

"Terra!" the shrill voice called more earnestly, and it was getting closer.

"No, no, no," she growled and scrambled to her feet with no time to brush the grass from her skin.

Terra had always been a child of the earth, even when she was quite young. She had spent her childhood frolicking through the gardens along the brick paths and through the maze of greenery until her skin was golden under the rays of light. She would pluck petals of orange poppies and pink daphnes while avoiding her responsibilities as the eldest Princess. But then she began to grow up, and evasion was no longer an option. Her trips to the gardens grew less frequent until eventually she was fortunate if she managed even a single trip. Luckily for her, today was a day where she was able to sneak away to her favorite haven.

Unluckily for her, she had been discovered.

Her eyes landed on a nearby tree and she darted behind it, pausing to peer around the thin trunk. She spotted a woman in the distance traipsing her way along the pathway and muttering angrily to herself. The woman's linen skirt caught on a branch and she tore it away with an insulted gasp.

Terra seized the opportunity of the distraction and bolted deeper into the gardens. She knew these paths like the back of her hand and she couldn't help but grin as she wove through the maze. In a moment's notice, she was already hidden far away from view and in an area where no one would dare look for her in fear of not be able to navigate their way out.

Slightly out of breath, Terra stopped next to a beautiful fountain that spouted water into a mosaic pool. The marble base pictured four intricately carved dragons holding another base on which a beautiful woman was posed. The woman was dressed in the same style of chiton that Terra was wearing and had flowers adorning her hair in a crown. She was the goddess of the harvest and would bless Terra's kingdom with a plentiful bounty, or so the stories foretold.

"Terra! Where are you?"

Terra cursed and glanced around fearfully before realizing that there was only one more place she could hide. Lifting up her hem, Terra dove straight into the water of the fountain.

The cold water shocked her system and caused gooseflesh to appear on her limbs, but she refused to surface. Deciding that being found was much worse a fate than her suffering in the ice-cold water, she remained just under the surface and only dared to allow a few bubbles to escape her lips. Through the ripples, Terra could see her follower put her hands on her hips while she surveyed her surroundings. Just when Terra's lungs were about to burst, the woman stalked away. She finally surfaced and crouched behind the centerpiece to gulp in air greedily.

Once she made sure that the coast was clear, Terra lifted up her now drenched skirts and threw her legs over the stone ledge. A puddle quickly began forming around her on the path and her sandals squelched beneath her toes. "Tricked again," she muttered wryly to herself and started to wring out her hem. An irritated clearing of one's throat sounded behind her. Whirling around, Terra came face to face with an elderly woman who scowled at her with such venom that one may have believed that Terra had just killed her favorite pet. *The gods hate me,* she thought to herself.

"Ms. Astrid," Terra choked out. "I didn't see you there."

"Were you overcome by the effects of the hot day and needed a refreshing dip in the fountain, Princess Terra, or did you merely trip?"

"I tripped," Terra immediately lied.

"Your mother wishes to speak with you at once, although you may need to gather yourself in your bedchambers prior." Ms. Astrid peered down at her in disgust.

"I shall do so at once, thank you Ms. Astrid." Terra quickly turned on her heel and nearly ran away from the harrowing woman. *That could have gone a lot worse,* she mused.

Terra hurried back into the palace and towards her chambers while leaving a trail of water behind her. She had made it to her hallway without running into anyone, but as soon as she was about to enter her room, a gasp behind her made her pause.

Cassi, her handmaiden, was standing dumbfounded. "What did you do?"

Terra's eyes flickered to the obvious puddles that she had left in her wake. "I went for a swim. Can you help me clean up?"

Hesitating, Cassi shook her head and headed inside while muttering under her breath about the shenanigans that Terra had somehow again found herself in. Cassi closed the door behind them and ushered her quickly into the marble room where a clawfoot tub rested before too big of a puddle formed. Terra stripped off the heavy fabric of her chiton and tossed it with a loud *plump* into the empty tub before leaning to unclasp the leather sandals on her feet. Cassi wrapped her in a towel and began to comb through her hair. Terra's long brown waves reached the small of her back, and detangling the wet mess was no easy task, but, eventually, Cassi finished and patted her shoulder.

"What would I do without you?" Terra pecked her fondly on the cheek. With the towel still wrapped around her, she stepped out into the main room of her bedchamber. The room was very open and what it lacked in furniture or personal objects, it made up with its view. The room led out to a wide balcony that overlooked the entire city that lay below.

The realm of Solaris was nestled against the soft shore of the sea. All of the buildings had a brilliant white exterior that reflected the light that graced the city most of the year. The breeze that commonly swept through the open aired palace and courtyards brought with it the scent of the rolling waves and a tinge of salt.

Terra had never minded the sea and the hustle and bustle it brought into the port city, but she was definitely more of the earth than the sea. It was obvious by the many potted flowers and plants she had snuck from the gardens over the years so that she could be surrounded by comfort, even while she slumbered.

Cassi opened the wardrobe resting along a wall and began to sort through fabrics for Terra to see.

"This one." Terra stepped beside her and pulled out a beautiful dark-blue chiton accented with gold jewelry. She dropped the towel and, with Cassi's help, the girls arranged the flowing fabric until it fell on her frame perfectly. The neckline was a deep v-cut and the back of it was entirely open to show off her slender shoulders. The deep blue was representative of the royal family of Solaris and Terra knew it would make her mother, and the court, happy to see it. Cassi handed her the leather sandals to put back on and hurried her on by pushing her towards the direction of the throne room.

Servants stopped to bow their heads respectfully to the eldest Princess as she passed them in the halls despite the many, *many*, times that Terra had begged them not to. It had taken Cassi years to stop and even now she still would depending on the company present. *It's not like mother would have their heads or anything*, Terra considered wryly to herself. The Queen was intimidating without a doubt, but Terra knew the softer side of her mother, and her mother could never be as cruel as to punish a servant for something Terra specifically requested of them.

Armed guards stood outside the double wide doors that led to the throne room, their circular metal shields polished and gleaming. They quickly stood aside to allow Terra access and the doors swung open to reveal a cavernous room full of the nobility that made up the court.

They were all dressed similarly to Terra in a multitude of colors and they all had on expensive jewelry to showcase the power of their wealth. They were the elite of Solaris, merchants and tradesmen who had paved their way into the good graces of the royal family through their social influence and their deep pockets.

Terra never cared for the court. She felt as if they were vultures constantly circling over their prey and waited for them to die before striking. But, through Terra's lessons and the training she has had to take over the throne, she understood the importance of playing politics with the court, even if it was the last thing she could ever imagine wanting to do.

Without giving them a second glance, Terra walked down the blue carpet where the Queen was perched alone upon her marble throne at the end. The King's throne rested beside her, devoid of any life and Terra kept her eyes on the woman before her.

Terra was a spitting image of the Queen. They both had luxurious chestnut brown hair that fell in deep waves down their backs and slender faces with the same prominent cheekbones. Terra shared her mother's button nose that curved up slightly at the end that could make her look young and innocent, but at other times it painted her as mischievous and daring. Both of the women had wide smiles and were very beautiful with their brown skin darkened by the sun. Terra had heard many compare her mother to the goddess of beauty and have even claimed that she was a goddess sent to earth in order to seduce mortal men, but Terra believed that it was entirely silly.

The only difference between them were Terra's eyes. Instead of inheriting her mother's deep brown eyes that were like two bowls of honey swirling intently, she had been born with her father's deep green eyes that challenged even the most luscious of plants.

"Queen Clio." Terra stopped in front of the few steps in front of the throne and gave her a respectful bow. "You wished to speak with me?"

The Queen stood, her rich blue robes falling elegantly to the floor. She had matching gold accents on her shoulders and a belt of gold cinching the fabric at her waist. She also wore a sapphire necklace around her throat and a gold crown with sapphires embedded into the delicate structure, all of which symbolized the sea which allowed Solaris to thrive. The court fell into a hushed silence at Terra's presence and she saw the spectators craning their necks to try to eavesdrop on what was happening.

"You sure took your time," the Queen whispered before raising her voice to address the rest of the room. "Please, I would like a moment alone with my daughter."

With a lot of unhappy muttering and annoyed huffing, the court filed out of the doors and they were closed behind them, cutting off the Queen and the Princess from the rest of the world in a rare moment of solitude.

"What is this I hear about you jumping into one of the fountains?" Queen Clio smiled and adjusted the accents binding Terra's garb together on her two shoulders.

"I merely tripped."

Queen Clio gave her a commonly used look of hers that said, "I know that is certainly not the case, but I will pretend to believe you anyways" and she winked. "I would have hidden from Ms. Astrid myself if I could. She was on a rampage this morning and was scolding the staff in the kitchens to no end."

"Whatever for?"

"The desserts they were making had not nearly enough cherries on top, of course."

Both Terra and the Queen giggled at this, knowing full well that Ms. Astrid was notorious for her desire for perfection. She terrorized every person as much as she possibly could, but she was wonderful at keeping the workings of the palace running smoothly because of it.

The Queen sat back in her throne with a heavy sigh. She was weary and Terra could see it in her eyes and in the way she carried herself. It was as if the emotional burden of the King's passing had physically affected the Queen in a way that could never be undone. "I do have a favor to ask of you darling which is why I sent for you in the first place."

Terra sat down on the steps in front of the throne and smoothed her skirt over her lap. "What is it?"

"Arla has been *dying* to go to the port. A rare ship docked yesterday from the east and she has been asking to see it nonstop. Would you take your sisters to the port and maybe spend some time in the market this afternoon? It would allow me to focus on some important business with the advisers that has been calling my name."

"What business?"

The Queen waved the question off. "Nothing that you should worry about, you're not the Queen yet."

The smile didn't reach her mother's eyes. *What is she keeping from me?* Terra frowned, but tried to let the worry slide off her shoulders. *She would tell me if it was something urgent, wouldn't she?* As the eldest Princess and heir to the throne, Terra was involved in all matters with the kingdom in preparation for when she would be eventually crowned. "It builds confidence," the Queen would always tell the advisors when they would question her.

But now wasn't the time for Terra to worry, so instead she nodded. "I'll find the girls now and we'll go right away." She climbed back to her feet and planted a soft kiss on the Queen's cheek before turning to go. But she made the mistake of gazing at the empty throne and she couldn't help but pause.

"I miss him, too," Queen Clio said wistfully when she noticed her glance and she took one of Terra's hands in hers. "I know that his throne was empty often anyways, but it feels different now."

"It does." Terra cleared her throat uncomfortably. King Aster had passed a little over a year ago from an unknown illness. It had wracked his body quickly and rendered him weak and fragile. He could hardly walk a few steps without severe coughs wracking his chest until he sat himself back down.

Prior to the King growing ill, he had traveled often on diplomatic trips to far off lands and left the duties to the Queen which, now looking back, had helped her immensely when he did get sick. Terra had never been very close to her father, but she also hadn't had a bad relationship with him either. She had no choice but to remain stoic and strong for her mother and her sisters.

Terra kissed her mother one last time and went to find the three young Princesses. Terra was the eldest at eighteen and Calliope, Calli, was the next born three years later. Marcella was thirteen and Arla was the youngest at nine. Each of the girls were vastly different than one another, but they were all known to get into trouble and mischief over the years.

Calliope was the easiest to find. She spent almost all of her free time at the stables grooming and riding the beautiful stallions and mares. Terra wasn't so bad at riding herself, but she much more enjoyed walking than viewing the world from the back of a horse. Calliope was a mixture between the King and Queen. She inherited their father's dimples and dark black hair and she was tall and broad from all the physical work she did daily with the horses. She had at least three inches over Terra, maybe even more and it wasn't uncommon for strangers to mistake Calli for the eldest sister simply because of her height.

"Just because you're bigger, doesn't mean that mother loves you more," Terra would tease her and usually Calli would throw something relatively soft at her in response.

Luckily for Terra, Arla was in the stables as well. The youngest Princess was dangerously cute with her curly black hair and the Queen's button nose. She was a cheerful child and had the most infectious smile between the four sisters.

Most days, she terrorized the staff by pulling pranks and scaring the handmaids by jumping out at them from behind a door or a corner in the palace. If they would ask Terra where Arla had learned that from, she would pretend that she had no idea, but secretly knew that Arla had learned it from her over the years.

"I heard someone wishes to go to the port," Terra said as she walked towards the stall where Arla and Calli were. Arla's face popped over the stall door and she grinned.

"Can we?" she nearly shouted.

"We can!"

Arla squealed in excitement and looked at Calli. "You hear that? We're going to see the pretty ship!"

Calli laughed and patted the gentle mare's hindquarters that was next to her. "I suppose we can go now, is Marci coming?"

"I haven't asked her yet; I haven't seen her all day now that I think of it."

"She was in the kitchen earlier trying to perfect a new recipe that was giving her trouble."

"That's okay, I'll go get her!" Arla ran out of the stables before either of the two older girls could say anything.

Before long, a frazzled Marcella entered the stables following a rambunctious Arla. Similar to Calli, Marcella was a beautiful mix of both King Aster and Queen Clio. The one thing that set the two girls apart was a scar that cut through the end of Marcella's eyebrow from once burning herself in the kitchen as a young girl. The hair refused to grow there and as a result, Marcella's complexion appeared mysterious and intriguing, even for a fifteen-year-old.

"If we're going to go, let's go now while we still have daylight." Marcella released her hair from a gold clip and beckoned the girls on.

The four sisters began their journey towards the port. While many would have opted for a horse or even a carriage for the trip, the sisters enjoyed strolling out of the palace gates and through the cobblestone streets. At this late in the afternoon, there wasn't quite as much foot traffic or travel in general as there would be in the morning, but with the influx of docking ships as of late, the city was still busier than normal.

The four girls passed by hordes of people. Horses clattered by and wagon wheels bumped over the stones so they hugged the side of the road. Most Solarians all shared the similar dark hair and dark olive skin complexion that the royal family possessed, hinting at generations spent by the bright seaside. There were many, however, that did not share this complexion, and these were all folks that hailed from lands far beyond the ports of Solaris.

"Hurry up, we're almost there!" Arla screeched at her three older sisters when they reached the edge of the sea. Arla ran and clattered down the stairs leading to one of the many wooden docks in the port. The waves were choppy against the docks with the wind blowing strong and the spray brought the taste of salt to the girls' tongues which only made Arla run faster.

"You're going to trip over your skirt!" Marci scolded and hurried after her.

At the end of the dock sat a gorgeous ship with jagged sails rising tall into the air. It sat low and was slender, but the three ruffled sails gave it the look of an exotic fish that swam the depths of the sea. Terra allowed her sisters to wander towards it while she ambled down the dock in the other direction on her own. As long as she could still be within earshot, she knew that they would be okay. *Unless they managed to burn down the ship,* she thought. *Knowing Arla, she would find a way.* She glanced back at her sisters one last time before continuing.

Terra relished in the bright sun beating down as she strolled. She walked down the length of the dock until she reached a point where it veered towards the side out of view and the wooden platform cupped a stone wall differentiating the waterline from the land. There, she paused.

Far ahead of her down the dock rested a massive ship that, to her surprise, was flying Solaris colors along its mast. On deck she could just make out the gleaming armor of soldiers scurrying around as if they were preparing to depart.

What are all of these soldiers doing here? Terra racked her brain and tried to recall if the advisers mentioned anything about dispatching soldiers to sea in their last meeting, but nothing rang a bell. All of their soldiers were currently stationed in Solaris to do regular guard duty... or so she thought.

Her mind went back to what her mother had told her before. *"It would allow me to focus on some important business with the advisers that has been calling my name."* Did that have anything to do with this?

"Why, isn't it the Princess!" a voice called out.

Startled, Terra looked around until she found where the voice had come from. Two men were on the deck of a smaller vessel and were peering down at her with wide grins on their face.

"Don't be shy, we don't bite," the other man said, and his partner jostled him with an elbow.

"I'm fine right here, thank you," Terra called back and tilted her chin up. Her eyes glanced back at the ship in the distance.

Noticing where her eyes went, the first man to speak leaned on the ship's railing and jutted his chin towards the ship in the distance. "War is coming, haven't you heard? This is only the beginning."

"They say they're coming for the throne, now that the King is dead. No one is safe, you most of all, Princess," the other added.

Terra's mouth went dry. What did they mean that war was coming? A hand touched Terra's arm and she turned to find Calli looking at the men fearfully. "Let's go, please." Calli tugged on her arm again. Without hesitating, the two girls hurried away from the sailors whose cackles carried on the wind after them. It wasn't until the two of them were far away that Calli finally spoke again. "What did they mean Terra, that war was coming?"

Terra merely shook her head and a frown etched her face. "I have no idea."

Chapter Two
Orion

The mist hung heavy over the castle spires and dampened everything it could reach its tendrils to. The rainy season was soon going to cease so that the harsh winter could come, that much was clear. The air was becoming colder with each passing day and soon all of the leaves would litter the ground in brilliant splashes of red, yellow, and orange. Orion didn't mind the winter. For him, it meant that Wolf's Pass would become too treacherous for travel and the land would become quiet and muffled.

The incoming winter would mean that he would have even more solitude in his land, just the way he wanted it to be.

He whistled sharply and two wolf dogs, Milo and Silas, immediately came running to his side while the third was nowhere to be seen. "Ash!" he shouted into the mist and finally his other midnight black companion came trotting to his side as if she had done nothing wrong. Orion enjoyed the silence that the mist brought to his castle in the valley. It seemed to quiet the world, just like the snow did when it fell thick and heavy. Not that every other day wasn't usually quiet, but it still brought him a semblance of peace when he felt otherwise.

Orion's leather books clacked across the stone path that led back towards the castle entrance. His furry companions were always antsy if he didn't allow them to run daily through the thick forest surrounding the discreet castle. It had become one of their routines and some days they would be gone for hours since it wasn't like anyone was there to miss them. Neither his groundskeeper or housekeeper would notice it either way, and his unit of soldiers knew better than to leave their housing in the woods to bother him. The few times that the soldiers ventured to the castle unannounced, it didn't end well for them and now they avoided their King like a plague.

The three jet-black dogs tousled with one another ahead of Orion as he walked, each of them play growling and batting each other as they went. He took one last breath of the fresh air outside before entering the wide and tall wooden door that led straight into the main foyer.

The main foyer held two grand staircases, one going to one end of the castle, where his bedchamber and his study was, and the other leading towards the opposite end, where both Laurent and Edith resided. The main floor held the common rooms such as the kitchen and the dining hall, but he didn't frequent those too often.

The dogs followed hot on his heels while he climbed the stairs and he ran his hand over the smooth banister that had existed for generations. He passed portraits, sculptures, standing armor and other decorative pieces that he so longed to get rid of, but he knew Edith would have his head if he even tried. She didn't get cross with him often but when she did, he truly did fear her deep down as he would fear an angry mother hen.

"You can't throw away everything that reminds you of your family!" she had shouted angrily the last time she had caught him trying to get rid of a portrait. "These things are the only things you have left of them, and I will *not* allow it!"

Orion chuckled at the memory and remembered how quickly he had left the room in desperation to avoid the angry woman. She put up a lot with him, he would give her that. He would repay her for it in a heartbeat if she would accept any gift from him. Multiple times over the years he had offered to set her up with her own land and her own cottage wherever she wished, hoping that she would be able to have a family and a life like he knew she so wanted. Instead of accepting though, she flat out refused every time and instead chose to live in a nearly empty castle with his obvious brooding and Laurent's lack of social interaction. "For generations, my family has been bound by honor to serve the royal family on the throne of Valerian, and I'm not about to be the one to break the cycle," she had told him when he had presented her with a map of land that she could have to herself.

They all were bound by duty — Laurent, Edith, even the soldiers that kept the borders safe were all from bloodlines that served his family for generations. Even if he chased them away, they would all come back. So he put up with it.

Down the hall, Orion noticed Milo's tufted ears perk up and Edith stepped out from around the corner. "Speak of the Devil," Orion muttered to himself. She was dressed in a short-sleeved dress in a crimson red that was warm enough to ward off the cold spell happening outside but also allowed her to go about her day in the castle. She was middle-aged and had hair so blonde that it appeared almost white. Her pale blue eyes pierced into his soul every time she tried to discover what the King of Valerian was thinking.

"Good evening, Your Highness," she greeted him.

"Edith, what brings you over here on this fine evening?"

"To inform you that there was a letter for you. I put it on your desk in your study, but I don't think it should wait. Judging by the seal, it looked quite important."

Orion looked at her curiously and tried to gauge her expression but she masked it well. She either knew exactly what the letter was, or she at least had her suspicions. He suspected the prior, for she always seemed to know everything that happened within the castle walls. "I'll go take a look at it now, thank you." He continued past his bedchambers with the three dogs and instead went to his study where he immediately closed the door behind himself. His study held sturdy bookshelves with old tomes that rested now in dust and thick curtains that were usually drawn over the windows to shut himself inside. In the center was an old wooden desk strewn with papers and miscellaneous documents that spouted financial information or other important details he needed to help run the kingdom of Valerian. Periodically, Edith would sneak in here when she knew he was away and would organize it all so that when he returned, he would find the room cleaner than he had left it.

His three dogs all took up comfortable positions where they could. Ash turned in a circle on a large ornate rug on the floor while Silas rolled onto his back on the other side of the desk where he was hidden from sight. Milo hopped onto an armchair sitting across the desk from Orion where he could rest his head on the armchair and watch Orion as he took a seat.

He lit the lantern on the edge of the surface so that a soft light was casted over the messy papers. On top of the pile of papers rested a single letter with a brilliant blue embossed seal on it. Looking closer, he studied the seal but couldn't place who, or where, the letter may have been from. Frowning, he tore the letter open and began to read.

To his most honored King Orion of Valerian,

My name is Frederick Arnett and I am the head councilman of Solaris. We have not crossed paths before, but I write to you in desperation. Please accept my deepest apologies for being so forward, but I am writing to you in the hopes that we may negotiate an alliance between the esteemed realm of Valerian and my home of Solaris. We are looking for allies that would, in the heart of battle, help to defend our land. War is coming to the shores of Solaris as mercenaries wish to take the throne after the late King's recent passing. If I am being entirely transparent, Solaris is needing soldiers to help defend our borders and protect the ports on the Sapphire Sea.

I would not be requesting this if we were not quite so desperate. The integrity of our realm hangs in the balance. I can offer trade deals, an exchange of goods and wealth, and the hand of the eldest Princess: Her Highness Terra of Solaris and Heir to the throne. Please, I beg for you to show us your kindness and mercy.

Signed,

Councilman Arnett of Solaris.

Orion set the letter down on the desk and chewed the inside of his cheek thoughtfully, not quite sure what to think about the letter. It was not unheard of, of course, for realms to strike up deals with one another and to offer aid when it's needed, but for this councilman of Solaris to admit openly that they cannot defend their borders against a war, Solaris was truly in trouble.

The realm of Solaris was familiar to him, even though he hadn't visited the ports in many years. It rested along the shores of the sea and far to the south from Valerian. The same bloodline had ruled it for many generations, similar to Valerian, but clearly that was coming under threat. But why should he care? These mercenaries posed no threat to Valerian, nor was Solaris currently an ally where honor would bind him to help them in any way that he could.

There had to be a catch to this. Without any prior discussions with him, they were already giving him offers that, typically, would have come much later in the diplomatic negotiations between the royals of the two kingdoms. For them to offer him the Heir's hand in marriage must mean that there was more to it all that he wasn't being made aware of.

A small part of Orion wanted to discuss it with Edith and her opinion on the matter since she did handle quite a lot of the day to day matters of the kingdom —including taking care of meeting any requests from allies that Valerian had prior to Orion on the throne, but he already knew that she would tell him to do it simply at the thought of him taking a bride. The image made him frown deeper. Whereas Edith would be thrilled to have a companion other than himself, Laurent, and the gruff soldiers, Orion would loathe hosting a spoiled Princess calling the castle her home.

The idea disturbed him enough that Orion took the parchment in his hands and held the corner towards the open flame of the lantern. The edge was just starting to smoke and his stomach flipped. A voice in his mind seemed to beg him not to do it. A horrid feeling began to wash over him as if he was making a mistake, but still he didn't pause until a fervent whining near his legs finally made him pull the letter away. Ash was sitting at his side, looking up at him with her jet-black eyes. She whined again.

In his mind, he could hear what his mother would say about it all. She would chastise him for not opting to help innocent people for his own greedy reasons. To her, being a kind ruler would be more important than his selfish wants. *"This is not how I raised you,"* she would say.

Orion sighed and placed the slightly scorched parchment back on the desk. "What am I supposed to do, huh?" he murmured to Ash and stroked her thick fur right between her ears. She gave his hand a gentle lick and whined again as if she was answering his question. "Why does this make me feel guilty? Out of everything to feel guilty about, I shouldn't feel guilty about *this*."

Orion knew the answer. Deep down, he knew why he felt guilty. Here he was being given the chance to do good for

Edith, to give her something he knew that she's been yearning for. And he should do it, even if it was just for her. She had dealt with him all these years even when he had not always been the warmest with her. Without her, Valerian would have shrunk until nothing was left except Orion hiding away in his castle.

Orion got to his feet and walked over to where a map of all the kingdoms rested. There was Solaris, far to the south and far away from Valerian's more mountainous region. A trade deal with Solaris would benefit his people, that he couldn't deny. It was difficult already when winter hit for Valerian to get imports of goods from the more southern-based merchants that, usually, traveled the roads selling and trading anything they could get their hands on.

A soft knock at the door shook him out of his pondering. "Come in," he said gruffly and continued to study the map and Solaris.

Edith opened the door and closed it quietly behind her. He saw that she was holding a platter with two cups of tea on it. She placed it on the desk on top of his mess of papers and pulled a second armchair, the one that Milo wasn't snoring on, closer so she could drink the cup of tea she brought for herself. "Why don't you sit?" Even though she worded it as a question, Orion knew she meant it as a motherly command.

Orion relented and took a seat again with a weary sigh. "To what do I owe the pleasure?"

"I can do without the attitude." Edith smirked into her tea. "I came to let you know that Darren requested to speak with you."

Orion scowled. The Captain of his guard was damn good at his job, but he was demanding. "Did he say what was so important?"

"No, so I recommend that you go speak with him and find out." Edith averted her gaze, and he knew that she knew exactly what Darren needed, but was playing coy simply to force him to go play nice with his Captain. She always told him that he's too gloomy and that he needed to make friends. But Orion having friends? He had laughed out loud and merely walked away when she had told him that. Edith's eyes came to rest on the slightly scorched letter crumpled not too far from the tea tray.

Orion picked it up and held it out to her. "It's a request for an alliance," he explained. "From Solaris, the port kingdom in the south."

"And?" She took the letter from him and started to skim it, completely ignoring the scorched corner blackened from the flame. "Are you going to agree?"

"We would get trade deals which would be very beneficial for us. Their port has direct access to many of the far-off lands." *And not to mention, my mother would have wanted me to accept.* Orion sat back in his chair and took the cup of tea for him off of the platter. He sipped at the bitter drink while he waited for Edith's reaction to the marriage proposal.

Her eyes widened slightly and she reread the letter once more before placing it back down. "The Princess's hand in marriage..." she mused. "And what are your thoughts about that part of the offer?"

Orion's steely eyes met hers. "You already know how I feel." It had been a conversation that they've had before, one where Edith would push him towards taking a wife and where Orion would vehemently refuse to do so.

"But you'll agree?"

"I will agree," he said slowly. "But it won't be for myself. I'll send a messenger with a response to Solaris at once."

Edith nodded, satisfied with his answer and knowing not to push it further. She rose to her feet and gathered the china on the platter. She turned to leave with it but paused at the door. "Your mother would be proud of you. I also think it will do you some good to have a companion."

"Nothing around here will be changing," he answered in his most commanding tone, but Edith only smiled.

"Whatever you say, Your Highness." She left and closed the door behind her, leaving Orion alone once more with his mind.

He picked up a quill and a fresh piece of parchment. He held the quill just above the surface and waited for the words to come, but they wouldn't. Orion cursed to himself and twiddled the quill restlessly in his fingers. "This shouldn't be so damned hard to do. Nothing is going to change." He took a deep breath and forced the words onto the paper. This was his least favorite part of being a King, having to appear noble and diplomatic when most of the time, he didn't care at all.

In one page, he presented his terms for Solaris to agree to and wrote everything he could provide in exchange, protection included. He vowed in the letter that if they came to an agreement, no harm would become the royal family nor their shores. He even wrote that he agreed to take the Princess's hand in marriage as an act of good faith for their newfound alliance. He signed the bottom of the parchment and folded it carefully, sealing it with a bit of hot wax and the imprint of the official crest of Valerian.

Instead of feeling as if a weight had been lifted off of his chest, Orion only felt irritated. He felt that he was bullied into agreeing but that was, of course, absurd. His own guilt guided his decision and that blame rested solely on him. The study began to feel cramped as if the walls were closing in on him and he felt the need to get out, to get into the fresh air and out of the cursed room. The shadows warped at the edges of the space and in the darkest corners as if they were alive.

"Not now," he whispered into the air and whistled to his dogs. Immediately, all three heads perked up and they jumped up from their spots when they saw Orion put his cloak back on. He snatched the letter and beckoned them to follow him out of the study. They followed him closely and as soon as Orion stepped out of the castle, they took off running. They began to nip and play with one another, but they still made sure to stay close to their master.

Orion headed straight into the thick forest and they trotted ahead of him with their tongues lolling out of their mouths. The sun was beginning to set, but he knew this area better than anyone. He soon came upon Thorn Hall, the building that housed his castle guard so that they were near, but not too near. The wooden building before him looked plain and simple. The structure didn't have defensive barriers or turrets like the castle did, but then again they didn't need it. Two soldiers stood guard outside it and were mid conversation when they spotted Orion. They both quickly fell silent and snapped to attention. The soldiers knelt on a single knee and placed an arm across their chest while the other hand still grasped their long spears.

"Your Highness," they both said together.

"Where's the Captain?"

"I'm right here, Your Highness," a voice called behind him. Captain Darren was trudging out of the trees followed by a half dozen men, all of whom had their swords at their side and bows in their hand. Darren was young, far younger than most Captains would be. He wore his dark hair long and tied up behind his head and he had a thicker beard than Orion would ever allow himself to wear. He had a scar that slit through one eyebrow and another down the opposite cheek, making him appear older than what he actually was.

Orion held out the folded letter and Darren took it from him. "I need this delivered to Solaris immediately. I need you to send your fastest rider on the fastest horse."

"Maverick," Darren called and one of the men standing guard at the door approached. "Deliver this to the palace in Solaris, speed is of an essence."

Maverick nodded and immediately disappeared to prepare to leave.

"You summoned me Captain?" Orion allowed his annoyance to show, his voice growing even more bitter and unhappy. He *was* annoyed and unhappy. He had more important things to worry about than silly summons from a palace guard.

"I *requested* to speak with you," Darren corrected. "My men are beginning to grow restless. Guard duty is quite monotonous. They work the same shifts, in the same rotation, and do the same exact tasks each time. Wandering the border can get old quickly. They are needing a mission or a different task to get their spirits up."

"Is protecting your King and the kingdom's borders too *boring* for your men, Captain?" Orion couldn't help but speak with venom in his tone.

"No, your Highness."

"Would they rather save damsels in distress? Would that be more satisfactory to their liking?" Orion snapped his fingers and his dogs perked their ears, waiting for him to give them a command. "I didn't know protecting their King was so *boring.*"

"Your Highness, forgive me, that's not what I mea—"

"Save it." Orion brushed past him and called over his shoulder. "I'll have a *mission* for you soon, don't you worry. You'll be escorting your future Queen to Valerian safely."

Orion sighed and ran a weary hand through his hair. Just as he suspected, he immediately heard the excited tendrils of the soldiers gossiping to one another. A Queen? After all this time? "Nothing is going to change," he told himself. "Nothing."

Are you sure about that? A voice whispered in his mind and Orion grimaced.

"Now is not a good time."

It never seems to be a good time, Your Highness.

A foreboding breeze began to pick up, the dead leaves on the ground swirling around him. "We are done here."

As you wish.

Chapter Three
Terra

"You will obsess over this until you demand answers," Cassi pointed out.

Terra had just told her about what she had seen at the port and she had been tossing around the idea of asking the Queen about it for the last few days. She didn't even tell Cassi at first, but instead Terra avoided it as if that would make everything go away. She didn't know why, but she was scared to ask even though it was in her right as heir to the throne to demand council with the advisers and the Queen at any given time. "It would teach her how to rule the kingdom," Queen Clio had always told the council.

"I know, I really should," Terra admitted and wrung her hands together. She was seated in front of her broad vanity and Cassi was standing behind her twisting her hair into glamorous plaits. "But what if I don't like the answer? What if there is more that they've been hiding from me? This itself is a pretty big deal and they never mentioned even a word of it to me." Terra saw in the vanity mirror that Cassi opened her mouth to say something, but snapped it back shut. Her handmaid had an odd expression on her face and a rose tint crept up her neck and into her cheeks. Terra turned in her seat to face her. "Cassi," she said carefully. "Do you know something?"

"Not exactly," she replied hesitantly. "I just hear...rumors. The staff likes to gossip here, so it's hard not to accidentally eavesdrop."

"What did you hear?" Terra whipped around in her seat to face her head on. "Is it true? Is the realm being threatened?"

"I would talk to the Queen first; It could be just rumors."

Terra sighed. Her fear only grew stronger and she turned back around to face the mirror so that Cassi could continue to fix her hair. "I suppose you're right; I'll go speak with her at once and ask the council to call a meeting."

Wasting no time, Cassi finished up so that Terra could seek out her mother. She made her way to the Queen's private bedchambers where she knew she would be this early in the morning. Outside the intricate double doors were two armed guards adorned in heavy armor and each had the standard shield, spear, and sword on their person.

"Good morning," Terra greeted them and, without missing a beat, they stepped aside to allow the Princess to knock politely on the door.

"Come in!" the Queen's voice came from the other side and Terra slipped in. Whereas Terra's chamber was minimalistic and bare, the Queen's was the complete opposite. The room oozed elegance and the Queen's personality. She had beautiful tapestries, paintings, sculptures, and jewelry everywhere. On display on side tables and dressers were necklaces, bracelets, and rings that had been passed down through the family for generations. The Queen took great pride in her familial ties and the history of her bloodline.

"What do I owe this surprise visit to?" Queen Clio asked and took a drink from the cup of tea she held in her hands. "Would you like me to call for more tea?" The Queen's two handmaidens were standing off to the side and the Queen was still in her flowing slip that she had slept in, not yet having prepared for her daily duties.

"I was hoping I could speak to you." Terra swore she could hear the slight tremor in her own voice. She then started to feel the embarrassment beginning to creep up her cheeks which only made her more nervous. "Alone, please," she clarified.

The Queen looked at her quizzically for a brief second before speaking. "Ladies, I will call you when I need you. Please, give me some privacy with my daughter." The handmaidens left the room swiftly so it was just the two of them. "Let's go out to the balcony, it's a beautiful day."

Instead of facing the city and the sea, the Queen's balcony faced empty hills that cupped the city against the sea and they had all of the privacy in the world for obvious security reasons. Terra missed the direct wind off of the sea and the view of the sparkling water from her own balcony, but she also enjoyed the change of scenery on her mother's when she visited.

"What's troubling you, my dear?" Queen Clio sat on one of the cushioned loungers. Terra took a seat on the matching one and realized that she was noticeably stiff and uncomfortable. She tried to relax her posture and told herself that it was entirely silly for her to be this worried.

"The other day in the port," Terra began carefully. "I saw something that concerned me. I saw Solarian ships preparing to leave the port with countless soldiers and-" She hesitated and took a deep breath. "mother, is there a war happening with Solaris?" Terra immediately expected her mother to laugh, to tell her that it was preposterous and that there was no truth to any of that. Except instead, Queen Clio coughed on her tea and Terra could see that she had turned pale once the coughing subsided. "mother, is it true?"

"Terra..." Queen Clio put her cup back down.

Terra stood up abruptly and walked to the edge of the balcony, her body humming with shock. She felt hurt and betrayed that this was kept from her. She felt like a fool, for not noticing that the council had been preparing for war for gods knew how long without her ever realizing. She was supposed to be a stoic leader, one who would one day lead her people with wisdom and kindness, and she had already failed. So easy was it for her to never notice, or to even catch a hint of this until now. What type of Queen would she be because of this? "How long? How long has this been going on and how long has this been kept from me?"

Queen Clio started to say something, but Terra couldn't hold in the wave of anger that began to bubble over. She wouldn't look at the Queen. "You expect me to take over the throne and to lead but you keep me blind to this? How am I supposed to learn? How am I supposed to rely on my council, when they have already failed to mention something of the upmost importance? How will I know how to properly lead when you're gone, mother?"

Terra felt her mother's soft hands upon her shoulders and one moved to her lengthy braid to stroke it gently. "Terra, sweetheart, let me explain."

She took a calming breath in, composed her features and turned to face the Queen.

"It's been a... struggle...to say the least since your father passed. Since your father died, there have been many threats made against Solaris." The Queen sighed and walked back to her seat. "The court has been very unhappy with my decision to not remarry, as has the council. I fear that some may even be working to undermine me as we speak. But the greatest threat has been from mercenaries that see your father's passing as an opportunity to take control of one of the region's most prized ports. There could be a lot of money made in their eyes, and they are entirely right.

"If one of these rival kingdoms were to invade Solaris, our military wouldn't stand a chance. Some of our biggest allies are no longer our allies, and instead they want to take the throne themselves just like everyone else seems to. The council has dispatched ships to protect our waters as we fear we are growing closer to an attack."

"I wish to meet with the council, I want to hear it from them and I want to ask more questions." Terra walked past her mother and paused in the doorway that led back into her bedchamber. "I will summon them this afternoon and I would like you to be present as well, but I understand if you're not." Without a second glance at the Queen, Terra left before the Queen could see the angry tears brimming in her eyes,

Back in her own bedchamber, Terra sent one of the many servants to pass along a message to all the councilmen to meet in the adviser's room in the afternoon, making sure to mention that it was an urgent matter that must be discussed immediately. Once this was taken care of, Terra sent out a message that Cassi's presence was requested. Not too long after, her handmaid returned.

"The talk with the Queen went well I assume? That didn't take too long, they must have been just rumors," Cassi said in a chipper tone, but once she saw Terra's expression, she faltered, and her voice went to a whisper. "Is it true? Is Solaris going to war?"

"We haven't yet, but there's a chance we might. I'm meeting with the council this afternoon to get all of the details."

Cassi seemed bothered by this but she wouldn't say as much. She was frightened as well, Terra knew. Solaris was her home just as much as it was hers. "Why don't you spend some time with your sisters until then? You need a distraction while you wait. You'll drive yourself crazy if you lock yourself away in your room today." She started to swipe any imaginary dust on the vanity.

"I know, but I don't want to worry them. I don't want them to find out about any of this, at least not until I know more."

"Then don't tell them yet, but instead go enjoy yourself."

Reluctantly, Terra listened. Cassi was right, the longer she wallowed in her twisting thoughts, the more she would end up with false assumptions about her kingdom's situation without having any confirmed facts to back it up. Cassi departed with an apologetic smile. "Ms. Astrid will have me punished if I leave her waiting much longer."

The rest of the day dragged by. Terra tried everything to keep her mind off of what was to come, but everything she tried failed in the end to keep her distracted. She was painfully aware of the minutes turning into hours. She first tried to wander the garden, but instead of soothing her mind, she found it only made her more agitated. She even went to the stables to bother Calliope, but eventually Calli had shooed her away due to her intense pacing of the cramped quarters and her lack of answers as to what was on her mind. Afterwards, she tried to relax on her own balcony with a cup of fresh tea, but the beautiful silence was drowned out by the anticipation coursing through her body.

Terra wished that Cassi was able to talk her down, to keep her calm while she waited for the afternoon meeting but, unfortunately, Cassi had other duties she needed to attend to besides taking care of the Royal Princess. Terra could have summoned her back if she truly wished, but she would never do that to her. Just when Terra could take no more, she finally went in search of Marci and Arla.

As expected, Marcella was hidden in the deeper confines of the kitchen and Arla was at her side, licking a colorful batter off a spatula while seated very unladylike on the counter. Terra dipped between the staff busy at work in the front portion of the sweltering kitchen and joined Arla on top of the counter. Marci was mixing a pink batter in a large bowl and had a small pan next to her with a dozen smaller circles to form the baked goods.

Terra snatched the spatula from Arla, which she responded to with a loud "hey!" and took a taste of the batter. Arla took it back with a scowl and continued her taste testing while Terra licked her lips. "That's really good!" she said to Marci. "What is it?"

"A lemon and cherry mix I'm trying to make into a cake. So far, I haven't been able to get the right mixture and amount of ingredients, but I think this time I might have gotten it," Marci replied and swept a loose strand of hair off of her forehead. She took the spatula back from Arla and used it to scrape every last bit of batter into the baking pan except a very thin layer that refused to budge.

"What're you up to today?" Arla asked Terra. "I was bored so I came here to bother Marci."

"More like to eat everything I'm making," Marci muttered and Terra laughed.

"I've been trying to find something to do all day myself," Terra explained and dropped her voice. "I have a council meeting later that I can't miss so I can't stray too far."

Marci barely glanced up from what she was doing. "What is the meeting about?"

This question quieted Terra, but she tried not to let her expression betray her emotions. "Nothing too important, just a few odds and ends. Speaking of which, it's about time that I head to the meeting room. mother would have my head if I was late." Terra hopped off the counter and stuck one last finger in a mixing bowl to swipe another bite of batter, much to Marci's dismay. Her sister's fake angry shouts and Arla's giggles followed her as she darted back out of the kitchen to meet the council.

Taking the long way, Terra wandered until she was completely out of time. She paused outside the closed doors when she arrived at the meeting room. Her nerves threatened to get the best of her and her palms had started to sweat so she wiped her hands on her chiton before smoothing back her hairline to try to gather any escaped tendrils. Straightening her garb, she took one final deep breath and pushed her way into the room. The entire council of six was already waiting for her around the long table that held Queen Clio at the far end.

Nodding in greeting, Terra claimed her seat at the opposite end of the Queen so that three council members sat on each of her sides. She knew their faces well. They had been advisers prior to Terra being born so they have been around as long as she could remember, but that didn't mean she felt even remotely friendly towards them. But that meant that she already knew who she could trust wholeheartedly when the time came for her to take the throne, and who she had to watch out for. Her mother's careful guidance certainly helped as well. But now, she viewed them all as her enemies. Even the Queen was included in this negative view which made Terra feel guilty, but all of them, including her mother, had kept this from her and she took it personally. They were meant to guide her, not set her up for failure.

"Princess Terra," one member, Councilman Romulus, said. "I apologize if I speak out of turn for the rest of the council, but I don't think any of us quite understand why you have called us here on such short notice. What urgent matter can we assist you with?"

Terra folded her hands together on the table and looked the council straight in the eye just like her mother had taught her. Any sign of weakness and they would tear her apart. Instead, she must challenge them and continue to do so less they eat her alive. "I summoned a meeting because I deserve to know any, and all, information regarding the status of my future throne and kingdom. Unless the council disagrees with this statement."

"Your Highness," another councilman began. Evander was his name, Terra remembered. He usually was a quiet one, but that only made him more threatening in the world of politics. "With all due respect, you have been informed of everything that you are needing to know. I'm not quite su—"

"What about the fact that I discovered that we are dispatching a small armada of ships to defend our waters against mercenaries threatening war with Solaris, Councilman Evander? And what about the Heir to the throne discovering this, not from her esteemed advisors-to-be, but instead from watching the soldiers prepare to sail from the port firsthand?"

The council grew quiet and exchanged glances with one another. Queen Clio made no move to speak. She sat back in her chair with her head held tall and allowed her daughter to take control of the meeting which Terra was grateful for. She had to fight for the respect of the council whereas her mother already had it and she might as well start that fight prior to taking the throne.

"No one wishes to speak?" Terra asked and sat back in her chair. "So be it, I don't want to hear excuses as to why my council has already failed me. Tell me everything that we know so far about the mercenary threats."

Councilman Arnett cleared his throat and Terra looked at him expectantly. He was the official head of the council and had the most power out of all of them. He had served her father well, that much she knew, but as to how he will serve her... that has yet to be seen. "Currently, there are two kingdoms to the north that we believe are hiring the mercenaries to do their bidding. They would have to capture another kingdom as well in between us and them to fully expand their empire, but our sources say there have been negotiations already that could make the pieces fall into place for a full-on invasion of Solaris. Scouts sent by the mercenaries have been seen mapping out the shores and the best way to get into the port which is why we have dispatched ships to ensure they are not able to use the information against us."

"What actions are we taking to make sure an invasion doesn't happen? Besides dispatching ships to keep the scouts at bay?"

"That is where we are running into issues. With the numbers that our own scouts are reporting... we don't have enough men to defend Solaris if the mercenaries would launch a full attack."

Terra wasn't able to mask her surprise from the council at this piece of information. "What do you mean we don't have enough men to defend the realm?"

"Many of our past allies have chosen to rethink their alliances with Solaris since King Aster, may his soul rest in peace, left us. So we have been actively engaging advisors and royalty in other realms to offer alliances in exchange for their protection and numbers to boost our own. I actually received this letter back today with an acceptance." Councilman Arnett produced a piece of unfolded parchment from his lap and placed it on the table before him. "His Royal Highness King Orion of Valerian has agreed to aid us in our fight against the mercenaries under the condition that we agree to a few specific trade deals and agree that he is able to take Princess Terra's hand in marriage."

"*What?*" Queen Clio roared, but the sound was muted in Terra's ears as Councilman Arnett's words sank in. "You dare offer my daughter's hand in marriage without *my knowledge or approval?*"

"Your Highness, please, it was necessary- "

"I don't care how necessary you deemed it! This should have been approved *by me!*"

Terra sat frozen while Queen Clio and Councilman Arnett continued to argue with one another about his actions. The rest of the council began to jump in until it was an all-out screaming match and the long table was on the verge of being overturned in the frenzy.

Her mind swirled violently around the newfound information. The council offered her hand to a King that ruled a realm she had never heard of. *Me? Married?* She couldn't wrap her head around the possibility. For years, she had been groomed and poised to take the throne but never once had it crossed her mind that she would have to rule with someone by her side as her King. Her veins felt as if they were filled with ice and she began to grow lightheaded when her mother's voice snapped her back to reality.

"Terra?"

"What did you say?" Terra asked once she realized all eyes were on her.

Queen Clio tried to give her a reassuring smile, but it didn't make Terra feel any better. "I asked your thoughts about this. I won't force you to do it, but otherwise we will follow through with it."

"I-" Terra started but the sharp gazes of all the council members made her falter. No longer was she strong and able to withstand the pressure of the council, her facade was beginning to crack. Councilman Arnett had seen to that with his sudden information. "I have to go," she said abruptly and stood. She was slamming open the doors to the hallway just as she heard the Queen call out for her, but she didn't hesitate.

Servants watched the Princess scurry through the winding halls in surprise, but no one made a move to halt the Princess.

Terra didn't stop until she had managed to escape the confines of the palace entirely and she was among the familiar paths of the gardens. There, she let it out.

Frantic breaths clawed at her chest and embarrassed tears fell hot and fast as she let herself cry now that she was away from the watchful eyes of the council. *And away from my disappointed Mother,* she thought sadly. Oh, how the gods must be laughing at her. She kneeled in the grass off the path and dug her fingers in deep until she felt the cool soil against her fingertips. This grounded her, allowing her to get herself back under control and remain calm despite the overwhelming panic she was feeling.

"Princess Terra?"

Terra looked up from her spot in the grass and was startled to see Councilman Arnett standing over her. Embarrassed once more that he had caught her crying on the ground like a young child, she quickly wiped her eyes and got back to her feet.

"I wanted to apologize," he began. "For the shock of it all. I know it must be a lot to take in all at once, but I still wanted to discuss it with you and make sure you understand the importance of it all. Would that be alright?"

Unsure of herself, Terra nodded anyways and clasped her fingers together in front of her, waiting for him to speak his mind.

"Without the alliance with Valerian, Solaris will fall. There is no way that we can defend our shores against the mercenaries without Valerian's assistance. And when Solaris falls, your family will be slaughtered. They will wipe out every possible Heir to the throne, do you understand? Your duty is to the well-being of your kingdom and its people, is it not?"

Suddenly realizing the magnitude of what he was saying, Terra nodded slowly and her voice came out no louder than a whisper. "Yes, it is."

Councilman Arnett let out a sigh of relief. "Marrying an influential King from a kingdom that would save Solaris would be in the best interest of the realm and for your family. Sharing the throne would only be a small price to pay in the grand scheme of it all. Please, think that over and let us know what you decide. I hope you choose to do the right thing." With a small bow of his head, he departed.

His words invaded Terra's core and she already knew what her choice had to be, for there wasn't any other choice. He was right. Her duty was to her kingdom and to her family. If her sacrifice meant that they would be safe and protected against their enemies, then she had to do it, even if it meant sharing the throne.

After a few more moments, Terra went to find her mother.

Chapter Four
Orion

The arrow flew into the center of the target with such force that a loud *twang* echoed through the trees. Orion lowered the bow, satisfied with the shot.

"Your Highness," a voice said from behind him.

Orion grumbled, but didn't turn around. Instead, he took out another arrow from the quiver resting at his feet and drew the string back with the weapon aimed again at the center of the target. "What do you want, Captain?"

Darren was standing behind him in comfortable clothes and alone. "I received a report from the southern border today that I think you may be interested in hearing."

Another arrow flew into the target on the tree and Orion turned to face Darren. "Well, I don't have all day, what is it?"

"There have been two vicious attacks at two separate homes in the last three weeks. For the first one, the husband returned from hunting in the woods to find his wife and only daughter with their throats slit in their cottage and for the second one, an entire family of five was slaughtered in their sleep."

Orion frowned. Valerian was usually a very quiet realm, one with little to no outward problems. There was only one village that was the center of community in Valerian while the rest of the citizens resided in small cottages with their own acres of land away from others. To hear that there were violent murders taking place was very out of place. "Any idea as to who is behind this?"

"Not yet, Your Highness. It could have been a rivalry or a debt that needed to be paid, but I have my men keeping their ears open to see if anything happens again or if we get any leads."

"Good. If you have more reports of it, let me know. Otherwise, leave me the hell alone." Orion sent another arrow soaring into the red circle.

Darren smirked. The Captain of the guard was not fazed by Orion's mood swings, leaving him the only guard who was not intimidated by the King. "As you wish, Your Highness."

More arrows flew into the target one by one until Orion knew that Darren was long gone. "You'd think he would take a hint by now," he remarked to Silas who was standing watch nearby. The other two were nowhere to be seen, most likely gallivanting through the trees within earshot. He let out one sharp whistle and gathered his bow and arrows to head back to the castle before the sun had completely set in the sky.

He began to follow his worn path through the brush with Silas at his side when Milo and Ash sprang out seemingly from nowhere. Edith was waiting for him when he came into the foyer which he wasn't suspecting.

"A letter for you." Edith held out an envelope with the royal seal of Solaris stamped in wax on the back. "Regarding your new betrothed. I figured it shouldn't wait."

Orion internally flinched at this term. To him, it wasn't a pleasant one. It didn't signify love, compassion, or even harmony. Instead, it simply reminded him of an uncomfortable mundane task that he had to complete and one which he avoided even thinking about. That was all that this was: a task. "Thank you, Edith."

She handed him the letter and looked at him curiously. "Are you sure this is what you wish? You don't have to if you don't want to. I don't want you to do this just because you feel like you would be doing me a favor."

"That's not why I'm doing it," he lied. *That is exactly why I'm doing it,* he wished to say. But he never would. It would break her heart to hear him say it. At least with it being an unspoken thing between them, she could still be excited to have someone else to care for. She was already preparing for her arrival even though it hadn't been confirmed or discussed quite yet.

Already, Edith was preparing one of the many empty grand bedrooms and filling it with dresses and garments of all sizes and types so that the Princess would have anything she could ever need. Edith let it slip the other day that she had requested orders of fabric for her to sew the Princess new dresses and cloaks by her own hand. "I didn't want her to be cold when winter comes," Edith had explained simply. "Solaris is warm year-round. She has likely never experienced a winter like we have here.

And so, Orion allowed it. He would let Edith do whatever made her happy, he owed her at least that much. He didn't need a companion like she did. He didn't need a lover to keep him warm on the cold nights or a wife to dote on him. He would continue to tell himself that he was doing it for Edith, lest he back out on his own decision.

But now wasn't the time to think about that.

"Thank you, I'll read it at once." Orion passed by her while she still regarded him carefully and he went straight to his bedchamber. Inside the room, he had a stone fireplace with a gold-inlaid mirror above the mantlepiece. There was one plush chair in front of the hearth and a large rug that fought off some of the cold of the stone floor. In one corner, there was a simple wooden desk and chair where he kept ink and paper for the few circumstances where he would actually need to compose a letter outside of his study and this was where he left the unopened letter for now.

The four-poster bed in one corner was in a complete disarray. The heavy blankets were thrown heavily to one side and the pillows were knocked off the bed entirely. He usually had sleepless nights, but last night had been particularly bad. His dreams had been plagued by a deep memory that had been lost until the previous night.

The memory had been of the first time that Orion had seen the ocean. Why it had just now surfaced, he wasn't sure, but he suspected it had to do in part with the upcoming alliance with Solaris. The memory came back to him in spurts, the images twisting and filling out his mind's eye until the sense of deja vu became overwhelming.

Orion was scarcely a teenager at the time when his father had insisted that his eldest son travel along with him to a land in the northwest that rested along a cold shore of the ocean. He had been under the impression that it was a diplomatic visit, but when his father and him rode along the crashing shore to a decrepit shack weathered by the salt and the sea, Orion realized that he had been wrong. The memory grew clearer as he pondered it.

The late King of Valerian dismounted his steed and beckoned Orion to follow him as he knocked on the wooden door. Footsteps shuffled from deep within and the door creaked open to reveal a worn looking woman wrapped in dingy shawls. She took one look at the King and the young Prince at his side and a wide grin warped her face. "You received my message I see, please, come in."

"Orion, wait here," his father instructed him and made a step to enter the shack, but the woman held up one gnarled finger.

"Uh, uh, we will need the boy to do what you ask. He comes with."

Gulping down his fear, Orion nodded stiffly and followed them into the small structure. Jars of herbs and oddities lined warped shelves and Orion tried to distinguish what was hiding in the murky liquid while the King exchanged hushed words with the woman.

"Boy, come here," the woman commanded and Orion obliged. She beckoned him and took his hand in her withered one to lead him towards a massive cauldron holding a frothing liquid on a meager fire. Orion looked to his father for reassurance or understanding for what was going on, but the King only avoided his gaze.

"Drink." The woman poured a cup of the white liquid into a tin cup and thrusted it towards Orion.

Now, the King took a step forward. "Please, is this necessary? Do we have to involve the boy?"

"Everything comes with a price," the woman tapped her bony finger on her nose and gestured to Orion once more. "*Drink.*"

Orion wrinkled his nose and poured the liquid into his mouth, expecting it to be warm and possibly sweet, but was surprised to find it ice cold and bitter. He coughed and his throat felt as if it was beginning to swell as the air seemed to be sucked out of his lungs. He fell to his knees as the hacks wracked his body and he was somewhat aware of the King being handed his own cup to drink the liquid too.

Shadows danced at the edges of Orion's vision and the cold creeped deep into his bones. This was it, this is what dying felt like.

But then, as if none of it had happened, the feeling faded and his vision cleared once more until Orion was resting on his stomach on the shack floor. He rose unsteadily to his feet and stared in fear at his father. "What just happened?"

"There is always a price," the woman murmured and let out a soft chuckle. The King handed her a sack heavy with coin. "Pleasure doing business with you, Your Highness."

The memory faded and Orion shivered. Whether from the chill in his chamber, or from the memory, he wasn't sure.

Silas jumped up onto the bed and nosed his way under one of the blankets while Ash and Milo curled up on the rug in front of the fireplace. Orion hung the black cloak on a hook next to the fireplace and then sat in the chair to unlace his well-broken in leather boots. Tossing them aside, he was left in his plain white shirt and his black pants that smelled of trees and fresh air. He quickly lit a fire and grabbed the letter once more.

He sank back into his chair and watched the flames crackle while he contemplated. He wanted to open the letter, but he couldn't make himself do it quite yet so instead he waited impatiently while the room slowly began to warm from the flames. A low hum began suddenly in his ears and caused a sharp pain in his temple that made him instinctively rub the area tenderly.

Ash yawned dramatically and sat up into a stretch before coming to sit at Orion's feet. She looked at him with her deep black eyes and he stroked her mindlessly. "Hi sweetheart," he cooed, and she nuzzled his hand back affectionately. He sighed deeply and ran a hand over the stubble on his jaw. Ash whined and nuzzled the hand which clutched the unopened letter. She made his own impatience seem like a virtue.

"Fine, fine, I'll open it," he said to her and ruffed her ears. She let her tongue flop out in sheer delight and sprawled back in her spot on the rug.

Orion took a letter opener off of his desk and slipped it underneath the wax seal. With one clean cut, he slit open the envelope and took out the parchment inside. Right away,

Orion could tell it was the same man who wrote him the first time judging by his careful scrawl. Orion still believed that it was a bit odd that a councilman had been communicating with him about the arrangements of the betrothal, but not all realms handled diplomatic matters the same way.

He began to read the letter. In it, the councilman gushed about how thrilled he was that Orion had accepted the offer and stated how Solaris was ready to make final arrangements for the marriage at once. Really, they probably just wanted his aid as soon as possible. Towards the end, Orion stopped reading immediately. "'We look forward to your journey here to Solaris for the wedding ceremony and coronation. Let us know a date that works for you and we will make sure preparations are completed by that time. Signed, Councilman Arnett,'" Orion whispered and lowered the letter in disbelief. He couldn't help but laugh.

Travel to Solaris? They must be mad. Not only had Orion agreed to send soldiers to aid them, but he had even promised that no harm would come to their realm and in return they had the audacity to assume he would rule in Solaris. The offer was never to take the throne there, it was to have the Princess rule by his side in Valerian. Why would he give up the throne of his homeland for another in a foreign realm that was extremely warm and extremely busy?

"Foolish girl," he growled angrily and went and put the letter down onto the desk once more. Rage began to grow inside of him and his dogs could sense it. They began to pace and whine uncomfortably as their master paced back and forth himself. "Who do they think they are? Requesting me, *me* to abandon my realm and handle their mess of a kingdom for them? *Imbeciles!*"

The sharp pain in his temple grew as the roaring surged and Orion swept a crystal goblet off the desk's surface along with his ink in a fit of fury. The crystal shattered over the stone floor and the ink grew into a sloppy puddle, but it wasn't enough to quell the anger inside of him. The shadows danced at the edges of the room restlessly and his chest rose and fell rapidly as he surveyed the mess around him. Milo stood to his side with his ears back and he barked once which seemed to break the spell that Orion was under. He let out a shaky breath patted him on the head. He knew he let his emotions get the best of him once again and it never ended well.

"I'm sorry," he said to his dogs. "I'll clean it up." He bent down and started plucking shards of the goblet off of the ground until he felt a sharp prick. Wincing, he pulled his hand away to see droplets of red blood plunking on the stone floor. A deep cut ran along his thumb and forefinger that was already starting to create quite a mess. Orion cursed and went to find Edith even though he already knew she would chastise him. Ash, Milo, and Silas tried to follow him out of his chamber, but he commanded that they stayed and even though they didn't like it, they always obeyed their master.

Not very long after, Orion found her and Laurent in the main foyer chatting until they set their eyes on him. "Orion!" Edith said, startled by the trail of blood that was dripping from his hand and down his forearm. "What on *earth* did you do?"

"A goblet broke, and my ink well, too." Orion held his hand up sheepishly and Laurent immediately grabbed a rag he had in his back pocket to give to Edith. She rushed up the stairs and wrapped it around his hand to soak up the blood.

"Well, why did you go breaking a goblet?" she asked quietly. He wanted to lie, to tell her he didn't do it on purpose, but she could see it in his face that he was angry.

"They want me to go to Solaris," he said quietly. "They expect me to take the throne there."

Edith looked up sharply. Her blue eyes were unreadable for a moment before she went back to tending to his bleeding hand. "And what are you going to tell them?"

"I'm going to tell them no, of course. The Princess will need to live and rule here. That was what the offer was, not this. They approached *me* for an alliance."

"Then tell them that." She smiled softly and lifted the rag away to show that the bleeding had already begun to slow. "Wait here, I'll get the medicinal kit." Edith hurried away and Orion walked down the rest of the stairs to where Laurent was.

He looked weary, most likely from having spent the day preparing the castle and grounds for the icy winter that was on its way. He was an older man, older than Edith and it showed from the hours upon hours he spent outside in the elements. His dark skin was wrinkled from the sun and his hands were slightly gnarled and callused from the hard work that he did.

Laurent's age might fool those who weren't familiar with him, but Orion knew better. Laurent enjoyed the work that he did and wouldn't give it up for anything in the world. Even when Orion offered to help him with more difficult tasks, the soft-spoken man usually declined his assistance and sometimes even let a quick-witted joke slide out with the refusal.

"I hope you know that you have given Edith something she will never stop thanking you for," Laurent said with a conspirator smile. "She has always wanted a family.

"She deserved it." Orion shrugged his kind words off. "It's the least I could do."

"Still." Laurent crossed his arms and winked at him. "You have given her newfound meaning. I don't remember the last time I've seen her this excited. Thank you for that, even though she's dragging me along with her shenanigans in the process."

"Don't mention it," Orion mumbled just as Edith returned with supplies in hand. He didn't mind knowing that he had done something good for her, but he didn't want to have to openly acknowledge it if at all possible. One could claim that he was just being humble, but really it was due to his own selfishness.

"Let's get this bandaged up." Edith opened a jar full of a cream that would promote healing. She slathered that on after she wiped the excess blood off and wrapped gauze around it until it was fully secured in bandages. She patted his wrist not unkindly and gave him a knowing smile. "Let me get you some more ink."

Edith led Orion to a supply closet where she plucked a new inkwell out for him. She had many closets and hiding places like this throughout the castle. She was almost like a squirrel that way and Orion smirked at the comparison. She would constantly have supplies distributed throughout the castle so no matter what one of the three residents, or the many soldiers, might need, she would have inventory of it somewhere.

"Now go write that letter, Your Highness." Edith winked.

Orion nodded and took a deep and calming breath to compose himself before making his way back to his bedchamber where his worried pups were waiting for him. As soon as he walked in, they began to jump on him and yip excitedly. He gave them affection and rubbed their ears until they all finally calmed down.

"I'm okay, I'm okay, hush," he soothed them and, soon enough, they were all laying around his feet while he pulled out a fresh piece of parchment. Dipping a quill in the ink, he hesitated. He didn't know what to say really. As angry and annoyed as he was about this, he also didn't want to fully come across as furious since deep down, the Princess nor the councilman deserved it. Orion didn't have the energy to do it either.

The cries vibrated his eardrums even more harshly and he clutched his head in pain. It was beginning to grow to the point that he was starting to not be able to think straight. After this, it would escalate to him not being able to hear, see, or feel anything except the roaring in his ears. He had to do this now, and he had to do it fast.

Dear Councilman Arnett,
I'm afraid that there has been a misunderstanding here. My offer was not to come to Solaris, but for the Princess to rule with me here in Valerian. My family has ruled here for generations and I am not interested in giving up my throne here in my homeland. If the Princess is not able to rule in Valerian at my side, then I apologize but this agreement will be terminated,

Orion paused to dip the quill again, his mind flashing to the report that Darren had given him. Was traveling going to pose the royal Princess a threat if she travels to Valerian? The last thing he needed was to find that his betrothed had been attacked on the road and have to explain to Solaris how it had happened. There were too many unknowns. Darren himself would need to travel to Solaris to return with the Princess. He would trust no one else, not when crucial trade deals hung in the balance.

With winter fast approaching, Wolf's Pass will soon be too treacherous to journey through and there will be no passage until the spring thaw. I highly suggest that if the Princess will be ruling at my side, that the journey takes place as soon as possible. I will send my quickest messenger who will return with your answer. If this is satisfactory, I will then send my own escorts to Solaris to travel with the Princess to ensure that she is received safely here in Valerian. We do not have the resources, I'm afraid, to allow many extra heads to reside in the castle at such short notice before winter. Once the Princess has safely arrived, I ask that any travel guests return to Solaris.

Orion let out a long sigh and set the quill down. He let the ink dry before picking the parchment up and rereading it. "Firm, but not entirely rude," he said to his dogs and Silas yawned in response. "Nothing is going to change." He picked up the quill one more time, not thinking of anything else to add besides the closing.

If these terms are unsatisfactory or not entirely to your liking, I request a letter be sent at once otherwise I will be expecting company and will dispatch personal escorts as stated above.
With warm regards, King Orion of Valerian

As soon as he set the quill down, pain shot through his temples that made him groan in agony. The souls kept calling, their roaring growing louder and louder in his head until he couldn't take it anymore. He answered.

Chapter Five
Terra

Terra was thoroughly sick of weddings even though she had yet to attend one. Ever since she had announced a week prior to the council and the Queen that she agreed to the union with the King of Valerian, the palace threw themselves into planning the ceremony with such ferocity that even Terra was surprised at the progress.

They still awaited the King's correspondence agreeing to a date, but that didn't slow the preparations one bit. Chefs began to plan the feast, flowers were being groomed and trimmed, some of Solaris's finest tailors were summoned to the palace, and invitations were being drafted to be sent far and wide once a finalized date was selected.

Terra was quickly swept up in the glitzy whirlwind that had seemed to encapsulate everyone. The days blended together and left her barely any time to take a moment to let it all sink in. Each morning for a week straight she awoke groggy and each night she slumped heavy into her bed where she quickly fell into a deep sleep. Whenever it seemed that she might have a free second to catch her breath, she was immediately pulled elsewhere to have the final say on trivial details

The throne room had been transformed into the center for all the preparations. Tables and chairs had been transported in to allow staff members and the royal family some comfort and space to work through everything that was needed. Terra started every morning in this room and would never leave until the moon was in the sky. Some days, she simply forgot to eat or didn't have time to, and, on those days, she was more irritable than normal. Today was one of those days.

"They look the same," Terra said pointedly to the decorator's assistant who was holding out two identical cerulean blue linen napkins. Her stomach grumbled painfully and she ignored it. "Can you just pick one?"

"Your *Highness*, these are most certainly *not* the same!" the gentleman replied, almost offended. "You see this one? This one has a stem stitching while this one has a simple, yet elegant, backstitch. They are entirely different."

Terra sighed and pointed to the first one he had help up. "Then we'll just use that one." The decorator scurried off with a small *humph* and Terra rubbed the bridge of her nose wearily. *Sacrifices are needing to be made,* she reminded herself. Before long, another voice called out to summon her.

"Your Highness." A young handmaiden approached her and bowed.

"Yes?"

"We have finished samples of centerpieces for the feast. We would like your approval on a final design."

Terra let out another long sigh. "Okay, let's see what you have."

The handmaid led her through the throng of bustling people hovering around tables and carrying fabrics, glassware, flowers, and gods know what else between places. At a table at the far side of the room sat three versions of centerpieces. The first was a tall clear vase filled with decorative branches complemented by a spattering of orchids while the second was a simple golden vase with a blue and white bouquet that would sit low on the table. The third option caught Terra's eyes though, so she made the easy choice.

"This one." She touched the glass lantern delicately. Inside was a simple candle and placed around the lantern flat on the table were blue and white orchids.

"Wonderful choice, Your Highness, I will let them know this is the version you want."

A soft hand touched one of Terra's arms and she turned to find Cassi. "It's time for your fitting. The Queen is already waiting."

Together, the girls left the throne room and made their way to the second floor where a dressing room was held. Mostly, it was used for special events when one of the Princesses needed to be fitted for a new gown, so it was already prepared for such instances with mirrors, plush benches, and a place for supplies to be kept whenever a tailor might need the space.

Waiting for Terra already was the Queen, one of the most notable tailors in Solaris, and Arla. Arla was sitting on a bench swinging her legs beneath her aimlessly while the Queen was discussing a long piece of fabric that the tailor held in his hands. Arla had been thrilled when Terra told her about the marriage arrangement, as were her other sisters. They were finally being given a brother, they had joked with her. They didn't know the extent of it, however, and Terra wished it to remain that way. She rather them be excited for her upcoming nuptials instead of fearing for their own lives as the threat of war looms ever closer.

The Queen smiled when she saw Cassi and Terra enter the room. "There she is! I was afraid that you had gone missing."

"I was only lost among all the people in the throne room." Terra gave her a tight smile and kissed her mother on the cheek. She tried to be happy, even if it was for her mother's sake, but she was finding it rather difficult. "Will this be the last fitting?"

"What do you think Fernando?" the Queen asked the tailor. He was taking the wedding gown off of the mannequin and looked at it carefully.

"I think this will be the last one I will need," he agreed and motioned for Terra to step behind the divider in the corner. There, she stripped off her current clothes and Fernando helped her to slip on the overlapping fabrics. Arla, Cassi, and the Queen "oohed" and "awed" as Fernando helped Terra out from behind the divider and onto a circular platform facing the mirror. He fluffed out the skirts and allowed everyone to drink it in. It was created in the common chiton style of white linen robes, except this was far more precious than an everyday ensemble.

The wedding dress was clasped at Terra's shoulder with a bright gold brooch. It draped diagonally down her body, around her waist, and up her back to clasp together at the shoulder. The pieces were perfectly positioned to allow free movement in her arms and to show off most of her back. The trim was a beautiful gold pattern that matched the brooch at her shoulder, both details contrasting the stark white of the dress. There was enough fabric left that trailed long behind her to create an astounding train to the masterpiece.

"I think we're just missing one final touch," Queen Clio said and took the crown off of her own head before placing it upon Terra's. "This will be one of the most beautiful days of your life. You will be one of the realm's most honored rulers and I'm so proud of you." Terra grasped the Queen's hand and gave it an emotional squeeze. Little did the Queen know, Terra was fighting down the bile that rose in her throat. She wasn't ready to rule, not yet. But she didn't have a choice.

"Does this mean I get Terra's tiara?" Arla spoke up and everyone laughed, even Terra.

"Yes Arla, you would be able to take my tiara when I am crowned Queen."

A soft knock on the door startled the group and it opened to reveal the head councilman. "Councilman Arnett," the Queen said in surprise. "To what do we owe the pleasure?"

The councilman coughed uncomfortably when he saw Terra on the podium in her wedding attire. "I apologize for the interruption, Your Highness, but I am afraid that this could not wait. May we have a word in private?"

The Queen looked at him quizzically, but obliged. "Please, continue without me. I shall be back shortly."

Fear began to overcome Terra. She tried to focus on Fernando placing a pin here and a pin there as he went through final touches, but she couldn't focus. Was something wrong? Was there an attack? Were they too late?

Her heart began to beat faster and her palms felt sweaty, but she knew that if she had the gall to wipe them on Fernando's masterpiece, she would never hear the end of it.

"Fin!" Fernando shouted and did one last look around. "How do you feel?"

Terra snapped out of her thoughts just enough to give him a reassuring smile. "I love it, you did an amazing job once again."

"We'll get it back onto the mannequin and you can be on your way, Your Highness."

Once she was back in her normal attire, Arla gave her a kiss on the cheek and ran off to cause trouble elsewhere while Cassi and Terra left Fernando to finish up whatever he needed to. The two girls made it barely down the hall before a young boy, no older than twelve, caught them. "Your Highness, the Queen has requested your presence in her bedchamber."

Terra's heart skipped a beat. *Something* was *wrong.* "Thank you, I shall go there at once," she told the boy and turned to Cassi. "I'll let you know what happens."

Terra and Cassi parted ways and she went to her mother's bedchamber. When she walked in, Queen Clio was seated on one of her chairs and Councilman Arnett was standing tall with his hands behind his back. A sheen of nervous sweat covered the back of his neck.

"Princess Terra, thank you for joining us."

"What's going on?" Terra asked. They shared a glance, but neither said a word. "Was there an attack?"

"Oh, no, Your Highness. Nothing of the sort."

"Then what's the problem? Did Valerian back out?"

"No, the arrangement is still in place. That's not what the problem is."

Terra held out her hands and looked at Councilman Arnett and then Queen Clio. "Then what's the issue here?"

"Oh, just spit it out," the Queen grumbled and crossed her arms across her chest in an informal way that Terra rarely would see.

"There was a bit of...miscommunication in regard to the arrangement," Councilman Arnett grimaced.

"What type of miscommunication? Like about when the wedding would be? If we have to push it off, then that's fine."

Councilman Arnett cleared his throat. "Uh, no. There was miscommunication about *where* the ceremonies would take place."

"Is it customary to do the wedding in Valerian? That's fine with me, we can host the wedding there and come back to do the coronation here when the time comes."

The Queen sighed and threw Councilman Arnett an aggravated look before approaching Terra. "Honey, what he is trying to say is that there will not be a wedding or a coronation here. King Orion had agreed for you to be crowned Queen of Valerian, not to rule together here in Solaris. I will be remaining on the throne."

"Wh-what?" Terra asked in bewilderment. "But you said..." She pointed an accusatory finger at the advisor. "I don't understand." Terra floundered for the words to express what she was feeling, but none came. "How did this happen?"

"That is exactly what I would like to know." The Queen turned to face Councilman Arnett and her expression turned to ice. She was no longer Terra's mother, but instead she was the furious Queen of Solaris. "This is an egregious error; how did this happen?"

"Your Highness." Councilman Arnett began to sweat profusely and his voice warbled as he spoke. "It was indeed an egregious error on my part and I do ask for not only your forgiveness, but Princess Terra's forgiveness as well. None of the council members had realized what happened until we received correspondence from King Orion today."

"Is there any way to fix this? To convince him otherwise?"

"King Orion made it very clear in his letter. Either the Princess agrees to rule with him in Valerian, or the arrangement will be nulled." Councilman Arnett turned to face Terra with a grave, yet hopeful, expression on his face. "Princess Terra, what is your decision?"

"I—" Terra's mouth clamped back shut. Her mind flashed back to her conversation with the councilman in the gardens a week prior. *They will wipe out every possible Heir to the throne, do you understand? Your duty is to the well-being of your kingdom and its people, is it not? Sharing the throne would only be a small price to pay in the grand scheme of it all.* She took a deep breath. "My duty is still to my kingdom and my family. How long until I have to leave?"

"Within a week, I would assume. Any later and the journey won't happen until the spring thaw. The path is impassable in the winter. Once Valerian receives our letter, they will dispatch an escort to take you there safely."

"Okay, then we will need to arrange this quickly. I trust that you will be able to coordinate this so that I may spend my final days with my family?"

"Of course, Your Highnesses. I am at your disposal."

"Is there anything else I will need to know?" Her own words sounded false in her ears.

The councilman lifted a handkerchief to his brow and dabbed away some of the nervous sweat that resided there. "Yes, Your Highness. King Orion had made it clear that you may travel with an entourage as is customary for us, but they will need to return to Solaris once you arrive there safely. Your handmaid included."

This was unexpected. Not only was she to leave her home and family, but she couldn't even keep Cassi with her there? "That seems a bit odd. A Queen with no lady in waiting?"

"King Orion had stated that with winter coming, they would be unable to get enough necessary supplies to make it through the winter with so many people in the castle. He assured me that any needs of yours will be provided for, however."

"I see. Get to work then, I shall leave in two days." Terra turned on her heel and exited the room before either the councilman or the Queen could realize how badly her hands were shaking. *What have I gotten myself into?*

Excusing herself, Terra made her way slowly and calmly out of the bedroom and headed straight for the gardens. As she grew closer, the panic in her chest began to grow as well until she was running. She burst through the palace doors and immediately hid as deep into the gardens that she could manage. Once again, she was in the same situation she was a week prior when the council announced that she would have to marry. Only now, it was much, much worse. Once she collapsed beneath a pomegranate tree, she dug her hands into the rich soil. Tears streamed down her face and sobs wracked her chest so hard that she felt like she had stopped breathing.

There she stayed until the sobs finally faded and her breathing finally began to get under control. Her skirts were now filthy from the dirt but at this point, she really didn't care. She could feel her hair frizzing from sweat and she knew she looked like a mess. The thought almost made her laugh. She wondered what King Orion would think of her if he saw her now.

Terra laughed to herself and wiped her swollen eyes. "Gods, I'm ridiculous," she muttered to herself. "Everyone meet the illustrious Queen Terra. What a joke." Grabbing a fist full of soil, she tossed it angrily in front of her. Sighing, she lowered herself flat on her back in the grass and looked up through the leaves of the pomegranate tree at the bright blue sky without a single cloud.

Terra took another weary breath in and contemplated taking a nap right then and there, for the exertion of the past week left her exhausted, except a strong breeze picked up. It shook the branches and the leaves until a single pomegranate was cut loose. It suddenly fell towards Terra and before she even could process what was happening, it struck the ground a mere two inches from her face. She sat up and stared at it.

Terra couldn't shake the feeling the fates were taunting her or trying to teach her a lesson that she can't control the uncontrollable. That's when the idea hit her. "But I can control the controllable," she whispered. No, this turn of events weren't ideal. In fact, this was absolutely devastating. But this was all bigger than her, and she needed to embrace it and make the best of the situation. She would never forgive herself if she refused the proposal and her family paid the price of her refusal.

My duty is to my kingdom and to my family, she reminded herself, and nothing was going to change that.

The next week flew by faster than Terra could have ever imagined. She spent every second she could with her sisters, Cassi, and her mother but it still wasn't enough in the end. When she had broken the heart wrenching news to her sisters, Arla and Marci began crying while Calli held it together despite the tears Terra could see threatening to fall. They were beside themselves, insisting on sleeping in the same bed like they used to as kids all the way through Terra's final night in Solaris.

Terra didn't mind it though, it gave her a reason to keep herself composed when she feared that she might just crack into a million little pieces. She was lost without her sisters, she knew that. What she didn't know was how to be apart from them. *Or to be a Queen of an unknown realm,* she told herself almost bitterly. She couldn't help herself. With each passing hour, she couldn't help but feel resentment towards the King she had yet to even meet.

Her final morning in Solaris was the hardest. The escort unit had arrived the prior evening and was a formidable group of iron clad soldiers that put even their own palace guards to shame. The Captain, Darren was his name, led the entire military for Valerian and stated that he was there as a show of good faith from King Orion himself.

"We offer only the best for our future Queen," he had said daringly and knelt down on one knee when he had been introduced to Terra. She hadn't wanted to like him, for he was a painful reminder of the sacrifice that she was making, but his smile and humor was so infectious that it was difficult not to return his charming grin. Even when she dared to request that they don't leave right away in the morning so that she could have one more final meal with her family, he was more than happy to oblige.

Terra ate one final breakfast in the dining hall the next morning with her sisters and her mother as if everything was normal, but they all knew that it was far from normal. As soon as they finished eating, she would be whisked away in a carriage, possibly to never be seen again.

Her sisters and her all held hands as they walked with Queen Clio to the front of the palace where the parade of carriages was waiting. There were easily a few dozen Valerian soldiers that would journey with them along with two supply wagons full of gift offerings from Solaris. Then there was one lonely carriage in the middle of it all where Terra would have Cassi for company. At least, until they reached Valerian where she would then have to leave.

They all said their goodbyes, each sister wishing her well and giving her one last hug goodbye. When it came to her mother though, Terra held her the tightest.

"You will be the most wonderful Queen," the Queen whispered in her ear. "You are beautiful, smart, and such a compassionate woman. I am so proud of you Terra." She pulled away and ran her hand through Terra's hair one last time. "Have a safe journey and write to us. You will do great things and I cannot wait to hear all about it."

"I will." Terra sniffled and the carriage driver opened the carriage door to reveal Cassi waiting for her. Terra looked at the door hesitantly until Cassi gave her a comforting smile. Only then did she climb the stairs and allow the guard to close the door behind her. Through the window, she watched as the carriage pulled away and her family grew smaller. They clattered out of the palace gates and headed in the direction opposite of the shining sea.

There's no going back now, Terra thought as Solaris shrunk behind her until it had disappeared completely.

Chapter Six
Orion

"If Edith asks me one more time about what she should serve for dinner the first night that the Princess is here, I swear I'll go into the woods and never come back," Orion grunted as he lifted a large bale of hay off a cart and walked it past Laurent to stack it in the back storage area of the stables. The older man leaned on the handle of a pitchfork while watching Orion help him with the heavy bales so he could take a quick break.

"She's enjoying herself," he said pointedly. "Let her have this. She may never have the chance to dote on someone again and this is what she always believed was her purpose in life. You make it hard enough for her to dote on, just be glad her attention is turned away from you for once."

Orion slapped down the other bale onto the stack and wiped a hand over his face. His shirt was already drenched through from the strain. "I told her when I accepted the proposal that nothing is going to change."

"She'll make sure it does change, if she has any say. Just you wait." Laurent grinned and winked at him.

Orion scowled and hefted the final bale with another grunt. "I say one thing and she insists on doing the opposite. Why do women have to be so damn insufferable all the time?"

Laurent chuckled. "Oh son, you have no idea."

Just when he stacked the final bale of hay, two of his soldiers walked into the stables and stood at attention. "Your Highness," one spoke up nervously.

Orion huffed and swiped his damp hair back irritably. "What do you want? Can't you see that I'm busy?"

"All of Valerian's foot soldiers have been amassed and are awaiting the final command to depart for Solaris," the soldier said.

"Are you who was left in charge in the Captain's absence?"

"Yes, Your Highness."

"Then get the units to Solaris immediately and don't screw it up before the Captain returns, got it? The last thing I want is to get a late night report that my men are brawling with one another or that a patrol is lost in the woods somewhere."

"Yes, Your Highness."

Orion turned his attention away from the two soldiers, expecting them to leave at once, but instead they hovered awkwardly. "What is it?" he snapped. "Out with it."

This time, the other soldiers spoke. He trembled ever so slightly and Orion didn't recognize his face as anyone of importance. *Must be fresh meat*, Orion thought almost wryly. He pushed down the urge to intentionally intimidate the green soldier more than he already was. "There has been another report of an attack from the northern outpost. A gentleman went to call on his newly married daughter and her husband, but he found him in the barn and her in the cottage. There were no other witnesses, but there were tracks."

"Assemble a patrol at once to follow them. I want them found. I will not tolerate this senseless brutality among my people. Notify me at once when they are tracked down and, in the meantime, I want all prior reports to be placed in my study." Orion pinched the bridge of his nose when the soldiers nodded in understanding, but still didn't make a move to leave. "That means *go*." They both scrambled into motion and quickly left the stables. "*Idiots,*" Orion grumbled and turned to Laurent. "I take back what I said earlier, it's not just women that happen to be so frustratingly difficult."

"I know naught of being a King," Laurent sighed and heaved the pitchfork he was leaning against so that he could place it against the newly stacked hay. "But I must admit. I find the information of these horrific murders quite disturbing."

"I do as well. It must be stopped and the guilty need to be punished. I won't have my people live in such brash fear in their own homes." Orion's expression darkened.

"And that is what makes you a fine King."

Orion shot him an unamused look. "You only say that because you're old."

"I may be old, but that doesn't mean I'm unwise." Laurent chuckled and wagged a finger at him. "Now stop distracting me from my work. My boss is a damned jerk if I fall behind on my duties."

Orion couldn't help but grin and say, "As you wish, old man."

Once outside, the three wolfdogs came bounding from their spot where they had been digging a hole along the side of the stable. They were muddy and filthy from their escapades and Orion groaned. "Edith will have my head, is that what you three wanted?"

Not paying him any mind, they tore off back to the castle and Orion started to set on after them, but a deep pull in his gut made him pause. His instincts sensed that he was not alone, but when he turned around, there was no one else to be seen on the castle grounds. He frowned and turned his eyes to the tree line in the distance. Almost expecting to see someone, a soldier or patrol perhaps, to appear from within its confines, but he was confounded when no one showed.

He was just about to continue to the castle when a strong breeze halted him. It ravaged through the branches and the leaves to knock down the last of the leaves which then fell to the ground, but still no one was to be seen. Despite this, he knew better than to think he was indeed truly alone.

Without another glance, Orion trekked after his dogs while praying to the gods that Edith wouldn't smother him in his sleep for the mess he was about to inflict on her floors. Trying to be quiet, Orion and the dogs entered into the grand foyer and he began to nearly tiptoe towards his bedchambers. He had just made it to the stairs when a loud clearing of one's throat sounded behind him. He turned slowly to find Edith standing with her arms crossed and taking in the muddy paw prints that already made a path from the door to the staircase.

"I was just going to give them a bath, I swear," Orion implored.

Edith shook her head in disappointment, but he could see the faint trace of a smile hinting on her lips. "Here are the reports you requested," she said instead of reprimanding him and handed him a stack of paper that had been tucked neatly under her arm. She started to walk away after he took them from her and she called over her shoulder, "And I expect you to not make too much a mess so soon before our guest will arrive. The messenger that was sent ahead reported that they would be here in three day's time."

"Of course," he called after her, but she had already disappeared around a corner and was long gone. "See?" he said to Milo, who was wagging his tale excitedly while his two siblings were already racing back up the stairs. "You got me in trouble. Now let's give you three a much-needed bath."

Nearly an hour later and after the dogs managed to make a soapy mess of the bathing room in his room, Orion had finally been able to change into cleaner clothes and make it to his study with the reports from the border patrols. He sank into his desk chair with a heavy sigh, suddenly feeling much more weary than usual. The sun had already set and he lit the single lantern that threw dancing shadows across the walls and across the bookshelves.

The air was eerie and made Orion shift in his spot but he pushed the feeling away to focus on the papers before him. In explicit detail from the patrol's own mouths, the ghastly scene was presented before him. He could imagine himself there and saw it with his own eyes. Orion could see how the door was splintered and broken as if someone had kicked it in and he could see the furniture and belongings in disarray as the intruder chased the wife through the cottage. It wasn't until the intruder had her cornered in the bedroom against the window that he finally struck. Her remains had been left as is and the splatter of blood across the window and wall finished the barbaric painting of the gruesome attack.

The patrol noted that with how the cottage was in disarray, it almost appeared as if the wife had answered the door, but then tried to close it again for some reason. They also mentioned that it appeared that the husband had been attacked first, for if he had heard the scream of his wife, he would have went running towards her. Instead, he was found in a horse's stall nearly beheaded as if he had been attacked from behind unknowingly. The horses were all left as is, although incredibly spooked.

The most peculiar part of the attack was the knife that had been found near the wife's body coated in blood. At first the patrol had assumed it was her own until another soldier pointed to a spot outside the cottage where a bloodied handprint was seen along the exterior wall. From there, they could track a trail of blood away from the cottage and heading more east. There, the report ended. There wasn't another update on catching the culprit until Orion's men followed the trail unto its end. He grimaced and turned his attention to a detailed map of Valerian he had rolled up within the confines of the desk.

Rolling it out across the surface of the desk, Orion held the sides down with the lantern and the inkwell before marking out where the attack had happened according to the reports as well as the direction that the trail had been traveling. The northernmost parts of Valerian were full of treacherous ravines and steep mountains that many chose not to reside in. The cottage had been among this terrain and east of it rested nothing but open forest and the eastern border. From his knowledge, most of the Valerians resided south of the castle and to the west, mainly away from the foothills of the mountains. So where was the culprit heading? Unless there was a hideout somewhere, there was nothing that immediately stuck out as a possibility.

Orion set down the papers and rubbed his eyes. Something about these attacks didn't sit well with him, but he couldn't distinguish why. It was as if the problem was taunting him, teasing him to place the puzzle pieces in place and discover some great untold truth, but he was failing to do so. Perhaps if his mind was sharper and he wasn't so distracted with the Princess's arrival he would be able to piece it all together.

Already the Princess was making waves in the normal confines of his life and his role as King when she hadn't even arrived yet. He couldn't imagine what else her presence would manage to change, but he knew wholeheartedly that he would have none of it. So what if she arrived in three more days, it didn't matter to him nor should it for her coming here wasn't to impact him at all, but only Edith because she chose to let it.

Even the idea of having a spoiled Princess walk his halls made him irritated. He knew that he should give her the benefit of the doubt, for she might be satisfied with staying out of his way if he stayed out of hers, but he couldn't help but assume the worst. In his mind, he imagined a young woman that has been told she was beautiful all her life, so she never had to put in any real work. The imagined Princess was constantly flocked by her royal court so that she could be validated and complimented at every moment of every day. This version craved jewels and dresses and any other materialistic want that she could get her hands on.

But she's not her. The thought struck Orion and he scrambled to his feet. Without meaning to, he was comparing this stranger to her and he was already preparing himself to deal with someone who was conceited and entitled. A heavy cloud of regret settled upon his shoulders and he couldn't help but wince at the overwhelming feeling. He told himself for so long that he would never do this again, to never give in and to live by himself in the way that he so wished. For years, Edith had pestered him about it and he had continued to put his foot down about it until now. But why now? Why suddenly did he have a change of heart and do this for Edith's benefit?

He truly didn't know. It could have been the small grain of optimism that rested deep within him that thought maybe finally giving in would reap its benefits. Or, it could have been the voice in his mind saying that his Mother would have been disappointed in him if he hadn't helped the realm in need, when he was more than capable of giving them the aid that they so desperately needed.

Orion abruptly stood up and pulled himself out of the swirling maze of his own mind. He didn't want to think about his mother, he simply refused especially after the terrible nightmares that have been plaguing him as of late. This endless thinking would only make him irritable and snippy which, mixed with the exhaustion plaguing his body, would be a horrific combination for anyone that might cross his path yet this evening.

I should just go to bed, Orion told himself and went to gather all the reports into a neat pile that stood out among the strewn about documents still resting on the desk. He went to blow out the lantern when something in his peripheral vision made him pause. The shadows that the lantern was splashing along the wall were morphing and twisting until they seemed to form a corporeal figure made of shadows. Orion could see the barest of outlines in the shoulders and the head, but the facial features were nonexistent. The figure stayed where it was and didn't make any move towards him.

"What do you want?" Orion asked, any hint of friendliness or warmness in his voice was completely absent. He straightened so that he was no longer bending over the lantern in order to glare at the figure now in his study. "You should know better than to appear here uninvited."

Your Majesty, the figure's voice grated in Orion's mind. *You are needed at once.*

"I will come when I chose to." Orion crossed his arms. "You do not summon me; I am not a dog. I am your King, and you will treat me as such."

The figure seemed to cock its head. *I mean you no disrespect, Your Highness. I merely am trying to tell you that you are much needed there.*

As if the figure had opened a floodgate, the whispers began quiet and slowly grew louder and louder until Orion's vision began to blur before him. The room rocked one way, and then the other. He clutched at his head and gritted his teeth. They were angry and distressed, but why? "What have you done? They weren't like this last time."

I have done nothing, Your Highness. I am a lowly messenger, trying to pass along their cries for their King.

"This will wait, or you will feel my wrath. Be gone!" But the figure remained and refused to dissipate back into the far reaches of the room. Orion blew out the lantern swiftly and it was gone. Trying to maintain his composure, Orion hurried out of his study and back to his bedchamber where his dogs barely roused at his approach from their sleeping spots strewn about the room. He closed the door behind him and tried to steady his breathing. The voices were still there, still insistent but he didn't want to answer. Not now, not when he was so tired, and he had so much else currently in his day that was trying to fight to steal his attention.

He feared he didn't have the strength to maintain control, he realized. Usually, he never faltered in his power or his confidence but with so much going on, he wasn't entirely sure that he could manage it now. So he had to hide, at least for now.

Orion held the voices at bay while he stripped off his boots and his socks, his pants and his shirt until he was in nothing except his undergarments. Even when he crawled under the covers of his bed and his dogs all pounced on him to fight for their own space in the bed, he held strong.

Even as he began to doze off, he managed to hold strong against the wave pushing against the barrier in his mind. There were no cracks, no dents, no damage whatsoever. He was powerful. He was their King. Orion was a force to be reckoned with, and he wasn't going to let them forget that.

But once he fell asleep, the wall came crashing down. His dreams were flooded and they became warped nightmares that plagued him through all hours of the night.

He dreamt of his mother, this time she was beautiful and alive and breathing.

"Orion," she said, her voice familiar and foreign all at the same time.

"Mom?" Orion took a step closer to her but stopped. "Are you real? Is - Is this real? Are you really here?"

"Why didn't you save me?"

Orion took another step. "I couldn't. Mom, I couldn't do it. If there was any way, I would have I swear it."

"You could have stopped your father that day at the beach. You let him do this to us, to *me*. Only you could have stopped him from making that choice."

"No, no," Orion shook his head fervently and tried to reach out to his mother, but she only seemed to travel farther away. "I didn't know what he was doing. I was a kid, I didn't know any better! How could I have stopped him when I never knew the consequences of it?"

"You should have found a way. You should have done something." Her voice grew angrier now. "You could have saved me! But you let me rot!" Her face changed now. Gone was the beautiful woman who sang him lullabies and played the piano while she sang with him. In her place was the faceless figure with its scratching voice that pierced his brain every time it spoke. "YOU COULD HAVE SAVED HER," it screeched, and the shadows flew closer to him.

Orion stumbled back and fell backwards hard. He continued to scramble backwards as the frightful figure came for him.

"YOU LET HER DIE! IT'S ALL YOUR FAULT. YOU WILL PAY FOR THE REST OF YOUR PITIFUL EXISTENCE!"

A sob broke out of Orion's chest. "I didn't do it, it's not my fault. I didn't know what Dad was doing. It's not my *fault!*"

"Orion?"

He turned and saw his mother once more directly behind him. He got to his feet. She was so close to him that he could simply reach out and touch her but when he tried, his hand fell through into open air. He spun around and called for her all while the tears pricked at his eyes and the desperation clawed at his chest. But she was gone, just like she was in reality.

A painful roar ripped out of his chest and he awoke drenched in sweat. The dogs all lifted their heads with their ears pricked up, but they only watched as Orion untangled himself from his sheets. Tears that he had shed while asleep were now dried on his cheeks, but his throat still felt raw. His heart beat furiously in his chest and he paced while trying to regain control of his emotions. Guilt still ravaged him and he couldn't stop seeing his mother's face as she told him it was his fault.

Your fault. Your fault. Your fault.

Master. The whisper tickled at his mind and he closed his eyes. They would never let him sleep, not unless he did what they asked. They would attack as soon as he fell asleep, just like they already had. There was never going to be a reprieve from this. It would never cease to exist and he would forever be bound to their will.

In that moment, Orion had never felt so damaged.

Chapter Seven
Terra

"Is it ever going to stop raining?" Terra huffed and sank deeper into her seat. "It hasn't stopped in four days and it's freezing out."

"At this rate, I don't think so," Cassi responded and peered out through the carriage window. They were deep in the forest now, passing thick tree trunks and foliage that made visibility almost impossible. They were far from the sea now and far from the warmth of the south.

After nearly six days of traveling, the caravan still hadn't arrived. Heavy rains made the roads muddy and slick and slowed them down immensely. The air grew colder around them as the altitude got higher. They finally found themselves close to the southern border of Valerian yesterday and managed to cross early this morning, but they still wouldn't reach the castle until sometime tomorrow.

Terra was dirty, tired, and sick of sleeping in a makeshift canvas tent when there weren't any nearby inns for them to spend the night. There hadn't even been a place where she could buy clothes that offered more warmth than her thin garments did, resulting in her constantly being chilled and frozen.

"We shouldn't be too much farther from the village. Jasper said we should reach there later this afternoon if we pass out of the rainstorm," Cassi added and let the curtain fall back to cover the window.

Terra smirked. "Oh yeah? Is that all Jasper said?"

Cassi turned bright red and bit her lip. "Yes, that is all he said." Terra knew her friend well enough to know that she had a massive crush on one of the younger guards traveling with them, and she suspected he had one on her.

"I certainly hope he's right; I need a cloak if this is what the weather is going to be like. The carriage stopped rocking beneath them and Terra frowned. "We can't be there already, can we?" She opened the door to the carriage and was preparing to step out when the carriage driver appeared before her.

"Your Highness, please." He took an already sodden wool blanket from his driving spot and draped it across the mud to offer some reprieve from the filth. He held out his hand and helped Terra to a dry spot under a low hanging tree branch.

"What is going on?" she asked the driver and Cassi appeared behind her shivering.

"The carriages are being slowed down due to the current weather conditions. We're going to have you both ride ahead in order to get to the village quicker."

Darren appeared then as if he was summoned, sopping wet despite the cloak he wore to defend against the elements. "We'll split up and put you on a horse. There is a dry cloak we can give you until we can buy new attire for you in the village."

"You want Her Highness to ride a horse? In this weather?" Cassi asked incredulously and gestured at the rain falling down.

"It will allow us to get to the inn far quicker than we would if we had you remain with the carriages. Do you have any objection, Your Highness?"

Terra put a hand up. "No, that is alright. May I have the cloak?"

Darren left and shortly returned with a thin blue cloak that had just enough room to wrap it around her bare shoulders. She put the hood up and followed Darren to two plain brown mares. Their small group that would trek on horseback consisted only of the two women and six mounted guards. With a helpful hand, Terra and Cassi climbed into the saddles and the group set off at a brisk pace.

The cold seeped into her bones as the fat drops continued to cascade around them. The silence was deafening between the members of the group and it made Terra readjust restlessly in her saddle. She needed a distraction or to take her mind off how uncomfortable and how chilled she currently was. Spurring her horse quicker, she rode beside Darren.

"Tell me Captain. What should I expect when we arrive to the castle?"

"I apologize, Your Highness, but I don't believe that I am the right person to ask about that."

"You won't allow me any insight into what my future King is like? How cruel of you." Terra faltered back into silence, disappointed that he wouldn't give her any details. "I just wish we were there already. This journey has been a long one."

"I promise we will reach the village soon."

Terra remained silent and gave up on trying to wean anything else from the stoic Captain. Their group eventually crested a hill and revealed the edge of a cobblestone road ahead leading into the village. She was soaked to the bone and had to fight the urge to spur her horse into a speedy gallop until she reached the inn.

The village was quiet in comparison to Solaris. There were very few people out and about in the rain that was filling the cracks of the road and if they were, their heavy cloaks were pulled tightly over their heads to fend off the cold. A fine mist was hovering above the town and gave Terra an eerie sensation. Whereas the buildings in Solaris were bleached white from the sun and smoothed down by the salt in the wind over time, the buildings in Valerian were wooden structures and the town was full of hues of brown, black, and a bleak gray. No one looked their way as they clattered by, even though the guards looked even more out of place than what she did.

They rode past what appeared to be a tavern. Terra's eyes were drawn to the building from the boisterous noise echoing from inside and the thick smoke floating up through the chimney that only meant that there had to be a toasty fire inside. The front door flew open and a large man fell on his face on the road to reveal an angry woman behind him with her hands on her hips.

"You come in here again, I'll skin your hide, you hear?" she belted out before slamming the door again. The man groaned and stumbled back to his feet.

"It seems like a quaint town," Cassi mumbled and Terra grinned.

"It sure does." This place was clearly very different than her home and it made her want to explore. She wanted to meet the people, see the shops and secret nooks that the town had to offer.

They finally came to the inn and Darren helped her to dismount before shuffling the two women inside while the guards kept the horses. As soon as they were inside, Terra draped her drenched cloak tighter around her shoulder and took the soaked hood off.

"Wait here by the fire," Darren instructed and disappeared. Terra and Cassi gratefully sidled up to the fireplace without a word. The brick fireplace appeared sturdy and strong, the brick detail trailing up the wall and all the way to the ceiling. The room was lit by square lanterns and Terra could smell something cooking from further inside that made her stomach growl painfully.

Darren returned with an older woman who peered down at them through her clear spectacles. She had her grey hair pulled back into a soft bun and wore a long-sleeved gown that brushed the top of her leather boots peeking out from beneath the hem. She wore a shawl around her shoulders and appeared kind and warm.

"I will show you to your room, please follow me," the lady said and gestured for the girls to follow her and she led them up a creaky staircase to the second level. She opened one of the doors with a silver key to reveal two simple beds adorned with thick quilts. A circular woven rug covered the floor and a single window offered them a meager view of the town below. A small door led to their own bathroom with a clawfoot tub. Overall, it wasn't as exquisite as a palace, but Terra loved it all the same.

"Dinner will be served in the dining hall at 5 o'clock and breakfast will be available at sunrise as well. I will be back shortly with water for washing, I'm sure you want to fight off the cold. Please let me know if you need anything else." The innkeeper smiled sweetly and turned to leave.

Cassi immediately busied herself with lighting a fire while Terra watched the few villagers below from the single window. Once the flames were roaring, Terra gratefully sat on the rug directly in front of the flames and Cassi set their cloaks out on the two wooden chairs in the corner to dry.

Terra wrapped herself in towels after bathing a short while later and lounged in front of the fire while Cassi cleaned herself up. Just as Cassi was finishing, a knock at the door sounded and it was Darren having returned with the few belongings from the saddle bags plus a multitude of warmer Valerian clothes he had managed to acquire for them. He stated that he would see them downstairs at dinner and left them outside the door where Cassi could reach out and quickly snatch the parcels inside before anyone could see.

Finally warm and dressed in a long-sleeved cotton dress and leather boots suited for the rainy weather, Terra felt at peace. The clothes were a far cry from the light linen material that they wore in Solaris. The thick layers insulated her much to her surprise and the muted green color blended in with the dreary weather outside. The feel of the sleeves and the flowing skirts were foreign to her, but not entirely uncomfortable. "Now I just need a warm meal in my belly and I'll be happy," she said to Cassi and Cassi sighed dreamily.

"I wonder what they're making downstairs."

"What do Valerian people eat?" Terra realized she knew next to nothing about the culture of the realm. Certainly her kingdom and Valerian had to have their separate customs and culture, one being a port city and the other being a mountainous village, but how different could they be really be?

Cassi shrugged. "Beats me, I guess we'll have to find out. As long as it's not a dog or a horse, I think we'll be okay."

"Gross." Terra made a face at the image.

The time passed quickly and the girls nearly raced down their hall and down the stairs to the dining room on the first floor when it was time for dinner. Wooden tables were arranged neatly in the room and another roaring hearth made the space a comfortable temperature. Other travelers were already seated and talking amongst themselves. There were mostly men, Terra realized, but she could spot at least three other women among the group.

At a far end of the room the innkeeper was scooping out bowls of the stew and handing them to folks already in line and waiting. Without wasting another second, Terra stood in line and Darren and Cassi weren't too far behind her.

"Thank you," Terra said to the innkeeper when she handed her a bowl with a slab of homemade bread on the side.

"You're welcome, darling."

The trio scouted an empty table in the back corner and set their meals down to dig in. Terra ate and ate until she felt that her belly would burst. It was a thick and hearty stew with herbs, vegetables, and a savory meat source that could have been a dog or horse for all she knew, but she wouldn't have even cared. She mopped up the remaining juices with her slice of bread and sat back in satisfaction.

"I don't remember the last time I have eaten so much." Cassi groaned and rubbed her stomach.

"Me neither." Terra sighed and felt fortunate that there was enough space in the waistline of her dress for her to still breathe after having consumed so much.

Darren merely shook his head with a small smile on his lips. "The sun will set here soon, my room is two doors down from yours in case there is any trouble, but we should just turn in for the night so we can get an early start." Darren got to his feet. "I'll escort you ladies back to your bedroom."

Terra's heart fell slightly. She was enchanted by the people around her and wanted to stay awhile to eavesdrop on their fascinating conversations. This was to be her land, her village, her kingdom. She yearned to learn about their culture and discover what makes them unique from her own, but Darren insisted they turn in for the night which foils her plan. Unless…

"Of course." Terra gave him her best smile. As soon as Cassi and she had returned to their rooms, Terra started to hatch a plan. "Let's sneak out."

"Have you gone mad?" Cassi asked.

"Of course I haven't gone mad. Can you blame me for wanting to have a bit of fun? There's so much to see, so much to *do*."

Cassi scoffed and sat on her bed. "You definitely have gone mad."

"Why should we stay here all night, look, the sun is barely even starting to set!"

"You don't think Darren or one of the other guards won't notice us hanging out in the dining hall after we were instructed to turn in for the evening?"

"We've been traveling for days. We deserve a little fun," Terra insisted.

Cassi stared at her warily. "What type of fun did you have in mind?"

Terra bit her lip, unsure exactly where this plan was going. What *did* she have in mind? Then, as if a god had answered her silent prayer and plopped an idea in her head, she went to the window and pointed north. "There was a tavern not too far from here that we passed by earlier. I've never been in a tavern before and now seems a better time than any."

"You cannot be serious."

"I'm completely serious." Terra turned around and kneeled before Cassi. She took her hands in her own and looked at her pleadingly. "Please, I just want to have a bit of fun before you have to return to Solaris. I'm about to be a married woman and a Queen at that, I don't know how much more fun I realistically will be able to have from here on."

Cassi rolled her eyes and sighed. "You act like you won't find a way to create mischief while you rule over Valerian."

"Does that mean yes?" Terra grinned.

She groaned and fell back onto the bed. "Fine! We can go!"

"You won't regret it!" Terra squealed and got back to her feet.

"For some odd reason, I have a feeling that is not exactly true. How do you expect to sneak out without being seen?"

Terra frowned and tapped a finger to her lip. "I mean, there is a window…"

"We are *not* going out the window." Cassi sat back up and crossed her arms. "If we cannot walk out the front door like normal people, we're not going."

"Well, why can't we just go out the front door? What's stopping us?" Terra pointed out. "We have cloaks. We can just pull the hoods up and move quickly. Are they really going to recognize us?"

Cassi rubbed the back of her neck. "I suppose not. We'll wait until dark."

"Great," Terra said cheerfully and plopped onto her own bed. "I don't think I can have any beverages with this much food still in my stomach."

"Who said anything about beverages?"

Terra rolled her eyes. "You don't go to a tavern and *not* have beverages. That defeats the whole purpose of a tavern."

"I thought you've never been in a tavern before."

"I haven't, but you get the idea."

The two went on like this, joking and talking as the minutes passed and the sun set on the horizon. The shadows fell quickly over the town and Terra was buzzing with excitement. They threw their cloaks over their heads and positioned them so that if they kept their heads down, no one would be able to recognize their faces. Terra took out a pouch of coins that had been in the parcels and baggage that Darren had brought to them and hid the pouch deep in the pockets in the folds of her dress.

They were just going down the stairs when Terra noticed Jasper, the young guard that Cassi had a crush on, with another guard about to head up the stairs. *Oh no.* Cassi fell behind her to make room for the two men to come up on the other side, so close that their shoulders would brush together. Terra cursed under her breath and silently begged Cassi to hurry past so that they weren't caught.

Terra slipped by and just as she believed that they were about to go unnoticed, she heard Jasper say, "Cassi?"

The girls whirled around and Jasper was stopped on the stairs, looking at them with a confused expression on his face.

"Run!" Terra blurted. The girls darted across the foyer and slammed open the front door where they almost knocked over a gentleman who had been just reaching for the handle.

"Hey!" Jasper shouted after them, but the girls squealed and kept running. They ran down the street and veered off into a thin alleyway completely shrouded in shadows. Terra held her breath and clasped onto Cassi's arm, both girls hiding themselves against the stone wall pushing into their backs. Jasper and the other guard went running by and the girls looked at each other with wide eyes before bursting into laughter.

"I'm never going to hear the end of this." Cassi readjusted the hood of her cloak back in place. "I should know better than to let you drag me into another one of your schemes."

"Hopefully they won't think to look in the local tavern for a runaway Princess and her handmaiden, let's go!"

Soon, they were standing in front of the tavern door that was vibrating from the music and conversations coming from inside. Before she could chicken out, Terra took a deep breath and pushed open the door. She was immediately slapped in the face with the musty smell of rolled tobacco, sweat, and beer. Gruff men and pretty women in scandalous attire mingled among each other and Terra saw a man slam an entire glass mug of the brown-orange brew before belching loudly.

Eyes glanced at them as they walked to an open round table set against one wall, but no one made a move to approach them. Terra and Cassi sat down just before a young woman approached them. She had golden blonde hair that fell in thick curls and alluring red lips. Her dress neckline presented her décolletage for all to see and fell in ruffles down to her ankles.

"What can I get you?" she shouted over the loud music that a band was playing on a stage at the deep end of the tavern.

"Two beers please," Terra said and the woman left before coming back shortly with two glass mugs full of the brew. Terra pulled a few gold coins out of the pouch and handed them to the woman. "Cheers to one last adventure," Terra said to Cassi and held her mug up.

"To one last adventure," Cassi repeated and their glasses clinked. They both took a sip and immediately Terra made a face while Cassi coughed at the bitter taste. In Solaris, they primarily drank wine above all else and even then, Terra had little experience with alcohol. Barrels of beer were imported into Solaris only to be shipped elsewhere. *Probably to Valerian,* she thought with a smirk.

Before long, Terra began to feel a bit woozy and she could tell that Cassi was too judging by the flushing of her cheeks, but neither stopped. Both girls reminisced on old stories and joked about the trouble they have gotten into together over the years until their stomachs hurt from the endless laughter.

The time began to blur almost as much as the room did around Terra. The floor seemed to tilt and shift and yet they kept ordering mugs until Cassi grasped Terra's arm fervently. "We must dance!" She tugged at Terra until she gave in. They both twirled and leapt in front of the band until other patrons began to join in. One man whirled Terra into his arms and with a firm hand on her back, led her spinning around the tables until she was giggling senselessly.

"You dance pretty well for a traveler!" he shouted in her ear over the music.

"How did you know I was a traveler?" she asked him as he continued to lead her through the steps of some complicated dance that she wasn't familiar with.

"It's pretty obvious, everyone could tell as soon as you ladies came in. It's in the way that you hold yourself, you walk like nobility. So, what is a noble lady doing in a dirty tavern on a fine night like tonight, if I may ask?" The song ended and the man dipped her low, causing Terra to laugh again. She could feel the blush in her cheeks and she was disoriented from all the spinning.

"Maybe I came here to hear about all the dirty secrets that Valerian has to offer a noble lady like myself."

"Why don't we take a seat to rest and I'll tell you all about Valerian?"

Terra and the young man sat at a table and she could see Cassi still whirling and laughing in the arms of another young gentleman.

"The name is Caius, what is yours?" He asked while he placed another order for drinks.

"Terra." Another mug was slipped towards her and she took a drink.

"What would you like to know about Valerian? I was born and raised here; I can tell you anything you want to know."

Terra mused over the possibilities. "Tell me about the kingdom as a whole. Is this the only village in Valerian?"

"It is," he confirmed. "There is quite a bit of land, but it's all forest and mountains so this is the only village. The more north you go, the more mountains you will encounter. Others live separated from people of course, but most reside here in the south. There are well known trails that are travelled often where people will build a house to take a squat of land themselves."

"Interesting, I would have thought the kingdom had more cities."

"You would think." He lowered his voice. "If you ask me, there aren't more people because they're scared."

Terra leaned in closer, suddenly intrigued at his mention of something exciting. "Scared of what?"

"King Orion of course. They say he's not human, that he raises the dead to stalk the forest at night to protect his castle from everyone and anyone. No one has seen him in gods knows how long besides his loyal soldiers. Why would he need company, if he has the dead for that? They call him the Keeper of Souls. They say that those who dare enter his castle will never been seen again."

"The Keeper of Souls," Terra repeated quietly. "But how-" The door to the tavern suddenly burst open and, to Terra's horror, an angry Darren stood in the frame with Jasper behind him. "Oh no." Terra shrunk down to try to hide. She looked around for Cassi and found her on top of a table dancing. She was lifting her skirts up high and kicking her legs up giddily. "Oh *no*," she said louder and Caius turned to see Darren.

"Is he here for you?" He pushed his mug over to Terra. "You might need the rest of this then."

Darren's gaze immediately went to Cassi and he motioned to Jasper to grab her down from the table while he stomped over to Terra. "To the inn, *now*," he growled. Terra smiled at him sheepishly and drained the rest of her beer before taking Caius's too.

"Thank you!" she called to him as Darren escorted her away. She caught one last glance of Caius's unreadable expression. Jasper was quick behind them and had Cassi thrown over his shoulder where she kept giggling and hiccupping while telling him how handsome she thought he was.

Expecting to be scolded to no end, Terra was surprised at Darren's angry silence as Cassi sang and swayed side to side over the uneven cobblestones. It wasn't until they had once again reached their room that he finally spoke, and even then, it was only a few words.

"I hope it was worth the risk." He closed the door behind the girls before Terra could answer.

She looked over at Cassi who was already passed out and snoring heavily into her pillow. She couldn't help but smile at the memory of their wild and risky night that she would forever be grateful for.

"Yeah, it was worth it," she whispered into the dark.

Chapter Eight
Orion

"What do you *mean* that they lost the Princess? How much of an imbecile do you have to be to lose a royal?" Orion roared at the soldier quaking in front of him. The messenger had arrived early this morning before dawn even broke. Orion was already up, of course, not having slept much in the past few days from the ever-present twisting thoughts that invaded every crevice of his mind, but that didn't mean he wasn't still irritated at the messenger's presence.

The messenger spun a tale about how the Princess and her handmaiden had taken off into the night right under the guards' noses. Hours went by and they finally found them both intoxicated in a tavern. As annoyed as Orion was, he was also begrudgingly impressed. He didn't expect her to be so brazen as to slip away from the guards he had sent to escort her just to have a bit of fun. But, on the other hand, what type of Princess frequented a place like a tavern? To drink herself into a stupor and make an embarrassment of the crown as a whole? *A troublesome one with a lack of awareness of her title and responsibilities.*

A duo of soldiers walking out of the shade of the trees caught his eye. *Great, more people to bother me.* "Return to the group and ensure that the Princess arrives safely and sober," Orion growled, and the messenger fled at once. As if he didn't have enough to worry about currently. The Captain's second-in-command stopped before him and saluted him respectfully. "Your Highness."

"What news do you have?" Orion asked, forgoing any pleasantries. He didn't have time to waste on idle chatter, not today when the castle was about to be turned upside down at the arrival of the Solarian Princess.

"Two guilty are in custody at the eastern outpost," the soldier reported. "One evaded capture and I dispatched men to follow. We are interrogating the two in custody as we speak."

His interest piqued at this information. He was surprised to find that they managed to capture the suspects so quickly, even if one had managed to get away. The eastern outpost was even closer to the castle than the northern outpost and Orion could make it there quick if he left now so that he could question the individuals himself. "Saddle my horse, I'll leave at once."

"With all due respect Your Highness, but the Princess should be arriving by this afternoon. Should you not be here to welcome her?"

"I'll be back by the time the escort arrives. It is also not your place to question your King's decisions, I may add. Find Edith and let her know that I must ride at once."

Orion took a few steps past the guard, but the guard cleared his throat awkwardly. "She would have my head on a spike if I passed that message along to her."

Orion pinched the bridge of his nose and turned to face him. "Then get everything ready for me and I'll tell her my damned self, you coward." Orion didn't blame him, for he was frightened of telling her himself and he was hoping that his men would do the dirty work for him. *Today is not my lucky day I guess,* he thought wryly to himself. Without waiting for a further response from the guard, Orion continued on his way to his room to change for the journey. Once he was dressed in his worn riding boots and adorned his cloak and gloves, he commanded his dogs to stay put so that he could get there and back as quick as possible. Pausing at the door, Orion's eyes landed on the sheathed sword resting near his fireplace and he grabbed it, securing it around his waist just in case something happened on the road.

Edith was already waiting for him in the foyer and saved him the time to search for her in the castle. "What is this I hear that you are now leaving?" Her voice was shrill and her dissatisfaction with him was obvious.

"I will be back by the time they get here," he reassured her, his mouth suddenly feeling quite dry, and he moved to leave. She stepped in front of him and blocked his path to the door with her arms crossed.

"Orion."

"Edith, I promise." He put his hands on her shoulders and looked her in the eyes. "My duty as King comes first, but I will ride there and back by the time they get here, okay? Every moment I stand here, I'm wasting more riding time."

Edith scowled but moved to the side to let him pass. "You don't even want to imagine what I will do to you if you are not back here by the time they arrive."

"I'm sure you're scheming something magnificent." His mouth quirked and he pecked her affectionately on the cheek. "I'll do my best not to find out what it is!"

In the stables, Laurent had his horse ready and waiting for him. It was a large stallion with a coat so dark that the brown appeared almost black. He was a spectacular beast and Theos was his name. Orion had bought him in the village years prior when the horse was no older than a colt. He raised him into the young horse that he was now, a tough stallion that towered above the rest. He was a horse bred unlike any other, that much was obvious just by his stature.

Orion wasted no time and as soon as he was astride his stallion, he spurred him off at a rushed gallop.

The first hour passed by quickly. The sun rose higher in the morning sky and the cool air warmed a bit as the sun grew stronger. The second hour however, seemed to drag on. The road grew more overgrown and narrower with the pines and shrubs pushing against the invisible boundary separating the civilized road from the wilderness in the trees beyond.

The unknown hiding in the forest seemed to beckon to Orion and his skin crawled as a sixth sense told him that he wasn't alone. He pulled Theos back until they were moving at a steady trot and his stallion was breathing hard beneath him from the exertion of the ride. Scanning the shadows among the tree trunks, Orion knew better than to distrust the feeling in his gut telling him that he was being watched, but he saw nothing and no one. Theos halted at the gentle signal of Orion's hands and he listened intently to the sounds around him.

Birds chirped despite the oncoming winter, not having fled south for the harsh cold quite yet. He could hear the distinct sound of the breeze rustling through the leaves that have turned and fallen into piles on the ground. But there was nothing else out of the ordinary. There wasn't an obvious snapping of a twig, a creak of a bow being pulled back, or anything else that would signal that someone was lying in wait just out of sight but yet, he couldn't shake the uneasy feeling.

Orion was wasting time that he didn't have. With a frown, he spurred Theos onward and kept his eyes peeled.

Another hour or so later, he finally reached the outpost. It was a stone structure that was simple, yet formidable. It towered above his head and had a wall walk around all four walls for guards to constantly patrol at all hours of the day and night. Only one single gate, closed at all times, allowed access within. At the sight of Orion, the guards on duty shouted for the gate to be raised so that he could ride within.

A flat and dirty yard rested at the center of the outpost where soldiers were training and battling one another to practice their techniques and to fight against the boredom of being stationed at a boring outpost. Orion remembered that yard well. The first time he ever sparred with a real sword was in the yard, even though he was always better with a bow. But his father insisted that he learn how to use a sword, "for all real men knew how to wield a sword in battle."

Much to Orion's dismay, his youngest brother though had a natural talent with a sword

"You're just upset that I'm better than you."

"Whatever you say, Theon." Orion turned back to the practice dummy in front of him that was stuffed with straw. The youngest Prince stomped towards him with his chest held out until Orion turned back around with a sigh. "What?"

Theon withdrew his sword from the scabbard at his side so that the sharp end was pointing directly at Orion's chest. "I challenge you to a duel!"

Orion glanced around them and noticed that no one was there to see them or chastise them for what they were about to do, so he took a defensive stance with his sword at the ready. With a wild shriek, Theon swiped downwards with all his strength so that their swords clashed together loudly.

Strike. Block, Jab. Block again.

Orion ran through the steps and the moves that he was taught flawlessly, realizing that what he was being taught had actually stuck. With each blow and each swing of his sword, Theon grew angrier. Orion could see it from the fury in his eyes and in the wild slashes he threw at his older brother.

Orion showed his little brother no mercy. With one last powerful swipe, Orion watched in slow motion as Theon failed to raise his weapon fast enough to block the blow and the tip of Orion's sword cut a clean streak down his cheek. Theon cried out and fell to his knees. Orion, horrified, dropped his sword and went to comfort him, but Theon only pushed him away. He wiped away the tears streaking from his eyes and dabbed at the blood already beginning to drip from the slice in his cheek before he ran away. "I'll make you pay for this! You just watch!"

From that day forward, Theon had never looked at him the same.

Orion shook the memory from his head and focused once more on the task at hand. He dismounted in the middle of the yard where the soldiers had stopped sparring at the sight of the newcomer. It wasn't until one had realized who he was and saluted him that the others all stood at proper attention at well.

"King Orion," one soldier's voice carried through the silence and a sturdy body stepped forward. The soldier was sweaty and dirty, having been one of the men sparring when he had approached. "What can I assist you with?"

"I need to see the prisoners."

The soldier kept his features expressionless and gestured with the heavy sword in his hand towards the northern wall of the outpost. "They're being held this way. Please, follow me."

Orion and the soldier trekked through the yard and he was led into the depths of the outpost until they went down a few steps into a small dungeon area. There were five cells only that were spread out in a circle so that if prisoners insisted on talking amongst each other, they had to shout around large corners that prevented them from even seeing one another.

The two prisoners were at opposite ends in their separate cells looking ragged and worn. Orion dismissed the guards on duty and told them to make themselves busy elsewhere while he worked.

"But, Your Highness," one protested. "Wouldn't you feel better if-"

"I can handle myself just fine." Orion leveled his gaze towards him. "Do you commonly ignore orders from your superiors, or just your King?"

The shaken guard stumbled over a quick apology and scurried away so that Orion was left with the first prisoner before him. It was far too easy to make his men panic. Orion took off his cloak when he approached the cell and hung it haphazardly over a lantern hook in the wall. The prisoner appraised him with a scornful look but didn't make any move to speak. He was a gruff man, covered in scrapes and bruises over his already present scars. Orion cocked his head. He didn't seem to be a merchant, or a farmer. Not even a locksmith or a tradesman. No, he looked like a hired mercenary that worked for someone other than himself. *Or many someones, whoever is the highest bidder,* he amended silently.

Orion crouched down so that he was at the same level as the man on the floor. "Tell me," he began. The shadows in the depths of the cells and around him began to twist and turn until a thick cloud seemed to encapsulate both of them in a sphere. "Who hired you to kill all those people? Or did you do it for your own sick pleasure?"

The man didn't blink. He spit at the ground by Orion's feet before placing his head back along the wall behind him so that he once again stared off into space. The message was clear: he wasn't going to say a word.

"So, we're going to do this the hard way then." Orion smirked. "Just the way I like it." The prisoner jerked suddenly against the chains around his wrists and began to choke. The shadows were swirling around his neck and his bloodied face began to grow purple, but Orion didn't react. Even when the man continued to struggle against an invisible force halting all oxygen to flow into his lungs, Orion remained emotionless. He almost enjoyed it.

Finally, just as the prisoner began to pass out, Orion released him.

The man gasped for air violently and coughed so loudly that the sound echoed harshly against the stone walls. He looked at Orion with fear in his wide eyes.

"Start talking." Orion got back to his feet so that he looked down on the prisoner.

Even still, the man shook his head fervently and his mouth remained clamped shut. Orion merely shrugged. "Fine, I'll find out from your little friend over there. You're no longer needed." Orion began to walk away and over his shoulder he said, "Kill him." The man was barely able let out a shriek before it was abruptly cut off and replaced with the sound of his gurgling. The other prisoner had heard their exchange and watched horrified as Orion rounded the corner to his cell.

"Well? Start talking," Orion commanded and waited rather impatiently as the prisoner tripped over his words. Orion put an aggravated palm up and the prisoner fell silent once more. "I have no issue with ending your life right here, right now. So, unless you give me a reason to keep you alive, you will share the same fate as your accomplice. Do you understand?"

The prisoner nodded meekly and swallowed hard. Whereas the other man looked like a trained killer, this prisoner did not. He was dirty and weak, but young. He barely looked like a grown man and Orion almost wondered what had happened in his life to lead him down this path. He wrung his chained hands together so that the metal clicked together in a fashion that made Orion want to strangle him and just end it all right then and there.

"Let's try this again." Orion gritted his teeth. "Why are you murdering innocents? What is the reason? Nothing was taken, so greed wasn't driving it nor was paying off a debt. So why target these families?"

"I don't know," the man replied in barely more than a whisper.

Orion plunged forward and took the prisoner by the front of the shirt in order to slam him against the bars separating the two of them. "What do you mean 'you don't know?'"

"I can't say."

The prisoner was slammed once more against the bars so that his nose cracked and blood burst from the broken cartilage. Orion let the man fall back and he groaned miserably as the blood leaked down his face.

"I swear I'm not lying!" The prisoner implored. "I'm bound in a code of silence; I couldn't say anything if I even wanted to."

"You can murder innocent people, slaughter children and women in their own homes without thinking twice about it, but you can't betray your accomplices? Because you're 'bound by a code of silence?' Somehow, I don't believe you."

The man shuddered again and his fingers trembled when he raised his palms up defensively. "I physically cannot tell you. I could try all I want, but as soon as I would try to say anything about who hired-"

The man stopped mid-sentence and began to turn a vicious shade of purple as if Orion had wrapped his hands around his throat and squeezed, except he hadn't. He was doing nothing to the man.

Orion frowned and regarded the man quizzically. It seemed almost magical, how the ability to breath seemed to disappear as soon as the man tried to discuss any impertinent information. "Someone hired you to do this. What was the goal?"

The man opened his mouth to speak again, but only a squeak came out. He shook his head and looked pained.

Orion knew this wasn't going to go anywhere, that he could torture this man all he wanted, but he wasn't going to get any information out of him which is probably why the other man refused to talk himself. This unknown agreement had him at a loss. It must be some sort of blood magic binding him to the code of silence whether or not the prisoner wanted to speak out about what was going on. Orion's temper flared and he wanted to smash his fist against the bars in frustration. Here was another obstacle blocking him from discovering the mystery behind all of this.

But, again, he didn't have time for this. The Princess would be arriving to the castle soon and even though he wished he could use this as an excuse to not be there, he knew he would never hear the end of it from Edith. So, he had to end it and get back as soon as he could.

"You're useless to me," Orion told the prisoner and shook his head. "I need answers and you have none. The one that escaped will need to give me the answers that I seek, so there is no sense to keep you alive in the meantime, now is there?"

Realization at Orion's words slowly crossed the prisoner's expression and tears began to stream from his eyes. "Please, no, have mercy. Have mercy!"

"There is no mercy for monsters." *I would know.*

The prisoner continued to beg and threw himself against the bars while reaching his filthy hands out towards Orion who stood just out of reach. But Orion didn't listen and instead wiped the sweat and grit from his palms on his pants. A guttural yell followed him as he walked away until the man was permanently silenced, this time by Orion's unspoken silent command.

There was no room for mercy here.

Chapter Nine
Terra

Terra swore that she was cursed by the gods. Between the pounding headache rattling Terra to the core and the intense nausea that wracked Cassi, they were in for a long day of hell. Begrudgingly, both of the girls bathed and helped one another sluggishly get ready until Darren knocked at their door to summon them downstairs for breakfast.

Once they made their way downstairs, Terra realized how famished she was despite the throbbing of her mind. She gobbled down the cooked eggs and slices of bacon eagerly. Her stomach settled with the food and she nearly breathed a sigh of relief. Cassi, meanwhile, appeared green at the sight of the greasy food on her plate and Darren ended up finishing it for her before she made herself sick. He was kind enough to give each of the girls a full canteen of water to guzzle down, but that's where his kindness ended.

"We're about two hours or so from the castle," Darren explained as their meager group reconvened outside the inn. Jasper brought their horses to them and helped them mount. After Cassi was seated sturdily on her mare, Jasper stepped back with a face that may have been even more flushed than Cassi's was.

Their group rode out of the village on a road that led them into even higher altitude. About an hour's ride later they came across the rest of their caravan that had been waiting for them to catch up. "We had a bit of a late start," Darren said to the carriage driver and threw a glance at Cassi's direction. She was sliding off her horse and clutching her head painfully. She merely grumbled at Darren before handing her mare's reins to a guard and climbed into the carriage.

Terra dismounted and another guard took her horse from her. "How much farther do we have to go?" Darren handed her a canteen full of water and she took a grateful swig. Her head was already starting to clear and she began to feel a bit better as time went on.

"Not too long," he replied. "So don't get comfortable."

Terra joined Cassi in the carriage her friend was sprawled out on one side, quickly falling asleep to the rocking of the carriage. *So much for not getting comfortable.* Terra remained silent and let her sleep, instead busying herself by peering out the carriage window and watching the world pass her by. Her thoughts were fleeting, but very distracting. It was hard to wrap her head around the fact that she was about to arrive to her new home where she would live out the rest of her days. It was difficult to not think that she made a grave mistake when she agreed to come here.

Terra imagined living her life in sullen misery away from her family as the seasons changed and the concept chilled her to her core. She had a hard time telling if the sick feeling in her stomach was from the drinking or if it was from the nerves. *Probably both,* she admitted silently. Wishing that Cassi was awake to help console her or to talk her down from the panic rising in her chest, she instead sunk back in her seat and closed her eyes.

Soon the dirt road grew rather bumpy and jagged so that the carriage was tossed back and forth violently enough to rouse Cassi from her nap. Terra could see through the window that they were in a deep ravine with rocky crags reaching high towards the sky around them. *Wolf's Pass,* she realized. This is the ravine that would end up full of snow and disallow any travel to and from the castle until the spring thaw would once again grace the land.

The path remained treacherous and it slowed them down until the carriage wheels clacked over cobblestone instead of the dirt path. They had arrived at King Orion's castle. *To my castle*, she corrected herself. Through her limited window view, Terra immediately noticed the thick forest that lined the stone road until the trees opened up to reveal a sprawling stone castle. The same mist that hung over the village hung over the spires of the castle, reminding her that she was very, very far from home.

The carriage came to a stop and the driver opened the door to help her step out onto the ground. The entrance to the castle rested before them. A beautiful door adorned with intricate carvings rose tall underneath a pointed arch and standing before the door was a woman and a man waiting to greet them.

"Welcome, you must be Princess Terra," the woman said in a soft voice that was warm like honey before she dropped into a curtsy. The man bowed beside her as well. "I'm Edith, the housekeeper of the castle and this is Laurent. He is the groundsman, butler, and whatever else I may need him to help me with."

"It's a pleasure to meet you," he said in a deep voice. "I trust that your journey wasn't too harsh?"

"Not at all," Terra assured him, even though it was indeed a hard trip. "I am honored at the invitation and I look forward to spending my time here." A pretty lie, one that she said with ease much to her surprise.

Terra couldn't help but study the two in front of her curiously. Edith, she was not surprised to see, was middle-aged and would have reminded her of Ms. Astrid if it was not for the kindness that resided behind her piercing eyes. She seemed to be the type that would be terrifying if you were to cross her, but as long as you didn't, then she would mother you and fictitiously adopt you as one of her own.

Laurent, on the other hand, struck her as sullen and quiet. He was clearly older than Edith and she could tell by the way he held himself that he spent countless hours working out in the elements. But the crow's feet at the creases of his eyes told her that not only was he a hard worker, but he also always found reasons to smile as often as he could. She still felt wary about the two, but she chalked it up to simply being uncomfortable in a new place. There were no apparent reasons why Terra should be careful around the two of them, for they both were here to welcome her when the King still had yet to make himself known, so she chided herself for keeping her mental walls up.

"We have brought gifts from Solaris as a thank you and as a celebration for the union," Terra said and gestured to the wagons. She almost winced at the fake politeness that even astounded her. *All that training to be Queen really is coming in handy*, she thought.

"I can take care of it," Laurent offered and the guards immediately set to helping him. They began unloading boxes and crates full of delectable fruits and jewels that were the pride of Solaris to bring into the castle interior.

"You must be chilled, please, come inside." Edith led Cassi and Terra through the throng of bodies and through the front door. Immediately, the foyer left her feeling breathless. The cavernous ceilings revealed a large hand-painted mural of beautiful women and men lounging among the clouds high in the sky. Terra could see apparent symbols and hints that they were meant to be depictions of the gods and goddesses in all of their glory. Two grand marble staircases led to the second floor and to the further reaches of the castle. Two story tall windows allowed what little natural light that could poke through the heavy mist to illuminate the artwork inside.

Still the King didn't make an appearance. Terra didn't know if she should be insulted that he refused to even greet her, or if there was a plausible explanation for it. She was rattled out of her thoughts by one of the guards that had brought in a box full of pomegranates and their seeds. Terra opened the crate excitedly to show Edith the bizarre fruits, who then remarked that she had never seen one in person and that they didn't get many of them imported to this area.

"We use the seeds in our salads, our baking, and in our cooking in general," Terra explained. The maroon-colored fruits were packed snugly and she lifted one out to show housekeeper.

"I see you're already making a mess of my home," a voice said from the doorway. Terra's gaze shifted to see a young man that had just entered the castle standing amidst the chaos and eyeing the mess that was forming around them.

"I beg your pardon?" Terra was taken back by his tone.

"I said, that you are already making a mess of my home." He stopped before her, broad and tall and close enough for her to smell the soap on his skin mixed with the scent of fresh air and pine. He was incredibly handsome she found, even though his pale blonde hair was unruly and hung to his shoulders. He hadn't shaved in days and a dark stubble covered his jaw. He was wearing a plain white shirt with the sleeves rolled up past his elbows underneath a cloak. His dark pants were tucked into tall leather boots that had faint traces of mud and dirt on them and, despite what his plain appearance was telling her, she knew this was King Orion of Valerian.

The King reached past her to snatch one of the pomegranates out of the box and weighed it in his hand. "And what is this?"

"That is a pomegranate, a symbol of Solaris and a gift for you," Terra answered through her teeth and batted her eyes at him. *Who does he think he is?* "This *mess* is full of gifts for you. Do you treat all of your guests this way?"

"Please, Princess, accept my deepest apologies for my egregious behavior." He swept his arms out in a mocking bow. "How will you ever forgive me?"

Terra wrinkled her nose and crossed her arms in disdain. "You are absolutely *obscene*."

He leered at her with narrowed eyes before speaking softly. "And you are absolutely naive." His gaze moved to Darren who had just set a crate down. "We need to talk Captain." He tossed the pomegranate back into the box and headed for the stairs. "Until next time, Princess." Terra watched him go dumbfounded and quiet.

An embarrassed flush began to creep up her neck to her face and she was painfully aware of everyone's nervous eyes on trying to gauge her reaction. She couldn't succumb to the complicated emotions she was feeling, not with everyone watching.

"I apologize for that," Edith spoke up and gave Terra a rueful smile. "Why don't I give you a tour?"

She couldn't help but let her mind run rampant as Edith led Cassi and Terra through the dining room, kitchen, ballroom, and more on the first floor. She was appalled at the King's behavior and felt dejected that their first meeting transpired that way. Shouldn't he be excited to meet his bride and future Queen? He had regarded her with such intense loathing that she was concerned that she would burst into flames right where she stood.

Who was he to treat her this way? Terra couldn't let him bully her, or to embarrass her in front of prying eyes. He would soon realize that Terra would be a force to be reckoned with.

"This will be your bedchamber," Edith said and opened a door to reveal a beautiful bedroom. A four-poster bed with dark red curtains rested in front of a stone hearth and an exquisite woven rug covered the floor. A wooden vanity rested in one corner with a beautiful carved top to border the mirror. Intricate carvings matching the posts of the bed frame graced the edge where the ceiling and the walls met. She longed to run a hand over the heavenly work, but she resigned to place gentle fingers along the smooth bed post before walking towards the grand windows looking over the lush forest. Here, she looked at the tops of the trees behind a pane of glass and at home she could smell the sea and watch the waves roll from her balcony.

No matter what she did, this place would never be home.

"I hope that you will be comfortable here." Edith smoothed the cover on the bed in an almost motherly fashion. "This will be your home and I want you to feel that it is. Anything you ever need, please don't be afraid to come to me."

"Thank you. I will make sure to do that."

Cassi glanced out the window and her face contorted as sadness crept over her. "The sun is beginning to set, we will need to get on the road soon. I will make sure your things are sent here for you." She faltered slightly before slipping out of the room.

Terra stood with her arms crossed and glowered at the view when Edith came to stand beside her.

"He's not always like that."

Terra immediately knew who she referring to without her having to say. *Put on a good face,* she reminded herself. "I suppose that's good to hear."

"I hope you give him a chance. He's not a deplorable person, just…"

"Just not honorable?" Terra supplied and Edith winced.

"Not when he has a temper, no."

"How long have you known him? Any pointers on how to handle this apparent temper?"

Edith sighed beside her. "I've known him his entire life, I've worked for the family for quite a long time. He's a very detached individual as I'm sure you've realized. But deep down, he has a true heart of gold and I do hope he lets you see that side of him."

Terra nodded curtly. "We'll see." She turned away from the window and headed back to the door. He may have a heart of gold deep down, but she also knew deep down within herself that coming here was a mistake that she couldn't undo now. He proved as much. "I would like a chance to say goodbye to Cassi before they depart."

"Of course."

Back in the foyer, all that was left was Terra's small collection of personal belongings that she had brought with her. Laurent led the last small group of soldiers-turned-servants towards her chambers while Cassi waited for her at the door wringing her hands. The King and Darren were nowhere to be seen.

As soon as Terra looked at her, tears began to fall from Cassi's eyes and Terra couldn't stop herself from crying either. Cassi clutched her tightly and the girls both cried silently, letting the tears soak each other's dresses and neither of them caring. After all of these years, after all of their adventures and hours spent at each other's sides, Terra was going to be alone.

"It'll be okay." Cassi sniffled. "You'll be okay. You'll be happy and you'll be a wonderful Queen, I just know it."

Oh, how wrong she is. "What will I ever do without you?" was all that Terra could muster.

Cassi pulled away and wiped her face. "You'll be one of the most kind and powerful Queens that has ever existed, that's what you'll do."

"I'm going to miss you." Terra clasped her shaking hands together and Cassi took them in her own.

"And I you, but you are on to bigger and better things."

"Oh gods I hope so," Terra chuckled through her tears. "Will you write me?"

"Of course I will."

The girls hugged one last time. They held each other tightly and wished that they could never let go, but both of them knew it was time. Cassi pulled away first and with one last wave, she followed the remaining Solarians out the door that then slammed behind them with a deafening sound. Already Terra felt overcome by loneliness.

She felt a soft hand on her arm and Edith was at her side. "Are you hungry, Your Highness? I can whip something up quickly for you, whatever you'd like. I know leaving your friends and family isn't an easy thing to do."

"Please, call me Terra." Terra smoothed her long skirts self-consciously. Only yesterday she had been enchanted by the thrill of the material brushing against her skin and now she felt as if she was an imposter in her own body. She was meant to be the honored Queen and instead she was alone and blubbering like a child. "And I am fine, thank you. I think I may retire for the rest of the night."

"Of course dear, do you need to show me where your room is again?"

"I think I'll be okay, thank you Edith. You've been very kind." Terra left Edith and made her way back up the stairs and towards the hall that she knew held her bedchamber. Instead of rushing, she took her time and stopped in front of paintings, sculptures, and other pieces of art that were on display in the halls in order to distract herself from the dark cloud hanging above her head. They were beautiful, really. Similar to the mural on the ceiling in the foyer, they depicted the gods in all their glory. The artwork was in perfect shape as if they were specially preserved somehow, but she knew they had to be older than they looked. Who would have painted them — King Orion? There was no chance. She nearly laughed out loud at the thought but instead Terra sighed and went on her way.

In her bedchamber there were the few clothes she had packed, a few plants tucked precariously in crates, and what little jewelry that had been gifted to her from her mother's collection of family heirlooms but first she started a fire. Already the castle was growing colder as the sun set fully and it was only going to get worse with the cold stone walls and floor. She then started finding spots to place her plants where they may still get some sunlight through the windows during any sunny days that may come. *If they don't die first,* she thought morbidly.

Sometime later, Terra had nothing else to occupy her. She tried to cozy up on the chair in front of the hearth and she even tried to rearrange anything in the room to a way she might like. She considered soaking in a bath, but she was far too restless for that. She found herself pacing aimlessly back and forth across the room until she absolutely had enough. *Maybe Edith had a bottle of wine stored in the pantry.* Terra believed she could remember the way to the kitchen. A candelabra rested upon the mantle of the hearth and she snatched it before lighting it carefully to leave her room.

The hallway was dark and foreboding, its unfamiliarity making it even more menacing than what it realistically was. Holding the candelabra out, Terra started retracing her steps to get down to the first floor and to the pantry. She took a left and expected to see the balcony over the foyer, but instead it was another hallway. "Oh no," she groaned to herself. "Please don't be lost, you idiot."

Terra went down another hallway. And then another, and another, none of which led her to the foyer. She rounded a corner and froze. Ahead of her in the darkness were two reflective icy blue eyes staring at her just out of the reach of the light of the candelabra. Fear overtook her and she took a few steps back, but the thing didn't budge.

"Shoo!" she hissed and waved the candelabra at it threateningly. It blinked and took a few steps towards her. "I said shoo!" she repeated, but it kept advancing. Terra stumbled over the long skirt of her dress and fell backwards onto her butt with the candelabra still in hand. Before she could scramble to her feet, the creature stepped into the light and she saw that it was a jet-black wolf. *A wolf in the castle?* Her mind screamed. She couldn't compute what she was seeing, but she knew if she didn't react fast, she would be ripped to shreds.

"Ash!" a voice called and King Orion stepped around the corner ahead with his own candle casting shadows against the hallway walls. He stopped in his tracks when he saw Terra frozen in fear on the floor with the wolf in front of her. Whistling sharply, the King called the wolf who blinked at her once before turning and trotting to his side.

Humiliation flamed across Terra's cheeks at this brash man seeing her in such a vulnerable position, all over his apparent pet. She got to her feet and they faced each other in silence as both of them refused to speak first. She could see his jaw clench as he looked her up and down as if he was sizing her up. Terra stood tall and lifted her chin before doing the same to him. *Try me,* she wanted to say.

"What are you doing?" he finally asked when the silence grew to be too much.

Terra smirked at the small victory. "Exploring," she said simply. "Unlike you, I don't need a — wolf?— as my midnight companion to keep me entertained."

King Orion ignored the jab. "She's a wolf-dog and she's harmless. You were *exploring?*"

"Exactly." Terra kept her face emotionless. "Have a good night, Your Highness." She made sure to add extra emphasis on "Your Highness" just to irritate him. Turning on her heel, she strode the opposite direction of where the King stood. She had just rounded the corner when she heard "Princess!"

Terra turned and found that he had caught up with her. "Yes?"

"You're going the wrong way, wherever you are headed."

Terra's mouth fell open in astonishment but she clamped it back shut. "Thanks, I'll keep that in mind." She walked away again — stubbornly in the same direction that she had been heading — and this time he didn't follow.

I'll show him, she assured herself. *I'm not some child he can insult when he saw fit. No, he will learn to respect me or he will have to feel my wrath.*

Feeling smug with herself, Terra wandered until she finally found her way back to the foyer and she sent a silent prayer of thanks to the gods. In the pantry she found a small wine collection and she snatched a bottle, a corkscrew to open it, and a glass to bring back up to her room.

This time, Terra didn't get lost at all and was grateful to change into her chemise to sleep in. That's how she rested in the chair in front of the fire, in nothing but her slip and the bottle of wine at her side. She poured glass after glass and hoped it would take her mind off the intricacies of how King Orion managed to get under her skin. "This is going to be one heck of a long life," she sighed to the darkness. "Cheers to a long and happy marriage."

Terra raised her glass in a toast to the shadows and drained the last mouthful from the bottle.

Chapter Ten
Orion

Orion brooded in front of his fire, watching through his window as the moon climbed higher and higher into the sky. Sleep was far from reach due to the foul mood clouding him. His blood boiled and kept him wide awake. *Not like I sleep much to begin with,* he thought bitterly. His mind kept repeating the events of the day until he grew more and more irritated. Sensing his restlessness, the dogs remained alert despite the late hour. Eventually, he lost his patience and stood up indignantly to pace the confines of his room.

"Who does she think she is?" Orion demanded Silas who was laying directly in front of the fire. "I have friends other than you three, she doesn't even know what she's talking about. She comes into *my* home with an attitude and she acts so entitled, expecting us to pretend like it's not an issue!" He pulled at his hair. "I should have known that she would be a demanding Princess that believes the world should be presented to her on a gold platter. This was all a mistake. She is more trouble than what she's worth and I was right all along. What have I gotten myself into?"

Silas raised his head and a deep growl rumbled in his throat as if he was agreeing. He barked twice and let a half howl escape from his jaws which caused Ash to grow agitated herself. She jumped off the bed and pushed her body against Silas which then caused him to nip at her. "I should send her home, then I wouldn't have to deal with someone so insufferable. I have enough to worry about. I'll tell Edith first thing in the morning that the Princess needs to go," Orion continued to vent as he paced.

He couldn't help but feel overwhelmed by the innumerable things that demanded his attention. Not only was the Princess already being a thorn in his side, but he also had to face the fact that the captured criminals didn't lead him any closer to discovering who was behind the killings. As soon as Orion had returned from the outpost, he had quite the heated discussion with the Captain in his study that unnerved them both. The seemingly magical agreement that prevented the two men from speaking any of their secrets made the entire situation even more complicated. The only thing Orion could realistically do would be to find the third man and to execute him as a guilty party to the crimes. Even now, patrols were combing the countryside in search of the final suspect.

Ash trotted in front of Orion and sat on her haunches while staring at him with her bright blue eyes until he stopped pacing. "Don't look at me like that." She continued to stare with an unwavering gaze. "I didn't mean it," he grumbled and sank heavily into his chair as the adrenaline began to ebb. "Fine, I won't make her leave. Edith would never forgive me if I did." He put his head in his hands. He could hear Ash snort and Milo slunk to Orion's feet where he pawed at his knee for attention.

Orion grabbed his paw. "I know, I know, I wasn't very nice to her today and I should have been better. I don't know what came over me." Milo stared at him with his wise eyes and Orion couldn't help but feel guilty for his actions. He had let his anger and his stubborn side take over instead of his common courtesy when the Princess didn't deserve it.

"No promises," he muttered aloud. "But I'll try to be nicer. Come on, let's go to bed."

The sun woke Orion up too early the next morning. Instead of the usual gloom that the cold season usually brought, the sun was shining bright and turned his bedchamber from the chamber of a temperamental King to an oasis of cheerfulness. It disgusted him.

He shifted and uprooted Silas from his spot between his legs, but even his dogs were not used to being up this early so Silas immediately plopped back down. Ash followed him as he padded to the window to look outside. Overnight, a thick dusting of snow had fallen and coated all of the tree branches. *The first snowfall of the season,* he mused to himself and he was happy to see it. The fire had grown to nothing more than embers overnight and he could feel the chill seeping in through the castle walls. Just as he put on a pair of pants, he heard a tentative knock at the door.

Orion's mind immediately went to Terra and adrenaline shot through him. Did she really have the audacity to knock on his door this earlier in the morning? He scowled and flung the door open wide. Where he half expected Terra to be standing, instead stood Edith. He bit the inside of his cheek in embarrassment. *Of course it would be Edith.*

"I would like it very much if you could join Princess Terra for breakfast," Edith clipped and crossed her arms. Orion knew what she really meant was that either he was to join her, or there would be hell to pay.

"I would rather not," he answered, daring to test her. He was already moody over waking so early, so he might as well speak his mind even if there will be consequences to it.

Edith turned and was already walking away when she shouted over her shoulder, "It wasn't a request!"

Orion growled and closed his door. "So not only am I up at the very moment the sun rises," he lamented to the dogs. "But I have to now play the oh so gracious host at breakfast with the girl." He slipped a dark green shirt on and rolled the sleeves up haphazardly. "What have I done to the gods to deserve this punishment?" He then tucked his pants into his boots and stood up with a groan. "Don't answer that," he added to Silas as he went to his washroom to clean up.

Orion tried to hurry to get ready, damn well knowing that Edith would be knocking down his door at any moment if he arrived any later. "Stay," he commanded to the dogs when he was walking out of the door. Knowing that he hated when they silently begged, the trio watched him go with sad eyes. "I'll be back soon, I promise." He closed the door and could hear one of them howl softly as he headed down the hallway.

"So dramatic," Orion chuckled to himself. He made his way downstairs to the kitchen where on most mornings Edith would have a plate ready for him to eat while he leaned against the counters with a cup of black coffee. But this morning when he went to the kitchen, Edith handed him a plate and a cup before simply pointing to the door that would lead down a hallway to the dining room.

Orion was not surprised to see Terra already seated at one end and picking at a small plate of her own. He sat down at the opposite end and began eating his own plate of quail eggs, bacon, and sausage in silence. A few awkward minutes passed with neither of them saying a word until she finally spoke up.

"I would offer you a pomegranate, but you see them as purely a mess in your castle, so I assumed you'd rather not have one." Terra popped a few seeds in her mouth and gave him a wry smile. Orion met her steely gaze and bit the inside of his cheek to stop himself from blurting anything too crass. *Is this how we're going to start the morning?*

"I feel no personal inclination towards unnecessary things," he answered and stabbed a sausage with his fork.

"Or people you deem unnecessary?"

Expecting her to look away, he was surprised when she continued to hold his gaze with those green eyes as she took a drink of her own cup of coffee. Until this moment, Orion hadn't allowed himself to truly look at her. He had to admit that she was very beautiful, even though he was already discovering that she had a cocky mouth on her. She was going to give him a run for his money, that much was already clear. "Do you expect an answer to a question that you have already answered yourself?"

"You are quite deplorable."

"And you are quite exasperating, Princess."

Terra scoffed and took another drink. "Says the one who has yet to formally introduce himself, *Your Highness*. Your wolf gave me a better greeting last night than I have received from you. Where did you learn diplomacy?"

Orion folded his hands in front of him. "My sincerest apologies, Princess. Hello, I am King Orion and you are in my home, don't you forget that."

She stood and grabbed her plate and her coffee. "I need not reminding, Your Highness, you have already reminded me at every possible instance and this is only my second day here." She exited the room with her empty plate and left Orion sitting in silence. His jaw worked and he clutched the knife in his hand until his knuckles turned white. Something inside him snapped and he thrusted the knife deep into the wooden table where it stuck fast.

"Orion!"

He whirled to find Edith standing in the doorway with her own cup of steaming coffee in her hand. She was fuming, staring at the knife that he had just stuck in the table.

"I'm sorry," he apologized sheepishly and tugged hard until the knife popped out of the table.

"That was entirely uncalled for." Edith took a seat next to him.

"I said I was sorry, okay?" he retorted and moved to stand, but her hand caught his arm before he could.

"You are acting like your father, the way you treat her. Is that what you'd like to become?"

Orion huffed and sat back in his chair. "I am nothing like my father."

"Then prove it. She has done you no harm so stop acting like she's a monster and treat her like a human being."

Orion met her eyes and made the same promise he had made in privacy to his dogs last night, but clearly had broken this morning already. "I'll try to be nicer to her, but she doesn't need to be so aggravating to deal with."

"Well have you met yourself?" Edith sat back and laughed. "You are the epitome of aggravating! Play nice, otherwise this is only going to get worse. Now, we need to still go over the plan for the wedding and then the coronation."

Orion groaned. "Do we have to?"

"Yes, we do. Now, I know you insisted that there won't be any formal invitations sent out, but I really think you should at least consider a grand feast for your men. They serve you well."

"I don't want anything extravagant. I already would rather not be doing this again, let alone making it a big affair. I want it to be as quick and as painless as possible."

"We still need to do this the *right way* as much as possible. When would you like to have the wedding ceremony?"

Orion rubbed a hand over his jaw. "I don't know, a week from now, I guess? It doesn't really matter, does it?"

Edith ignored his last comment and nodded. "A week from now will work. I can make a beautiful feast for everyone after we have the ceremony, no matter what you say. Do you have any other special requests? Any music? Any certain foods?"

"No, we can keep it as simple as possible." *Even though I know you will find a way to make this more complicated*, he wanted to add.

"I will get the preparations in place then." Edith tapped the side of her cup of coffee thoughtfully. "I do need you to do one thing for me though."

"And what would that be?"

"I need you to tell Terra that the ceremony will be in one week."

Orion sighed heavily and leaned his head back until it rested on the back of his chair. "I knew you had to make this complicated." Edith tilted her head in a look that Orion knew meant he was walking a fine line.

"Is that a problem?" she questioned, daring him to give her the wrong answer.

"Not at all, I will do it at once." He stood and went to grab his plate, but she smacked his hand to leave it. He held both of his hands up before him defenselessly. "Okay, okay, I'll leave it."

Where would she be? Orion asked himself and began to wander the castle. The obvious first choice would be her bedchamber, so he worked up the courage to seek her out. Once outside her door, he cleared his throat and knocked three times before waiting patiently. No answer came, so he tried again. *Knock, knock, knock.* A few silent moments passed and still no answer.

"Well, what the hell," he mumbled. Either she was intentionally ignoring him, or she just wasn't in her room at all. In fear of angering Edith, he went with the latter. He considered that maybe she had gone outside, but she was a Princess from sunny Solaris, she wouldn't enjoy the cool air and snow on the ground, would she? He didn't really have any idea the type of person she was, he realized, so he had nothing to work off of.

Instead of wasting half the day wandering the castle in search of her, he went back to his room where the dogs were. All three were waiting on the other side of the door excitedly for him, sniffing him and rubbing him with their heads until he scratched their ears. "We need to find the Princess." Their ears pricked up in interest. "Go on, find the Princess," he urged and they immediately darted between his legs.

As if they were in the forest, the three canines split up the territory of the castle in an organized manner so that they left no area unsniffed. Ash would always lay back to ensure that Orion was following them while Silas and Milo would go as far and as fast as they could to wherever Orion had directed them. It worked well in the forest and it wasn't entirely useless in the castle either in a situation like this. It was an easy way to find Laurent or Edith if they weren't in their more usual spots.

A short while later, Orion heard Milo and Silas barking down a hallway and Ash ran ahead of him to disappear around the corner herself. When he rounded the corner, he could see the three dogs at the far end of the hallway and a frightened Terra sitting on a window bench in front of a large window. She had her legs drawn up to her chest away from the barking dogs with her skirts clutched in her hands.

"They won't hurt you," he called to her, but she didn't dare put her feet down. Her face had gone white in fear and he could see a slight quiver in her hands. "Down," he commanded the dogs and they obeyed, slinking farther away before lounging on the floor.

"How do I know that they won't hurt me?" Terra questioned and lowered her feet back to the floor. A peculiar expression crossed her face and a bit of the spitfire inside of her came back to the surface.

"Because I didn't command it." Orion leaned against the bare wall and crossed his arms over his chest. "Not much to see," he commented and nodded towards the window. The window faced the deep ravine that was Wolf's Pass. The higher angle allowed them to see the rocky crags and the trees lining the pass. The dusting of snow had already begun to pile a bit heavier between the sheer surfaces and would eventually be impossible to traverse for most travelers.

Luckily for him, he had a hidden path to the main road that no one else besides his people knew about.

Terra turned and gazed out the window herself. "It's a nice reminder of why I'm stuck here," she answered sarcastically before returning her eyes to him. "Is there something I can help you with, or did you just wish to disturb my solitude to prove a point?"

Orion opened his mouth to make a jibe back at her, but he clamped his mouth shut when he thought of what Edith might do to him if she found out that he was *not* being nice to her. "I came to tell you that the wedding will take place one week from now. Edith will be in charge and you can let her know anything you may need or wish to have."

A sudden wave of sadness crossed her face and before Orion could catch himself, he had taken two steps towards her. As soon as he realized what he was doing, a cold wave washed over him and he stopped. He didn't know if he involuntarily stepped forward to comfort her or what, but whatever his subconscious was trying to tell him, he didn't like it.

"Thank you." Her voice was now emotionless. "I will discuss it more with Edith. Is there anything else?"

Before Orion could answer, heavy steps drew his attention away. A breathless soldier rounded the corner and messily saluted him while he struggled to catch his breath. "Your Highness," the soldier panted. "Please, come at once. The Captain has caught the last man and has him at Thorn Hall."

Orion's chest tightened and he moved to follow the soldier at once. *They caught him.* "Apologies Princess, but I must go."

"Go where?" She quickly got to her feet and began to follow him. "I want to come with you."

"You don't want to come, I promise you that." *Please,* he almost added but he turned his back to her and quickly strode off after the solider with his dogs at his side. Instead of remaining where she was, however, he was surprised to see Terra following them as they hurried from the castle to Thorn Hall. Even when they plunged into the woods, Terra wordlessly followed. Voices grew louder and more fevered as they approached Thorn Hall. As soon as they broke through the trees, they were met with a chaotic sight.

Energetic soldiers circled around a man sitting on the wet ground with his hands chained together. Some threw kicks and knocked him over just so he could struggle to seat himself upright once more. The men jeered and taunted him, but the prisoner's face remained passive. He was filthy and bloodied in torn garments. As soon as the soldiers saw Orion, a hush fell over the crowd and they parted to let him in.

Orion looked the man up and down and the prisoner met his steely gaze with his own emotionless one. "You have caused me quite a bit of trouble, did you know that?"

The captive man hesitated before nodding once stiffly.

"And do you have anything to say about what you are being accused of?"

He opened his mouth as if he was going to speak, but them clamped it back shut so he could shake his head no.

"Then so be it." Orion turned to the crowd of soldiers. "Fetch me a sword."

A strangled cry echoed through the group and Terra pushed her way forward so that she stood right next to Orion who had forgotten that she was present as soon as he saw the chaos ensuing with his men. "What are you doing? Doesn't he get a fair trial?" The vexed Princess demanded, her face flushing a bright crimson in her fury.

Ignoring her, Orion faced the prisoner once more. "You are to be executed for your crimes. Do you wish to say any final words?"

The prisoner hung his head low and shook it once.

"No!" Terra shouted and grasped Orion's sleeve with a clawed hand. "You can't just *kill* a man in cold blood!"

"This doesn't concern you," Orion growled quietly.

Terra gripped his shirt tighter and he pried her fingers loose. "You can't do this, please."

Orion looked at the Captain who was nearest to them. "Restrain her."

Darren did as he said and took her roughly by the arms, tugging her away and pleading for her not to watch what Orion was about to do, but she refused to listen. He felt her gaze heavy on his back as he faced the man in front of him.

"May the gods forgive you," Orion called loudly. In one swift motion, he swung the sword with enough force that he cut through the man's neck cleanly. A sick thud echoed through the quiet and Terra was deadly silent now, no longer fighting. With each passing execution, it never seemed to get easier.

But a job was a job.

"You're a *monster*," Terra seethed, now being free of Darren's grip.

Orion stepped to her so that they were nose to nose. "A King must make painful choices," he said dangerously quiet. "You can make me the villain in your story all you want, it won't change a damned thing, Princess."

Fire burned in her eyes and in her words. "I *hate you.*"

"Good." *I do, too* he wanted to say, but he choked down the words. *I had to do it, he deserved a fate worse than death.*

A soft voice tickled Orion's ear and he clenched his jaw. *Murderer...* it whispered. *Monster.* "Captain, escort the Princess back to her chambers safely."

As if he had suddenly become possessed, Orion handed the sword off to a nearby soldier and plunged back into the forest. The voice continued to whisper in his mind while he wove through the trees with his three companions in tow. He couldn't help the trembling in his hands as he finally burst into the castle. The voice grew even more impatient, heightening until it was more than just one calling for him, begging for his attention.

Master...

Orion's stomach rolled as he headed to the hidden staircase that would take him down into the depths of the dungeons that lay hidden in the ground beneath the castle. He wasted no time to even wash the blood off of his hands and his arms from the execution. Instead, it began to dry, and he nearly laughed at the painful reminder that it provided. The desperation overtook him once more and he hurried along even more, pushing away the image of the blood and Terra's expression as she called him a monster.

The worst part? She was right.

The air grew even colder until he could see his breath in front of his face. His dogs followed close at his heels. Orion walked past the now empty cells with chains that had once all been filled years ago before he became King of this castle. The torch thew shadows against the walls that almost seemed to join and form menacing figures that would disappear if one would look directly at them.

At the far end of the dungeon sat a heavy stone door with almost archaic writing surrounding a carving of a bident. Orion placed his hand against the bident, closing his eyes and listened to the roar of the souls in his ears. A black light sprang from the writing and the symbol lit up and the dungeon seemed to vibrate beneath his feet. Dust shook loose from the cracks in the stones and the heavy door creaked open.

Orion swung it fully open and a blast of freezing air blew back his hair and his cloak. Before him sat an abyss of darkness and the final words he heard sent chills down his spine.

"Welcome home."

Chapter Eleven
Terra

"Maybe if I'm lucky, he won't even show up."

"Terra!"

"What? It's the truth." Terra brushed her hair back with her hands and sighed. Edith, I'm so tired, how much more do we need to do? It's not like either of us particularly want to be there."

Edith sat across from her at dining table with parchments scattered haphazardly around them. They contained notes and details that they still had not finished up in regard to the upcoming ceremony. "The wedding is tomorrow; we need to make sure that we have everything ready." Edith raised a pointed finger. "Even though neither of you want to be there."

Terra fought the urge to slam her head down onto the table in defeat. The last few days had been filled with Edith pestering her with details. Terra thought it was an absolute waste of time, but she insisted. It was clear that Orion had nothing to input himself, so it was all on Terra to decide. The stress had bogged her down and even though she wrote home pretending to be excited for the preparations for her family and Cassi's sakes, it was becoming too much for her.

As if we'll even acknowledge each other tomorrow, Terra thought bitterly. Not a single word had been exchanged between the two of them since the execution happened. Her dreams have been haunted with the images of the man's head being severed from his torso and rolling to the ground as if it was a piece of fruit that fell out of a basket. The reminder of it made the bile rise in the back of her throat and it only made her angrier knowing how much of a monster that the King of Valerian was.

Every morning like clockwork, they would eat breakfast together and every day neither of them would say a word. He would disappear almost as quickly as he would appear Her days had been filled with unspoken tension brewing stronger between them and spending time with Edith instead to plan the ceremony.

Edith also had begun to plan the coronation they planned another three weeks from tomorrow, giving them once again enough time, as Edith would say, "to make it as special for Terra as possible." The thought made her want to dive off the edge of Wolf's Pass in all honesty. She didn't understand why they didn't just get it all over at one time.

"It's tradition," Edith would say every time Terra would make that very suggestion.

Terra almost just wished they would do it all at once and get it over with. Why hold two separate events for nonexistent guests? "It's tradition," Edith would say every time Terra would ask her that very question.

"Can I go take a nap?" Terra asked. "I'm going to start dozing in this seat."

"There will be plenty of time for beauty rest, we still have more to do," Edith scolded. "Besides, there is a present waiting for you yet."

Terra perked up at this. "What type of present?"

"A surprise type of present."

"But what is it?"

"It wouldn't be a surprise if I told you, now would it?" Edith smirked and piled all the loose parchments papers into a neat pile. "I suppose we've been at this for too long this morning, I can take you now."

Terra followed Edith to the second floor with a spring in her step. Instead of going in the direction of her chambers, they made their way down an unfamiliar hall until they reached a plain door. Edith swung it open and ushered her in. In front of them on a stuffed mannequin sat a white flowing gown that was breathtaking, but Terra was perplexed.

With a preliminary glance, it appeared to be a wedding dress with its white fabric, but that certainly couldn't be the case. Terra had brought her dress with her from home with full intent to wear it. Terra had tried the chiton on in the privacy of her bedchambers the other night when she felt particularly homesick. She had just written a sorrowful letter to her sisters and her mother telling them how much she missed the sun reflecting off the deep blue waves on the coast and how much she missed being able to simply walk down the corridor to hug them when she felt lonely. Instead of cheering her up, the chiton only made her break down in sobs that ended with her hiding it back in her wardrobe where it would remain safe.

"Is this a wedding dress?" Terra asked Edith. The dress on the mannequin had a lace up bodice that fed to a swooped neckline and fell into long sleeves full of an intricate lace detail. The skirts flowed long on the ground and in a long lace train behind it.

"Yes dear," Edith beamed as Terra stepped up to the dress to feel the fabric. "It is a present from King Orion himself. I already made sure all the measurements are correct and it will be perfect to wear tomorrow."

Heat flared through her chest. "Did the King pick it out himself?" she asked. He couldn't help with any of the preparations, no, but he could try to dictate what she would wear?

"Well, no," Edith admitted. "But he was aware and supported the decision."

"I have a dress already." Terra dropped the fabric and turned to Edith. "One that is in Solarian style and was created for my wedding. I showed it to you earlier this week."

Edith wrung her hands and her face turned red in embarrassment. "Yes, and it was beautiful, truly, but in Valerian it is custom for your husband to pick it out himself."

"Is it not good enough for you?"

Terra turned and Orion stood in the doorway with his arms crossed. He had on his cloak and Terra could smell the crisp scent of snow on him from recently having been outside. Although she had not left the castle since the execution, she recognized the smell every time he returned for dinner.

"A *wedding dress,* are you serious?" Terra said incredulously. "I am expected to adhere to all your *prudish* traditions and expectations, not even being able to have my family here to see me wed, and you are dictating what *dress* I wear?"

"Yes," Orion responded with a straight face.

"I didn't ask for any of this. I never chose to marry such a brute. Who are you to tell me what to do? You're nothing but a murderer, Your Highness, and I think the last thing you should be concerned about is what I wear."

He scoffed and took a few steps towards her. "Don't patronize me, Princess."

"Tell me I'm wrong." Terra crossed her arms across her chest. "Tell me you didn't chop a man's head off without a fair trial, or even a chance to defend himself."

Orion was suddenly dangerously close to her, his frame towering above hers. She almost regretted the accusation she let out of her mouth as she swallowed hard, but not quite

"He was a murderer; did you know that? He slaughtered innocent women and children in their homes for the rest of their families to find. The last thing *you* should be concerned with, is how I run my kingdom. That man deserved a fate worse than death."

Terra's jaw worked as the truth began to sink in, but her temper could no longer be reasoned with. It was far, far too late for that. "What could be worse than death? You condemned him without even giving him a chance to defend himself."

"There are many things worse than death, Princess," he growled. "I would know.

"You are un-*bearable*," Terra seethed. "You may be King and you may give yourself the authority to send a man to his death without ever considering there may be more to the story, but that does not mean you get to control me the way you do with everything else in your life."

But before he could respond, Terra snapped. The anger became an ugly beast that roared in her ears so that there was no going back. "Do you really think I care? You have taken *everything* from me!" She stepped towards him with an accusatory finger jutting forward. "I gave up my home, my kingdom, even my family for you and instead of being compassionate or even understanding, you undermine me at every step and make my life a living hell. I gave up everything for you and you have done *nothing* in return."

Orion opened his mouth to say something, but Terra threw her hand up to cut him off. "You will let me finish! You have not said a word to me all week, nor have you even acknowledged my existence. You not only took away my home and my family, but then you damn near forcibly removed my best friend and confidant to completely isolate me. Just because you despise the world does *not* mean you get to treat people this way!" Terra finally snapped and before she could realize what she was doing, she slammed her hands into the mannequin on which the dress rested to send it toppling onto the floor. It crashed down and the sound caused Edith to flinch, but Orion barely even breathed.

The silence between them was deafening. Edith awkwardly hovered in the corner of the room while Terra's chest rose and fell rapidly. Everything from the last week bubbled to the surface. The loneliness, the anger, the frustration that she had been feeling became too much to bear. Embarrassment began to creep up along her neck as she grew red. She waited for him to speak, to say something, anything really. She wanted him to fight back and to tell her that she was wrong. She wanted to hear him say it, to throw anger right back at her the way she threw it at him. But instead, Orion said nothing. He appeared calm and collected with his face completely unreadable which only angered her more.

"As long as it's on your terms, you clearly don't care. I will live the rest of my days despising you," Terra seethed. "I see it every night now, did you know that? I see his blood stain the dirt beneath him and I hear the sick sound of his head falling off of his body." Storming past him, Orion stepped aside and let her go. "I do too," she almost thought she heard, but she quickly hurried down the hallway. As embarrassment began to claw at her throat. There was only one place for her to go. Terra made her way to the foyer and thew the doors open wide and to step outside.

Immediately, Terra was blasted in the face with a type of cold air that she had never felt before. It violently ripped through the cotton material of her dress fiercely and caused her long skirt to swirl around her legs. She slammed the door shut behind her with a heavy slam and fought to breathe through the frosty air. The last week, she had not dared step outside among the white powdered snow and even now, her body screamed at her to run back inside where it would be toasty and warm. *You will* not *go back,* she chastised herself. *You won't give him the satisfaction.* She forced herself to take the first step forward and then the next. Time alone is what she so desperately needed. At home in Solaris, whenever she felt overwhelmed, she would steal away to the garden to gather her thoughts. But here, she had nothing. *Or anyone.* She strode forward until she stepped onto the sheath of unshoveled snow covering the ground. Her boots prevented the cold from penetrating into her toes at least momentarily and she took the chance to run.

Where she was heading, Terra had no clue. The grounds were a complete mystery to her, but she knew she would break if she spent even a single minute more in the castle under their judgmental gazes. The wind loosened her hair from her long braid and soon it was blowing every which way in the breeze, but she no longer cared. She couldn't feel this anger and this loneliness any longer, so she prayed to the gods for the cold to make her numb.

Ahead, Terra noticed the tree line almost beckoning to her and without hesitation, she plunged into the forest that Orion spent all his time in. She twisted through the thick trunks and fought her way through the twigs and branches that clawed at the fabric of her dress. Her strands of hair kept catching but she kept pushing forward, going deeper and deeper into the woods. Soon, the elevation began to change and she found herself hiking upwards where the air grew even colder. She couldn't feel.

She didn't want to anymore.

After maybe a half an hour, a flurry began and the snowflakes fell large and soft to cover every possible surface, including her hair and her body. Terra's hands trembled from the cold and her body wouldn't stop shivering as the wind began to pick up. She had to stumble across one of the patrols of the soldiers sooner or later, right?

Her boots sank into deeper snow and the crunch sent shockwaves through her. The temperature was dropping and the world was starting to freeze around her. *And so am I,* she realized when she tried to fumble with a lace on her boot. *This was a mistake.* Even if she wanted to turn back now, she didn't know if she could even find the castle. The trees around her were looking identical and in a single frightened moment, she realized she was lost. Terra's breath condensed in the air in front of her face and she stuck her hands underneath her arms to try and keep them warm. Her teeth chattered sharply so that her entire being trembled. She had to go back.

Fading light tossed shadows across the trees, the sun was already beginning to set. If she didn't hurry, Terra would never make it back before dark. She grew more weary and soon she found herself almost stumbling through the snow. The cold was sapping all the strength that she had, and her fear began to warm into desperation. Among the trees she heard what sounded almost like a howl. Her mind went to Orion's wolf dogs and even as much as she didn't want to see him, the wolves could mean that she was close.

A bit further ahead, Terra thought she had spotted movement among the trees but when she turned, there was nothing there. She felt the breath of movement behind her and she whirled around again. "Hello?" she called out. "Is anyone there?" No answer came and she continued on, keeping her eyes open. Again, she heard what sounded like a howl again and that's when the realization hit her. There might be more than just pets in these woods.

Her chest tightened and she tried to hurry on, but the sun was setting too quickly. She was barely able to see anything before her except the flurry still raining down from the sky and the dark shadows that appeared to form frightening shapes around her. A log appeared out of nowhere and her boot caught, upending her into the snow and drenching the already damp material of her dress.

Tears began to prick Terra's eyes as she tried to haul herself back to her feet, but she only stumbled again. She dragged herself to the log and sat down on it. She tried to blow warm air onto her frozen fingers, but she was only able to produce a small and ragged breath through her shivering. "Why did I do this?" she asked herself and she began to cry harder. The tears seemed to freeze as soon as they touched her cool skin. "Why did I leave home? I should have never come here." She threw her head in her hands.

Movement in front of Terra startled her and she quickly raised her head to see a shadow slink through the trees. Her heart began to beat faster and she tried to peer through the falling snow and the oncoming darkness to distinguish what the animal was. A shape appeared behind her right side and she gasped before seeing that it was a black wolf dog. The wolf dog pressed its body up against her and Terra cried even harder, moving to wrap her hands into the warm fur.

A tall figure appeared before and she whimpered in relief. He had come for her. Orion was utterly furious. "Are you *trying* to kill yourself?" He growled and undid his winter cloak around his shoulders to throw over her own. It was toasty warm from his body heat and she drew it closer around her freezing body. "Or," he continued and pulled a pair of woolen mittens off of his hands. "Are you just trying to make sure Edith kills me, so you don't have to?" He put the gloves on her hands almost tenderly and stood before her in nothing but a tunic and a pair of his pants. The snow settled on his dirty blonde hair and she could tell he had been walking a while by the tangles in it. The stubble on his chin seemed as if it had grown tremendously since she last saw him as well as the dark bags under his eyes.

He looked haunted, she realized.

But he came for her. Why?

So? We don't care, Terra chastised herself. She tried to answer him instead with a not-so-nice response, but she couldn't get her lips to form the words.

"Save it," he cut her off instead and lifted her into his arms. "We need to get you back to the castle before Edith murders me. She's been worried sick." He began walking with her and let out a sharp whistle for his wolfdogs so that all three of them would follow.

Terra's mind could barely form a thought around her violent shivering. Orion hugged her closer and didn't stop until they finally left the shelter of the trees where the castle was then waiting for them.

As soon as they both entered into the foyer, Edith shrieked. "You had me worried *sick!* We need to get you out of those clothes dear, before you catch your death." She reached for Terra's gloved hand and began escorting her towards her bedchamber, reprimanding her the entire way. "And *you!*" she called out and pointed a finger at Orion. "You get yourself cleaned up at once as well, mister." Terra looked back and now that they were in the light, she could see he was as disheveled as she felt, if not more so. He was soaked through, but he watched them until they disappeared from view.

Once in her bedchamber, Edith started a fire and practically pushed Terra towards it while demanding that she strip that instant. Soon, Terra was bundled in a fur blanket in front of the flames while Edith insisted on making her a hot cup of tea, worried that she would grow ill from the exposure.

"How foolish of you," Edith grumbled as she strode from the room.

Just as the shivering began to stop, there was a soft knock at the door. "Come in!" Terra called, thinking it was Edith with tea. The door creaked open and it wasn't until Terra turned in confusion at the silence that she realized it was Orion in her doorway. He was freshly bathed and looked clean and warm, despite his cool features.

"I apologize if I'm disturbing you," he said, and Terra saw his eyes flick to her bare collar bone peeking out above the edge of the blanket. She blushed and drew the blanket tighter around herself, blatantly aware of the fact that she was bare skinned besides the one piece of fabric that could accidentally slip away at any moment.

Still feeling slightly annoyed with him, she turned and faced the roaring fire. "What do you want?" Terra asked. "A thank you for finding me?"

"Well, that would be a good start, don't you think?"

"Thank you for finding me," she deadpanned. "Also thank you for being the reason I left in the first place."

"You can't blame that on me."

Terra turned and narrowed her eyes. "Oh, I'm so sorry your Highness. No, me leaving wasn't your fault, but thank you for the night terrors and the trauma you have already put me through in my short time here. Don't you worry, I'll never forget it."

"I told you not to come!" Orion shouted and gripped his hair in frustration. "I knew what was going to happen and I asked you not to follow, but you did anyways!"

"How was I supposed to know you were going to *cut off someone's head?*" Terra got to her feet and jutted a finger into his chest. "Even though he needed to pay for his crimes, you didn't need to punish him by slaughtering him!"

Orion merely shook his head and glanced down again at her. Terra flushed and drew the blanket in once more as she turned to face the fire. A stressed silence hung between that was interrupted only by the crackling of the fire. Finally, she spoke. "Why do you do this? Why do you shut people out? You are always pushing people away when they get too close." *What are you hiding?* She wanted to ask.

She could feel him hesitate behind her before stepping closer. "It's complicated," he admitted softly. "That would be a very long story and today is not the day for that." He was quiet a moment more before asking, "Did you mean what you said?"

Terra thought back to the harsh words that left her mouth, tossing them over in thought now that she was relatively calmer before nodding. "Yes, I meant it."

This seemed to bother him, and he closed the distance between them until they were again almost touching, but not quite. "I'm sorry that I have made you feel that way, that was never my intention."

Terra turned and looked at him stunned. Was this really happening? Was King Orion saying these words, *apologizing* to her? She cleared her throat awkwardly. "I appreciate the apology."

His eyes again stole another look at her, but this time she thought he was staring at her mouth instead of the flash of skin peeking out from the blanket around her shoulders. *Good,* she thought to herself. *I hope it bothers him.* But he didn't look away. For a moment, Terra thought that he might lean in and kiss her. Her heart fluttered and she could feel her heart thumping in her throat. Her mind considered the possibility and wondered what it would feel like to press her lips against his, to feel his hands on her waist, to feel his hair between her fingers, but she just as quickly shook the thought from her head as it had formed. Seeming like he was reading her thoughts, Orion took a step backwards.

"Does that mean you forgive me?" he smirked and the smile tugged at something deep within Terra that she immediately shoved back down. "After all, tomorrow we are getting married."

"Nope," she replied and returned to her spot on the ground by the fire. "It doesn't. Have a good night, Your Highness." She sensed him behind her yet, hovering in the doorway but not immediately leaving. After a few more silent moments, she finally heard the floor creak and the door then closed softly behind him. She let out a deep, draining sigh and adjusted the blanket around her shoulders. He was complicated, that was for sure. There was more to him than what a person could see on his surface level, but would he let her ever see the deeper side of him?

Do you even want to see the deeper side of him?

Terra scoffed at her silly thoughts. Of course he wouldn't let her see that part of him, nor did she even know if she wanted to. He had kept up his stoic facade since she had met him, unless it was Edith who pushed him to make things right. *It was probably her that made him come look for me.* Anger still boiled deep inside her. Anger at him, and anger at herself for getting into this situation in the first place. She wanted to make him as mad as she was. No, she wanted to get *revenge*. A thought began to bloom in the back of her head as a scheme swirled through her thoughts. Since she was still so irritated at him, why should she let him get away with everything so easy?

Terra climbed to her feet and made her way to her wardrobe. She creaked open the doors and pushed aside the dresses to reveal the white and gold wedding chiton that her mother had made for her. She couldn't help but smile wickedly. *If I can't win, then I'll get even.*

Chapter Twelve
Orion

The only thing that Orion found worse than waking up at the crack of dawn, was to wake up to Edith pounding maliciously on the door to his bedchamber. "Rise and shine!" she called in a singsong voice from the other side. "Big day today and I am *not* dealing with your attitude, so breakfast and coffee are waiting for you downstairs!"

Silas groaned from his spot along his legs and his jaws opened in a yawn.

"Yeah, me too buddy," Orion grumbled and rubbed his eyes with the heel of his palms. "The day just started and I already want it to be over." The night prior had left him feeling drained and irritable.

The fear he felt when he realized that Terra must had been caught out in the snow invoked his inner most protector. He would have torn through the skies and hell until he found her which only baffled him more. He couldn't put to thought the feelings that she gave him.

And Orion absolutely hated it.

To make matters worse, Terra's words still rattled through his mind and haunted him throughout the night. *"Why do you do this?"*

Because I'm a monster, just like you said. And it is safer for you, he wanted to tell her but would never dare.

Realizing that he had been deep in thought, Orion shook his head and hurried to get ready before Edith came looking for him again. He put on a plain shirt and pants to at least eat breakfast first. Assuming that he would not be seeing Terra anytime soon, he whistled for the dogs to follow him and they excitedly bumped their way through his legs and out of the bedroom as he closed the door.

Laurent was in the kitchen when Orion walked in. "Good morning, sir," Laurent said and took a sip of his coffee before sliding Orion's own across the counter to him. Laurent glanced at the three dogs wandering and sniffing through the kitchen. "Edith would have your head if she saw they were in here," he commented with a knowing smile.

"It's an important day for them, too, right?" Orion grinned and took a bite of the buttered bread on the plate Edith had left for him.

"This is still something you would like to do, right? This is not something you have to do."

"Now you sound like Edith," Orion joked to hide his obvious discomfort and took a first drink of his coffee. He sighed happily and quickly drained almost half the cup. "Even though it's a ruse, she still is taking it seriously. But, I suppose, she is right. You know what my father used to say."

"'What is a King, without his Queen?' Your father did have a point there."

"And I cannot have a Queen without a bride. And she isn't half bad, even when she decides to be a pain in my ass so here we are." Orion shrugged nonchalantly and went back to eating. Laurent looked at him funny and it made Orion set his fork back down with a sigh. "Yes, Laurent?"

"You know I never give my opinion unless asked for it."

"Are you wanting me to ask you for your opinion?

"Perhaps."

"Pray tell my good friend, what is your opinion?"

"My opinion is that Princess Terra is more than 'not half bad' and you know that as well, you just won't admit it." Laurent leaned in and lowered his voice conspiratorially. "She is not like the others."

The kitchen door opened just in time to save him from answering and Edith entered with a silver tray balanced precariously in her hands upon which sat an empty teacup and kettle. She stopped in her tracks and her head whipped to face the three dogs snuffling their way around the kitchen. "Are those *dogs* in my kitchen, Orion?" she nearly screeched.

"I don't know what you're talking about." Orion drained the last of his coffee before darting out of the kitchen lest Edith smack him. The dogs came running quickly on his heels, frightened of Edith themselves.

Impatience lingered at the back of Orion's mind as he made his way back to his bedchamber and it was a feeling he couldn't get rid of. It was impatience for the ceremony today and impatience for today in general. He already wished it was all finished so he could leave, go to the woods or elsewhere as long as it wasn't *here*. Even after the incident of last night, the woods would still be a welcome reprieve. Ideally, he would not be overcome with emotions and reminded of the fact that his actions almost caused Terra to not just be injured but *die*. Edith had been in hysterics and clueless. Her and Laurent scoured the castle in desperation with no luck. Edith blamed him for making her so upset, and he knew that she was right. If Terra wasn't in the castle, then that only left one place. Before Edith could protest, he had dashed out to the forest with his dogs hot on his trail.

Guilt still rocked him. He couldn't help but blame himself for it all happening. Ash had found her first and sent Milo racing back to Orion while Ash stayed with her. When Orion first saw Terra with her head in her hands, he thought she was too far gone and that he had been too late. Relief had overwhelmed him as soon as she lifted her head and it took everything in him not to draw her to him. He would have never been able to live with himself if she had been lost out there when it was his fault she was there in the first place. He was fortunate, too, that nothing else in those woods had gotten to her first.

Again, he realized his thoughts turned to Terra and it frustrated him. Why did he feel this way about her? She was nothing to him except an inconvenience.

But yet...

Orion's mind fluttered to the memory of her resting beside the fire with nothing except the simple blanket draped over his shoulders. Just the sight of her made something deep within him awaken, and even now he fought to push it away.

"Why do you shut people out?"

Because I have to.

Realizing he had too much time on his hands and that it was only giving him more opportunity to contemplate intricacies of what was happening within him, Orion diverted his path and instead went to peek inside the grand ballroom where Edith had prepared the ceremony. Hiding in a far wing on the first floor, the room was normally empty and had once been used often to throw grand parties and galas for the nobility at every possible chance. Now that those days were far behind them, the room remained mostly empty and instead filled with dust as the years passed.

Now, though, it would finally be put to use. He reached the double wide wooden doors and opened one to reveal the expansive room before him. Large multi-story windows cast natural light across the rectangular room and illuminated every corner of it. The windows gave a breathtaking view over the gorge that hugged the one side of the castle and showed the snow-covered trees as far as the eye could see.

Large crystal chandeliers hung from the ceilings and would be used to illuminate the gold marble floor at night. The decadent walls were a soft maroon color with gold trim to match the flooring. This color theme, however, appeared to be the direct opposite of the ceremonial decorations that were held in the middle of the grand room. Leading straight from the doors to the center of the room were blue colored lanterns with unlit candles and further rested an altar at the end with an archway.

The archway was an extravagant rectangle shape with greens and baby blue flowers entwined in a vine formation around it. The colors reminded Orion of the sea and of the earth, both which also reminded him of the Princess herself, even if he wanted to deny it. It was as if Edith managed to embody Terra completely and create a spitting image of her.

"This is a bit much, don't you think?" he asked his dogs. Milo and Silas began playing with one another in the wide-open space as an answer and Ash simply looked at him as if to say "no, it's just you, you crazy person, you."

"Whatever you say," he said to Ash and whistled for the boys. They came prancing and finally exited the room with another call from Orion so that he could shut the doors. He still felt jittery, anxious even, as he went back to his bedchamber to pace aimlessly. Whereas Terra would be kept busy all morning by Edith, Orion instead was left with his own thoughts and with nothing but extra time. What was there for him to do? He supposed he could get ready and get dressed, but what was the point? Then he would be pacing by himself in his bedchamber with *still* too much time on his hands.

"I can't win, can I?" he complained to the dogs and threw his hands up in the air before sinking into his armchair in front of the fireplace. "If I left the castle, Edith would have my head on a spike."

He couldn't recall the last time he spent so much time in one place. Orion knew that his own mind was always his worst enemy, even more so than the physical ones. As if his enemies heard him summon them, the familiar whisper trickled in one ear and wove its way deep into his mind. *Not today*, he thought angrily. *You can bother me any other day except today, I don't have the time for this.* Much to his surprise, the voice listened for once and fell silent which relieved him. He was already stressed enough and the last thing he needed was to have to take care of the others today.

Something else tickled his mind while he chewed on the inside of his cheek thoughtfully. It was the strong sense that he was forgetting something important, but he couldn't quite grasp what it was. Was it something that Edith asked him to do? Orion frowned, unable to conjure up what was causing the uncomfortable feeling. He had to figure it out eventually, so instead he began the process of getting ready.

Before long, he was dressed and cleaned up to the point that even Edith would approve. His hair was smooth and combed and he had even shaved, trimming the scraggily hairs until he looked well-groomed in comparison to any other day.

Orion wore a pitch-black tunic with red rubies inlaid in the buttons to compliment the red threading woven throughout the material. He had black riding breeches tucked into his shiny black riding boots that he never wore. Instead of wearing clothes for a commoner, he was now dressed like the King that he was. He regarded himself in the mirror and smoothed back his hair. *I look like my father*, he couldn't help but think.

Orion quickly looked away from his reflection as the stark realization set in. He looked like the person that he hated most in his life. *Am I becoming him too?"*

Suddenly, he finally remembered what he had been forgetting and what Edith would hang him for if he forgot. "Come on," he called to the dogs and left his bedchamber.

Much to his disdain, he passed countless soldiers and staff now roaming the corridors to aid Edith with preparing for the ceremony. He made his way to an older room hidden away in a wing far from his own bedchamber, one that he had not been in for years and where the object he needed would be.

Orion creaked open the door and commanded the dogs to wait outside before closing it behind him quietly. The old parlor sat just as it had when Orion was a child. There were chaste couches resting around one of the most elaborate fireplaces in the castle. A grand piano sat in one corner and Orion walked over to it to run a soft finger over the dust covered surface. A hidden memory suddenly surfaced and he was transported back to his childhood.

"Mom," young Orion cried, running into the parlor with tears streaming down his face. His mother had been sitting at the piano playing a soft melody and turned around just in time to catch her eldest son in a hug.

"What is the matter?" she asked softly and had stroked his hair while he had sobbed hard into her chest. "What happened?"

"Theon ha-had left the stable doors open," Orion had blubbered. "And - and father asked us who it was but I- I didn't want Theon t-to get hu-hurt so I said it was me."

His mother frowned and took his chin with a thumb and forefinger to scan him over. A black eye was already beginning to form and she let out a weary sigh. "That was very brave of you to protect your little brother like that, dear. Should we make you a cup of tea? Would that make you feel better"

Orion shook his head. "I should have never said it was me, Theon should have admitted what he did. It's all his fault."

"Some mistakes get made. As long as we learn from our mistakes, it's okay to make them Orion."

"I hate father!" Orion had shouted and wiped his tears away angrily. "I wish he would just leave and never return!"

"Shhh don't say that darling. Your father loves you very much."

"He wouldn't always leave us if he did. He would be here to love us and to go riding with us and tuck us in at night. Instead he keeps leaving. When is his next hunting trip?"

Tomorrow." His mother grimaced at the confession. "But Orion, that does not mean he doesn't love you."

"I wish he were dead."

Orion was brought back to the present and he quickly took his hand off of the piano surface. His heart ached at the memory. His mother had been beautiful and one of the most compassionate women that had cared deeply for her family. He could almost still smell her familiar scent of vanilla and see her glowing smile.

Single handedly, she had raised Orion's three older sisters along with his two younger brothers while his tyrannical father was constantly absent from his throne. It was better that way, Orion had realized growing up. His siblings and even his mother was constantly walking on eggshells when he was present, which just wasn't a way for children to live. "We all make mistakes," he reminded himself. "Even mother made them."

Orion left the piano and looked at the portrait of his mother that still hung above the hearth along with a portrait of his father. In the painting, his father looked gruff and as lifeless as he had been in person whereas his mother's essence seemed to be trapped in her own. Her eyes glittered as if she was about to make a joke and her cheeks were frozen in a soft smile that might transform into a large grin at any moment. *If only it were true*, he thought wistfully. He almost wished he knew what she'd think of Terra and their upcoming nuptials. But now wasn't the time for him to sulk, so he went to the glass case in the corner to grab what he had come for.

Orion lifted the glass display and resting on a satin cushion was the King's royal crown that was passed down from father to son for generations. It was a beautiful thing, he had to admit. Rubies were inlaid into the twining metal and represented the blood that his family had sacrificed in order to build their kingdom. It was quite ironic, really.

A small voice in his head urged Orion to start a family, to once again have others to love and to cherish, but he knew what consequences could come from that. Edith and Laurent are definitely his family, but he would never let them become the type of family he once had. He knew that Edith secretly hoped that Terra would be different, that she would be the one to finally convince Orion to have his own legacy, but he thought otherwise. Just as Terra had said, he was a monster.

Orion donned the crown and found a dusty hand mirror resting on one of the tables. He blew the dirt off and found himself looking even more like his father. "I will not be my father," he told himself with conviction. "I will *not* be my father." But instead of feeling soothed by saying the words out loud, his reflection seemed to mock him, to ask "are you so sure about that?"

"You are acting like your Father, the way you treat her. Is that what you'd like to become?"

The words that Edith had said to him that morning in the kitchen still shocked him. His mind was plagued with the fear of becoming like him and it made his head ache from the strain.

"I will not become him," he whispered again and set the mirror down with a sharp inhale. Who was he becoming? He was a stranger to even himself. Orion wasn't sure how much time had passed, but he felt like he took longer than he had thought.

But he couldn't dwell on this now, he had to go.

Laurent found him just as he left the parlor room. "Your Highness, it is almost time." He looked Orion up and down and drank in his appearance. "You look very handsome, sir. Are you ready?"

"As ready as I can be," Orion answered.

Side by side, Orion and Laurent wove through the corridors to the ballroom. Laurent swung open the massive doors for him and as soon as Orion stepped inside, he nearly faltered. The entire aura of the room had transformed. As the sun had begun to set, the brilliant sunset casted different soft colors through the windows and highlighted the archway perfectly. Edith had lit the lanterns and placed soft rose petals down the aisle for their entrance. Even Orion had to admit that it was romantic. It left a strange lingering feeling within him.

Soft music floated through the air as a harp player strung the instrument softly off to the side and soldiers dressed in their best uniforms waited in their seats to witness the ceremony. All it took was a generous offer of a feast and plenty of ale.

Edith was standing beneath the arch with a weathered book placed upon a podium in front of her. In it were the words that she would recite to officially join Terra to Orion during the ceremony. Edith made a quiet noise of approval at his attire when he approached her and she looked as if she was about to cry.

"You didn't get my attitude today, so I don't get your tears," Orion teased her quietly and kissed her on the cheek. She was dressed in one of her finest gowns for the occasion as well. The stitching was immaculate and the red complimented her well. Even though this was a small affair, Orion knew that it meant a lot to both Laurent and Edith.

Expecting Terra to not be very far behind him, Orion was agitated as the minutes ticked by and there was no change. He still stood awkwardly in front of a crowd of his men who whispered conspiratorially amongst each other. The sun seemed to set even more while they remained as is and just when Orion was contemplating sending out a search party, the doors creaked open.

Everyone in the room immediately straightened and looked at the entrance, the soldiers standing at attention.

A flash of white appeared first as a foot stepped through, then a leg, then a torso, and then the rest of Terra. Orion's gaze focused on her and a feeling of disbelief washed over him. "She didn't," Orion muttered under his breath. Terra slipped through the doors and walked slowly over the rose petals with a smirk on her face while Orion stood dumbfounded. The wedding dress that Edith had bought for her, the one that they had fought over, was not what Terra was wearing, no.

Instead, she was wrapped in the fine fabric of her dress from Solaris.

Annoyance flared hot through his chest and it mixed with a tinge of admiration for the gall she had for daring to disobey so outwardly. He supposed he deserved it, and the more he lingered on it, the more he felt the urge to laugh at the whole situation. *She sure showed me.*

Terra appeared to feel the same, for when she reached the end of the aisle and stopped across from him, he could see the growing smile plastered on her face. She held a bouquet of flowers in her hands and she didn't meet his eyes, but Orion couldn't help but glance at her. Her still-tanned skin looked smooth among the folds of her dress. He couldn't help but be distracted by the sight, almost too distracting for the words that Edith was saying were muted and nonexistent.

Laurent subtly cleared his throat and Orion's attention snapped back to the ceremony happening right in front of him. He took the rings from Laurent and repeated the words Edith instructed. He then placed a black band with a purple amethyst in the center of it on Terra's slender ring finger and he could feel the electricity shoot through him at the gentle graze of his hand against hers. Abruptly pulling away, he placed the thick black band on his own hand.

"May the gods bless your union," Edith recited to close the ceremony and beamed at them both. "Now, let's feast!"

The mass of soldiers cheered and clapped, officially ending the ceremony. As everyone began to mingle and converse amongst each other, staff that Edith had hired from the local village burst into the room with glasses and mugs balanced precariously on trays. Terra quickly grabbed a flute of champagne and the handmaid gave him one as well, curtsying politely before hurrying away.

Staff begun to clear the aisle and archway in order to set up tables and chairs for the feast. In a blink of an eye, the room was converted. Edith beckoned them to their spots at the head table.

Orion swept his arm out and invited Terra to go first. Without saying a word, she picked up her skirts and he followed after her, his eyes resting on the bare back that the gown had to offer. Terra turned to look at him and he quickly averted his gaze. He almost wanted to smack himself, what was wrong with him? Since when was her beauty so hypnotizing?

They took the right two seats at the table, their shoulders almost touching while Laurent and Edith took their own so that both Edith and Terra sat side by side. Two young servants soon appeared with wine in hand to gill the goblets before them before disappearing once again.

"So, Princess," Orion said under his breath to Terra. "You're quite daring to be wearing that. If you would ask one of the more suspicious bunch of my men, they would even say that you have cursed our marriage before it had even begun."

Terra shrugged and her familiar smile tugged at the corner of her lips. "In my culture, this style of dress is indicative of a happy marriage."

"Is that so?"

"No," Terra grinned and took a drink of her own wine. "But you believed it was."

Orion sat back in his chair and shook his head. "We're enemies, remember? Maybe you should be cautious of what games you play, Princess."

"We're enemies, don't you forget. You're just scared that you'll lose."

Before he could make a snarky remark back, the servants returned with steaming hot dishes and the feast began. Deciding to allow himself to at least enjoy this part and to let the electricity between them simmer, Orion dug in.

There were plates of rich soups, stuffed duck, venison lathered in a rich gravy, roasted vegetables and much more. The wine kept coming and soon he knew that he needed to slow down lest he becomes too inebriated.

Terra, however, did not. The new bride kept requesting to have her goblet refilled and she was beginning to sway in her seat. She and Edith were whispering quietly with each other before bursting out into uncontrollable giggling. A band struck up in the corner and began to play upbeat music that made the guests dance jovially as they drank.

Orion took advantage of the distraction and snapped his fingers under the table until the dogs, who were let in once the feast had overall finished, slunk to him happily. He snuck some of the scraps left on the table underneath the table and allowed them to enjoy the feast with them.

"Dance with me."

Orion turned to Terra in surprise. "You want me to dance? What happened to us being enemies?"

"In Solaris, it's customary to share a first dance, but usually it's not quite as fun as this." Terra gestured to the drunken soldiers clapping and enjoying themselves on the makeshift dance floor. "Besides, I like to keep my enemies close. Unless the issue is that you can't dance and you're too scared to make a fool of yourself."

"Oh Princess, you underestimate me." Against his better judgement, Orion took her hand and pulled her to her unsteady feet. The challenge, he decided, was just too good to pass up.

Orion could feel the guards' eyes focus on him and his new wife. He spun her and pulled her close, causing her to let out a small gasp of surprise. "My mother taught me to dance a long time ago, but I was very good."

Before he could lose his nerve, he danced. The two of them twirled and spun across the ballroom floor. Her skirts swirled elegantly, and the soldiers gave them space to cheer them on. He felt her every breath, her every smile at the sensation of floating in his arms. It was an intoxicating feeling.

The song came to a close and just on the last beat, he pulled her once again to him and dipped her until her hair brushed against the ground. Terra's face was flushed a crimson red. Either from the wine or from their proximity, he couldn't tell. He swallowed hard and tilted her back up before clearing his throat. "Like I said, don't underestimate me."

"One point for you," she said in a hushed tone of admiration. Her green eyes sparkled and she looked at him like she had never seen him before.

Before his emotions could betray him, Orion hurried back to the table and left Terra in the middle of the dance floor where she was immediately swept into the arms of one of the soldiers to continue to dance.

Hours passed and still everyone celebrated. Orion watched Terra spin around the room again and again as everyone yearned to twirl their new Queen. It wasn't until Edith laughed so hard that she fell right out of her chair onto the floor that he decided it had gotten late enough. Orion and Laurent immediately jumped out of their seats and helped her back to her feet.

"Oh, forgive me, I fear I may have had too much wine," Edith hiccupped. "I should turn in for the night, Laurent can escort me back to my chambers." Edith looped her arm through Laurent's and they were on their way, Laurent holding her steady as she stumbled off.

Terra finally found her way back to her seat and looked like she was ready to turn in as well, even though he knew she would never admit it while the stronger of his men still continued their boisterous drinking.

Orion looked at Terra with his hands on his hips and when she noticed him looking, she scowled. "What are you looking at?" she slurred.

"Someone that I think needs to go to bed," he said not unkindly and stepped towards her. "I'll help you, let's go. I don't always have to be the enemy."

She looked thoughtful for a moment before answering. "No, I suppose not."

Reluctantly, Terra took his outstretched hand and hooked her arm through his to heavily lean on him. Together, they left the ballroom where the guards had begun to drunkenly sing a tavern song and they headed up to the second floor where Orion commanded the dogs to "go to bed" so that they would be waiting for him in his own bedchamber. Neither of them said a word to each other until they arrived outside Terra's door. She let go of him and leaned her back against the corridor wall heavily.

"Listen, I wanted to apologize for the things I said again," she said and placed a steadying palm against the wall. "I shouldn't have called you a murderer when the man deserved punishment and I can't help but feel guilty for it."

Orion's chest tightened and he willed his voice to remain steady. "Please, don't worry about any of that. It's already forgiven."

Terra nodded and swayed a bit to one side before righting herself once more. "So," she began. "Is this where we spend the night together as husband and wife?"

Orion looked at her in complete shock, that so-called expectation never crossing his mind. "Why would you ask that?"

She shrugged and looked away bashfully. "Because that's what husbands and wives do, I don't know." *Because it's expected for a wife to give an heir*, he imagined her adding.

He regarded her thoughtfully, feeling bad that this was a thought of hers at all and that it was never one for him. One of her long strands of hair had fallen in front of her eyes and before he realized it, he brushed the strand back with his hand and tucked it behind her ear. She sucked in a sharp breath. "You're not a monster," she said softly. "And you're not the villain in my story." Her eyebrows knit together in a frown. "I don't know what you are yet."

Gods. Orion bit the inside of his cheek and the flood of emotions made him feel sick to his stomach. *What the hell is wrong with me?* Before he would say or do anything he would regret, he pressed a tender kiss to her hand. "Goodnight Princess." Before she even had a chance to say anything in return, he hurried away out of sight.

Something was happening to Orion, something that he didn't like. This girl had begun to expose a soft spot within him and she was breaking down his walls. He was starting to tread dangerous waters.

He couldn't let her in, and he couldn't expose her to what he was. Her safety was more important than his feelings and he couldn't put her in danger. He could end up hurt.

Or worse, she could.

What the hell was I thinking?

Chapter Thirteen
Terra

Another dull day, Terra huffed and stared out her bedroom window at the flakes of snow that had begun to flutter from the sky. The coronation ceremony had been held that morning and had only lasted maybe a mere half an hour where Edith recited more traditional script from the same large book she had used for the wedding. This gave Terra the rest of the day to stare forlornly out of a window as if she didn't already do so every other day. Her new crown was already cast aside, the silver thing sitting upon the mantle of her fireplace and mocking her from a distance.

"You call yourself a Queen?" it seemed to say.

Terra thought back to the night of the wedding and cringed at the memory of asking Orion if he was to spend the night in her bed. She had never meant for the thought that was crossing her mind at that moment to slip out of her lips, but the wine certainly didn't help the situation.

Or maybe it was the way that he spun her around the dance floor that bothered her so. It had taken her breath away and had made her think that maybe, just maybe, they were reaching a new level of their relationship. They were getting along and had multiple sweet conversations that gave her the impression that they were getting somewhere.

But then Orion put his wall back up as quickly as it had seemed to disappear.

Ever since the night of the wedding, he had managed to steer clear of her. Well, besides the awkward breakfasts that Edith forced them to still share. A word would never pass between them and usually Orion would finish first, disappearing into the woods or elsewhere while Terra would fight against the overwhelming sense of embarrassment that threatened to smother her.

Even now, the embarrassed tears were there, still threatening to let loose and she wrangled the inner turmoil back together once again in order to hold herself tall. Terra was a Queen now, even in privacy she had to be strong. She couldn't allow herself to falter or to let her emotions make herself vulnerable. *I'm starting to act like Orion,* she thought almost wryly to herself. But it was true. She couldn't be a weak and young girl to him anymore, she was now his wife and a Queen and he needed to treat her as such. Well, as soon as the awkward silent treatment stopped.

If her mother was there right then, Terra knew that she would tell her that she needed to be the bigger person and confront Orion about what had transpired between them. If she took the step to try to find an understanding, it would make her life a lot easier. But, of course, her Mother wasn't here and even in the letters that Terra would write her, she would never dare let her mother be privy to her current predicament. It would only worry her mother if she were to know that this wasn't a dream come true and the more that her mother worried about her, the less she would be focused on protecting the throne.

But the thought was still there. She had to talk to him about it and get the air cleared up between them. Orion and she couldn't keep merely existing in each other's worlds and the effort was leaving her drained. If Terra was ever going to be happy here, then something with them needed to change. She didn't need romance, she didn't need a husband or a lover, but she needed a partner. Yes, eventually she would need to give the kingdom an heir, she knew that, but Orion has made it subtly clear that an heir is not on his radar anytime soon, and she planned to keep it that way as long as she could.

That left only one valid option that Terra could see: try to make amends.

Terra sighed and hauled herself to her feet to go find him, but not before she grabbed her cloak. If he was not in his room, he would most certainly be out in the forest. She first stopped at his door and knocked softly. Only silence on the other side greeted her. "I really didn't want to go out in the snow," she grumbled to herself but clasped her cloak over her shoulders anyways. She hadn't been outside since the incident in the last blizzard and she still was slightly frightened of ending up lost in the wilderness once more. Her body screamed at her not to go when she took the first step outside, but of course she was never very good at listening.

Terra had barely made it to the tree line before one of the dogs came bounding towards her. She was finally beginning to be able to tell the difference between the three, mostly due to their personalities and not their identical midnight black fur. Ash, the only female, was the only dog that was overly friendly with her and would rush to greet her (like she just did). Silas, she could tell, did not like her and would always steer clear of her while watching her with careful eyes. Milo was neutral and didn't rush to greet her at every chance like Ash did, but he wasn't completely against attention from her like Silas. She was genuinely curious about Orion's story of how he came to have the three wolf dogs, but he would never talk to her long enough for her to ask.

"You shouldn't be out here."

Terra, who was rubbing her hands vigorously, raised her head to see Orion appearing through the trees with a bow in his hand and a quiver slung over his back. "And why would that be?"

"Because, Princess, there are dangerous things in these woods that you would be no match up against."

"Ah, ah, ah," Terra waved a playful finger at him that she hoped would disarm his steely attitude. "*Queen.*"

Orion's jaw ticked, but he didn't correct himself and he didn't appear to be amused by her correction. "What can I do for you?"

"I wanted to talk." Suddenly, her throat felt tight and her mouth went dry. She was nervous, she realized, but why? Because he might laugh in her face? Because he could disagree with everything she might say and make her life a living hell as a result? He quirked an eyebrow but remained silent. Terra shifted uncomfortably and drew her cloak around herself tighter.

"I don't like it when you completely avoid me," she finally blurted out. "I already feel alone here and I feel like you're punishing me for something I didn't do. You refuse to be even in the same room with me besides every morning just to quick eat."

His face remained stoic and he leaned against a tree with his arms crossed.

"I know we didn't start off in the best of places, but I thought we were beginning to make progress. I know I called you some pretty horrific things, and in my defense, you weren't very nice to me either, but what happened for us to end up like this? I don't expect you to treat me like your wife," Terra continued. "But I am your Queen and I want to find a common ground where I don't feel quite so miserable and alone here. We have to be able to, I don't know, work together I guess?"

"And what do you suggest?" he asked carefully.

Terra's brain froze, she hadn't thought about this part. She knew what bothered her and she knew that she wanted their dynamic to change, but into what? How would they go forward to try to be partners, maybe even friends? "Could we start by spending more time together? I spend every day alone and I fear I may grow a bit mad if I keep it up."

After a thoughtful moment, Orion nodded and Terra let out a silent sigh of relief. "We can do that."

"I've always wanted to learn," Terra said softly and pointed to the bow he still had in a hand. "Maybe you could teach me."

Orion looked at her in surprise. "I could do that, but not today though. The weather may turn ugly today and I wouldn't want you to be stuck out there in it. I know you have a fondness for disappearing when there's a blizzard, but I would not advise that." His mouth quirked.

Terra couldn't help but smile herself. "I'll try not to find myself in that predicament again. I will leave you to… whatever it is that you're doing then." She rocked on her heels, not quite sure what else to say before she turned to leave.

"Terra!"

She turned in astonishment and a warm feeling like honey flowed through her. He normally didn't call her by her name and it sounded foreign on his lips.

"Why don't you take Ash with you? For company," he clarified.

Terra gave him a small smile. "Sure. Let's go," she said to Ash and called her along. Ash bounded after her, sending snow flying in her wake.

Grateful to leave behind the baffling encounter, Terra couldn't help but feel unsure about the exchange. He was quick to joke with her, but he still seemed standoffish in comparison to the wedding.

"What should we do Ash?" she asked the dog, suddenly needing a distraction. The longer she was here, the more she found herself talking to the dog as if she would one day respond as a human would. "What type of trouble can we get in?"

Ash panted with her tongue flopping out the side of her mouth while she trotted next to Terra. Terra wished that she could answer and be a true companion, but she supposed it was better than not having anyone at her side.

"We could bother Edith, let's check and see if she's in the kitchen." The two of them made their way out of the cold and to the warm kitchen to find Edith wrapping her own cloak around her shoulders.

"Where are you off to?" Terra asked her as Ash slunk around her legs with her head down as if she was trying to make sure Edith didn't notice her sneaking in the area.

"I'm off to town before the weather turns. I should be home before dark though, so no need to worry."

"Isn't the pass full of snow already?"

"Pah," Edith waved a hand. "I'm a seasoned veteran when it comes to these winters. Besides, we have our own secret way to get to town that the villagers aren't aware of. It allows us to move quicker and with less eyes watching our every move." She winked conspiratorially and moved to leave.

"Can I come with?" Terra questioned, hoping that Edith would finally say yes one of these times. Edith had taken a trip to the village maybe two or three times and each time she insisted that Terra stayed, put much to her dismay.

Edith shook her head. "I'm afraid not dear, I wouldn't want you to try to weather this storm. It's a far cry from the warmth of Solaris. We will go when the weather clears up."

Terra smiled to hide her disappointment. "Safe travels." She snapped her fingers at Ash and the dog followed her out of the kitchen and back towards her bedchamber. "There goes that plan. We could explore since the castle is empty, there is plenty I haven't seen yet. What do you think?"

Ash wagged her tail and her tongue lolled out of her mouth again in delight.

"Works for me," Terra laughed. She quickly hung up her cloak to dry in her room and the two went off looking for more trouble.

Most of the first floor Terra had grown quite familiar with. The rooms were mostly common spaces instead of hidden gems like the other floors could potentially hold. So she began with the third floor, one that she knew to not be occupied and which could be housing many treasures of the unknown.

The third floor was discernibly unused compared to the other two. There was a lack of life in the dusty rugs and lanterns, but there wasn't a lack of history. Terra could see it in the paintings that lined the halls and in the scuffs on the corners of the doorframes. This floor was once lived in and was used more than maybe even the other floors, that much was obvious. She wondered what secrets she may find.

Ash ran ahead of her, snuffling the rugs and doors while Terra peered in each room. Many of the spaces were now empty she found, full of only dust and memories that were long gone. She heard Ash barking down the hall so Terra closed the door and went to investigate what Ash was getting so worked up about. At the end of the hallway, Ash waited for her expectantly and wagged her bushy tail before disappearing from sight once more.

"Ash?" Terra called. She reached the end of the hallway and discovered that there was another staircase, this one being a small spiral one that led steeply upwards. "There's another floor?" Terra mumbled to herself. She heard a faint bark from Ash that echoed down the stairs and climbed up after her.

Instead of leading to another long hallway, the staircase led to a short hallway with only one wooden door at the end of it. Ash was sniffing at it and scraped one of her front paws at the stone floor. She turned to look at Terra as if to say, "what are you waiting for? Open it already!"

"Okay, okay!" Terra exclaimed and opened the door. It creaked open heavily and Terra sneezed from the plume of dust that followed. It was a bedroom, she saw, one frozen in time as if its occupant disappeared one day and had never returned. A gorgeous ballgown lay draped over a chair at a vanity full of brushes and colors of makeup reflected in the giant mirror. The bed was unmade and its blankets were still haphazardly twisted from someone having slept in it. Terra saw a hairbrush on the vanity inlaid with gold. She picked it up and noticed bright red hair still in it.

This must have been one of his family members' chambers, she thought to herself while she snooped around, looking at the little trinkets and decor that rested throughout the room. Terra walked to the window and threw open the drapes, revealing a single door leading to a small balcony. She dared to open it and stepped outside under the falling snow. With a start, she realized she was on the roof of the castle and could see what seemed like the entire realm around her. It took her breath away to see the vastness of the forest below her and the flurries falling from the sky into her hair. It may not have been Solaris, but Valerian was beautiful.

Terra shivered and stepped back inside. She closed the door again tightly and drew the shades until they sat exactly the way they had before she disturbed them. "Let's keep going and see what else we can find," she said to Ash and the two traipsed back down to the third floor again. Yielding nothing else exciting, Terra travelled back down to the second floor. Most of the second floor she had seen as well, but there were parts she knew she had not visited prior.

Ash sprinted ahead of her and Terra followed the dog as quickly as she could down a few hallways until she found herself in a wing that she had not seen before. "This could prove interesting," she murmured to herself and began opening doors to see what she could find. Most of the second floor were guest rooms that Edith kept tidy (just in case she would always say) and rooms for storage, except for this wing. This wing, similar to the hidden fourth floor, held dusty bedchambers that were now long abandoned

Ash whined at a door so Terra left the room she was peeking in and instead went to the one that the dog was wagging her tail at. "You have a keen sense," she commented to the dog and swung the door open. Ash yawned as if she was suddenly bored and trotted down the hall where a cushioned window seat rested in front of a window. "Suit yourself." She climbed up and put her head down on her paws before letting out a huff before Terra entered the room. The beauty of it all overcame her. Many of the rooms in the castle were breathtakingly beautiful in their own way, sure, but nothing else was quite like this.

Terra was in a once extravagant parlor room and she looked around in awe, taking in the plush chaise lounges, the piano resting in a corner, the expensive woven carpet, the two empty display cases along one wall, and finally her gaze landed on the portraits hanging above the fireplace.

There was a King and a Queen pictured and the King looked quite familiar. It wasn't until Terra studied it for a while that she realized why. The man pictured was an older version of Orion. They shared the same sharp jaw, the slender nose, the pale hair, and the stormy grey eyes. The woman, on the other hand, had long beautiful black hair that fell in waves down her back. She had soft brown eyes and a rounded face that looked feminine, kind, and very pretty. Terra's eyes were drawn up to the crest of her head where she saw the same silver metal crown with rubies that now rested in her bedroom. With a start, she realized they must be Orion's Mother and Father. What happened to them though, she wasn't sure.

"Ash!" a voice from outside the room called. Suddenly panicked, Terra peeked her head through the door and realized that it was Orion calling. His voice echoed as he called again, and she knew he would come around the corner at any moment. For some reason, she felt embarrassed by the fact that she was snooping around the castle and invading what could be a private space for him judging by the portraits. Instead of helping them grow closer, this could only drive a deeper wedge between them. She closed the door quietly and looked for a hiding spot, darting behind the heavy drapes right as she heard the parlor door creak back open.

Heavy boots strode across the stone floor and Terra held her breath. She could hear him fussing with something but couldn't place it. Seconds ticked by slowly as if they were hours and the entire time Terra was praying to the gods that he wouldn't throw back the drapes to discover her.

Instead, she heard him sigh and say, "Really? You can't leave me alone for one day?"

Bewildered, Terra thought he was addressing her and that he actually had found her hiding place, but before she could decide what she should do next, the footsteps grew more faint. "I'll be right there," she heard him grumble irritably before hearing the door click back shut once again. She heard his muffled call for Ash and then he was gone. Too afraid to move, Terra waited silently until she was completely sure he was not coming back and then let out a shaky breath.

That was a close one, she thought to herself. Who was he talking to? Something doesn't seem right and she was stumped by what just transpired. There was only one way to find out the truth. Against her better judgement, she decided to make the foolish decision and follow him. He had said "I will be right there" so he had to be meeting someone, but who?

Gathering up her skirts, Terra snuck back out of the room and scurried down the hallway as quietly as she could. Moving quickly, he was clearly in a hurry to reach whoever it was that he was meeting. Ash was at his side and paid Terra no mind even though Terra knew that there was no way that Ash at least didn't hear her following them.

Terra was calculating and hid around corners until the coast was clear, but never giving him too much space where she might lose him. This wasn't the first time she had done this, just the first time with him. Growing up, her sisters and her were always sneaking around the palace and playing games of hide and go seek that could sometimes last hours. Terra felt her heart ache at the thought of her sisters. She missed them horribly and even though she wrote them letters almost daily, it wasn't the same as being with them in Solaris. But now wasn't the time. She had to focus.

To her surprise, Orion hurried down to the first floor and instead of going out the front door, he snatched one of the lanterns hanging in the foyer and veered down a different hallway with all three dogs now at his side. Terra leaned over the banister and before continuing after him, she made sure that no one was in sight. Orion disappeared through a door that Terra had never noticed. She could hear his boots against stone and it sounded as if he was on a staircase. *Another hidden staircase?* Giving him a little longer of a head start, she finally worked up the courage to pull open the door. She was hit in the face with extremely cool and damp air from a passage that led downwards.

Taking a nervous gulp, Terra followed. The darkness was indescribable. It seemed to hug her tightly and smother her. She could hear water dripping from an unknown source and she climbed further down into the darkness. Finally, she felt the stairs end and she reached flat ground. She crested a corner and could see Orion walking with his lantern ahead with his dogs following him. The light from the lantern illuminated his surroundings just enough for Terra to realize that she was in a moldy dungeon resting below the foundation of the castle.

Is there someone down *here?* Terra thought in horror. *Were there prisoners down here that he was coming to see?* Her mind flashed to the execution, but that didn't mean that Orion was fond of torturing captives. She kept one hand against the wall and crept forward towards his light but not wanting to get too close. He stopped ahead and the lantern showed what looked like a giant stone door with something inlaid into it. She could hear him speaking softly before it swung open, making her stop dead in her tracks.

A low rumble seemed to shake the stones beneath Terra's feet and smaller bits shook loose from the ceiling and walls. A horrible feeling overcame her and she froze, unable to move even a single inch as the feeling of dread consumed her. She was stuck in silent horror as Orion, the lantern, and the dogs disappeared through the doorway. The door swung back to close and only then was Terra able to finally breath again, except now she was stuck in complete darkness beneath the earth. With her limbs shaking, she shuffled onwards, determined to get to the door before the last remaining bit of her courage dissipated entirely.

Terra finally rested a quivering hand on the door and she could feel markings engraved into its surface, but she wasn't able to make any of it out. She felt around the surface, desperately trying to feel for some sort of doorknob or handle, anything that would allow her to open it. To her dismay, there was nothing. She slammed her fists against the cold stone in frustration.

There was no way for her to open the door and Orion was gone.

Huffing in defeat, Terra slunk her way back to the staircase by feeling her way along the wall. By the time she reached the top of the staircase and was once again met with beautiful light, she vowed to herself that she would return soon and find out what secrets lay behind that door.

Chapter Fourteen
Orion

"You're going to poke an eye out with that thing, and it won't be mine." Orion darted a hand towards Terra and seized the arrow that she was holding out of her hands. "You have to be more careful."

Terra huffed and a plume of her breath rose in the cold air. "I *am* being careful." She snatched the arrow back from him and strung it in the elegant bow she held in her slender hands. "I can't *shoot* the bow unless I *point* it, now can I?"

Orion stepped away from her and crossed his arms over his chest, watching her as she drew the arrow back with a shaky hand and let it release. The arrow cleanly missed the makeshift target hanging on the tree before her and instead flew far into the brush outside of the clearing to be lost forever. Terra groaned and closed her eyes. "Did I just lose another one?"

Orion couldn't stop himself from smirking when he answered, "You sure did."

Her face turned an angry shade red and she took a deep breath to calm herself before she stomped into the brush to search for yet another lost arrow. Orion chuckled and looked down at Ash resting at his feet. "Do you think I should tell her that I still have a few more?"

Ash considered him briefly with her all-seeing eyes before resting her head onto her paws again.

"You're right," Orion said and turned his gaze back to Terra cursing amid the foliage. "I'll wait a little bit and then tell her." He trudged through the packed snow to a log where their cloaks were resting and to where the quiver was obscuring a few more arrows as well.

Orion took his sweet time taking an arrow out, holding it in front of his face and noted the intricacies of the arrowhead. He ran a finger over the smooth wood carved to perfection and the fletching. He could hear Terra cursing as she tore through the brush trying to desperately to find any of the arrows. It took her a while but as soon as her head popped up from a large shrub, she saw him holding the arrow and he swore that she was about to chuck the bow at his head. Orion held it out and she stomped back into the clearing while declaring him dead with the glare in her eyes the whole way.

"I hope you have more where these came from," Terra muttered. She placed the arrow firmly against the bow string and pulled it back again as best as she could.

"No need to worry Princess, I do."

"*Queen*," she corrected irritably and let the arrow fly. Instead of soaring wide of the target, it impaled itself mere inches from the center and stuck fast. Terra looked at him with a smug grin on her face and waited for him to say something.

Orion ran a hand over his jaw thoughtfully, approaching the arrow in the target and inspecting it closely. "Subpar," he finally said and shrugged at her. "Could be better."

Terra gripped the bow with both hands and he couldn't help but grin, waiting for her to lose her cool and throw the thing at him. "You are so *aggravating*!" she growled.

Orion raised his hands in a "don't blame me" gesture. "You're the one that asked for me to show you how to shoot a bow, *Princess*."

Terra's jaw clenched and he could hear the heavy breath she sucked in. "Yes, so why don't you actually *show me*," she said through gritted teeth. Orion sighed and yanked the arrow out of the wooden target. He took the bow from her and, in one fluid motion, he drew the arrow and let it fly so that the arrowhead plummeted hard into the direct center of the target.

"See? Easy." He and handed the bow back to her.

"That isn't what I meant."

Finally giving in, Orion decided to stop patronizing her. "You need to straighten your back when you shoot." He stood behind her, having her draw the arrow back again and touching the small of her back. "You need to be stiff here, it'll give you more control." He moved his hand to her right elbow and raised it so that her arm was parallel to the ground. He was so close to her that he could smell the faint scent of her soap. She smelled like a field of flowers and honey, a sweet scent that he had never noticed before. "Now try," he said softly and tried to focus on the task at hand. She shifted uncomfortably, but took a calming breath in.

Orion took a step back and Terra let the arrow go. It sailed straight and landed not too far off from where his shot had been. She whirled around and looked at him with an expression of pure delight on her face. "Did you see that!" she shrieked. "Soon I'll be even better than you!"

Orion laughed. "I wouldn't go quite that far, it'll take many, many years of practice to get to where I am."

"You underestimate me!" she called over her shoulder as she tried yanking the imbedded arrow out of the target but failed. Orion went to help her and noticed her peering out deeper into the woods. A cold breeze picked up and flurried the top layer of snow resting softly on the ground.

"This forest gives me a weird feeling," Terra admitted quietly and retreated back to the center of the clearing — back to safety.

"These woods aren't safe." Orion handed her the arrow. His mind strayed and he thought of the danger that she would be in if she wandered out here alone again. Even here at the edge of the forest and with his patrols, her life was in more danger than he would have liked to admit. Him, on the other hand, not so much. But a pretty and defenseless maiden like herself? She would be slaughtered if it would come down to it. "Never come out here alone. Even my men don't like traveling too deep into the woods."

She looked at him with wide and frightened eyes that still held a hint of curiosity in them. "Why? Are there some horrible monsters that stalk these woods? Or would a pack of wolves bigger and more ruthless than your dogs tear me to shreds?"

Orion sensed the fear in her tone despite the smirk on her face. "Wolves," he pondered. "Yeah, something like that." *Oh, it's so, so much worse,* he wanted to say.

"I'll keep practicing then. Whether it's to become better than you or to be able to protect myself, you'll never know." Terra knocked the arrow once more and took aim. She adjusted her grip and her stance to follow his instructions and again hit the target almost dead center. "You know..." she started to say and pretended to study the shape and make of the bow in her hands. "I've been thinking, maybe we could make a few changes around here."

Orion barked out a laugh. *"Changes?* What type of changes? What, do you want a bigger room? More finery? Dresses, jewelry?"

Terra's face turned red in embarrassment and her eyes narrowed at him. "No," she said harshly. "I don't want more *things*, I'm not like that."

"Then what, Princess, does your heart desire?" Orion could see her chew on the inside of her cheek and she avoided his gaze. He sighed and stepped directly in her line of sight with his arms crossed. "Terra."

"Friends," she blurted. "I want...friends. Company, anyone really."

"You have Edith." He frowned and turned his back to her to slip the arrow back out of the target. "And if you need more responsibilities to help keep you busy, I can have Edith teach you to balance the books and help handle other paperwork necessary to help the realm maintain itself."

Orion could hear the quiver in her voice as she said, "At least let me bring Cassi here, I need my friend if I can't have my family."

"I said *no*." At the venom in his voice, the dogs grew antsy. They could sense his unease and the sadness that Terra was trying to hide. Ash whined and stayed where she was near the log, cowering into the snow while Milo hovered not at his side, but close enough so that Orion knew he was there. Silas slunk between his legs to stand stiff and silent while waiting on a command or direction from Orion.

Orion was even surprised by the own malice in his voice, but he could not let her win with this. He depended on his secrets remaining secrets. He couldn't afford the risk, even if he hated to see the hurt look she had on her face.

"I am your *Queen*," she growled defiantly. "And that means I have a say in what happens in this castle whether you like it or not. I am not asking for much."

Something snapped inside him. It was a hellish beast, springing forward and clouding his mind with a thick black cloud until every rational thought was muddled into nonexistence. The fury rose from deep in his belly until it clawed up his throat and through his mouth. "Let's get one thing straight," he breathed quietly. "I don't care who you are, where you came from, or even what your favorite color dress is. This is *my* kingdom and I am the *King* of this kingdom. You can defy me as much as you want, I really do not care but don't you for one *single second*, think you are in charge of my realm or my castle. I do what I have to for this realm. I have sacrificed much for my people."

The words hung heavy in the air and the feeling remained in Orion's chest, pressing on his lungs and forcing him to fight the urge to gasp desperately for air. Terra's emerald eyes seemed to grow cloudy and dangerous as if they were a storm that would reach out and smite him with an electrical bolt where he stood. "I am only here," she finally said softly. "Because you brought me here. Because I needed to protect my family and protect my kingdom against those who wished both harm. I am here because you made a promise to protect my people. You live in an empty castle inhabited by forgotten memories and the ghosts of the past, and you act like I don't know sacrifice? That I have not hurt and bled for my people?" Terra shook her head. "And here I thought we were reaching a middle ground. But yet you still prove that you are brash and unfeeling."

Orion chose his words carefully, keeping his voice controlled and keeping the monster inside of him at bay. "I have done more than you think. Write your family and ask them. Ask them how I have returned their gracious gifts with gifts of my own, unbeknownst to you. Ask how I have even written your Mother and have assured her that I would take care of her precious daughter. I have done all of this, and more, without your knowledge because no matter how crucial you believe yourself to be to my realm, I have run this realm long before you came along and if you would leave, I would run it long after you were gone as well. Do not underestimate me, Princess."

Terra's jaw twitched and she crossed her arms but didn't say a word. After a terse moment in which neither of them spoke through the heavy tension hanging between them,

Terra quickly spun to face the target where she unleashed another arrow to slam into the bright red center. Her chest rose and fell rapidly and a part of Orion wanted to apologize, to go to her and tell her he should have never let those words leave his mouth, but the monster wouldn't let him. The beast held his heart in a tight grip and squeezed it tighter until he swore he could feel the physical ache in his chest. Silas slid out from his legs with an anxious growl, but Orion still didn't move.

"When I came here to be your Queen, it never crossed my mind that you would hate me so wholeheartedly. I didn't expect an instant romance, no, but never once did I think I would be spending my nights alone, crying myself to sleep in a bed that even after all of these weeks, still doesn't feel like home. Never once, did I think I would give up everything for my family and live miserably in solitude. But yet, here I am." A single tear rolled down Terra's cheek and she dropped the bow into the snow before quickly brushing past to go back to the warm castle.

"I don't hate you," he whispered after her, but he was already too late. She was already gone.

The wind plucked up the words as soon as he said them and carried them until they dissipated into nothing. Orion stood still for a long while, trying to suppress the roaring and the agony filling his head. He wished he could tell her, to say the words and just let her in. But he knew she wouldn't like the darkest parts of him. Why would she? She even said it herself, he was a monster and she was everything he was not.

Terra was light and laughter, flowers blooming under the caressing touch of the sun and the birds flittering through the trees to gossip. She was the sweet nectar nurturing the bees and the butterflies and she was the smell of fresh rain spattering recently tilled soil. Watching her skirts sweep around her as she twirled on the dance floor the other night had left his heart wounded and aching. Even now, he wanted nothing more than to see the joy brighten her face.

But Orion? He was none of those things. He was the gloomy winter nights where even a crackling fire couldn't create enough warmth to penetrate the stiff chill. He was the sense of mourning when winter arrived to wipe out the beauty in the world. He was a leech, sucking out the happiness and the good until nothing was left except an empty void which is exactly what he was doing to her. How could he ever tell her that he wanted to let her in, to let her see everything he is and everything he will be?

Gods, what have I done?

Orion had to get away from it, he had to escape the overwhelming feeling of regret. He plunged deeper into the woods and shoved his way through branches that scratched at his shirt and through the untouched drifts of snow. Even his dogs didn't follow him as he hurried against something that didn't exist, in a race that he had already lost. Here, even the forest was quiet but the roaring in his head didn't stop. Orion clutched his head in his hands, gritting his teeth against the sultry whispers reaching for him, begging for him.

My King, they purred. *We miss you. Please, won't you return to us?*

"Get out of my head," Orion hissed, his breath growing more strained.

Don't you miss us, My King? We have been waiting for you. Oh, how lonely we've been without you here. It's been days.

"I said get *out!*" Orion screeched and fell to his knees in the snow as the invisible hands caressed his back, his arms, his face.

We can make you happy, they continued. *She doesn't understand you the way we do, she will never make you happy like we do. We will love you, even your darkest parts. Join us, My King. We will give you everything you have ever needed. You will never have to leave.*

"Stop, stop, stop," he pleaded and dug his hands deeper into the freezing snow that shot icicles through his fingers and up his arms.

Join us.
Join us.
Join us.

The noise grew louder and they grew more insistent until Orion knew he couldn't resist them any longer. As if he was in a trance, he rose to his feet as calm as ever and headed back to the castle. In the clearing, his dogs found him again and trotted after him while he didn't stop.

This is what he was and this is all he would ever be. Orion could never be happy; he could never be normal. *I could never be a good husband*, he thought bitterly. Clenching his jaw, he didn't stop or even slow until he made it to that retched dungeon door. Even the door purred to him, enticing him and drawing him in with such force that he didn't think he could deny it even if he tried with every part of his being. He placed an icy hand on the bidet symbol and a shock of electricity shot through him that made him almost cry out in pain.

An unnatural black light appeared once more beneath the ancient writing and symbols while the old stone walls of the dungeon shook from the unleashed power hiding on the other side of the stone door —*His* power hiding on the other side of the door. The stone grated against the dungeon floor and swung open to release its deathly chill in a rush. Orion commanded the dogs to stay and stepped through quickly on his own, not bothering to close it behind him for it always swung closed on its own from some unearthly property.

The inky blackness was unnatural in itself as if every particle of possible light had been sucked out to leave behind the darkest dark that ever existed. There was no sound except for his shuddering breaths and his boots hitting the stone floor.

Eventually, the floor turned to hard dirt beneath him and he began to see outlines of tree trunks and branches as if he had stepped outside under the moonlight, but he knew damn well that wasn't the case.

Orion pushed through the tightly knit branches and ignored the gashes covering his arms and hands as well as the voices nearly screaming for their King. This went on for a while until the trees suddenly ended and he stumbled into an open meadow. Sprawling before him was long grass that came to his knees and a distant river that he could just barely hear. Even farther away, so far that he could almost not even see it, was a lone cabin that appeared abandoned. At least it would be until he could reach it. He sensed that this time, he wouldn't be leaving that place.

He barely made it twenty paces before he heard a voice that shook him to his core.

"Orion."

He whirled and discovered that he was no longer alone.

"*Terra?*"

Chapter Fifteen
Terra

"Orion," Terra called again. She was quivering, she realized, shaking so much that she was afraid her knees might start knocking together. "What the hell is this place? And don't you dare tell me we're outside the castle, I'm not that much of a moron."

A slight breeze rushed through the tall grass and chilled her to the bone. She swore she could even hear tiny whispers surrounding her and speaking horrible things into her ears, enticing her to commit unspeakable acts. It felt as if a hand trailed a finger along the tender skin of her neck and she even felt the invisible hand brush back a lock of hair before she flinched away.

Orion was suddenly in front of her in a fraction of a second. He gripped the sides of her arms roughly and his stormy eyes were wild and feral. *"What are you doing here?"* he roared. *"You can't be here!"* Shadows morphed around them and she couldn't believe what she was seeing.

Terra tried to take a step back and release his hands from their painful grip, but he held fast. "I followed you, I heard you yell in the forest and I thought something bad had happened." *And I was waiting for an opportunity to see where the stone door led,* she thought, but didn't dare admit aloud.

"You need to leave right now," Orion growled and with one hand still gripping her arm, he started to pull her back towards the line of trees and back the way she had come.

"Why? What is this place?" Terra wrenched his fingers away from her flesh and stumbled away from him. Something about this place wasn't right, she could feel it deep in her bones and the odd sensation left her bewildered. The landscape around her appeared to have its colors muted and it made everything seem otherworldly. A stale scent filled her nostrils and she felt the hum of ancient power through the soles of her feet. But there was something else there. Something that felt almost dangerous.

Orion's eyes darted to the scenery around them as if he was combing for someone or something. Somehow, Terra knew in her core that they weren't alone here. She could feel it deep in her core and the feeling was unnerving. "Orion," she said again. "What is this place?" The cold breeze swished past her and ruffled the strands of her hair. The whispers filled her ears again and she felt an invisible fingernail trace a path on her jaw from under her ear to the middle.

Orion's wild gaze finally met hers and the shadows around them dissipated. "They're coming, we need to leave."

"Who's coming?" Terra asked shrilly. The panicked feeling she had managed to subdue began to break free. "Where are we?"

"There's no time!" he shouted in frustration and grabbed her arm again. Quickly, he began to drag her back towards the treeline and this time, she didn't fight him. She managed to throw one last glance over her shoulder and she saw a strong breeze rip through the grass straight for them. Just in time, they ducked among the tree trunks and Terra heard a mighty roar behind her. Whatever it was, it couldn't get past the trees she realized. The trees were a safe zone. But Orion didn't stop. He held on tightly and Terra was forced to follow.

The air grew darker and darker until she could barely see the outline of Orion in front of her. Just when she thought they would never find their way back, the stone door appeared out of nowhere, floating by itself in the midst of the trees. Orion placed his hand against it and it immediately swung open.

The both of them nearly tumbled into the dark dungeon before the door slammed shut behind them. It was pitch black, neither of them having had lit a torch on their journey through the door and Terra couldn't slow down her panicked breathing.

"Orion?" she called meekly and held a hand to her chest. She felt dizzy and sick to her stomach from the inky blackness.

"I'm right here," a gruff voice answered and she felt his hand on her shoulder. She immediately reacted by grabbing his hand and following the feel of it until she felt his sturdy chest. She threw herself into him and he wrapped his arms around her without hesitation.

"I'm sorry, I'm sorry, I'm sorry," Terra began repeating and tears fell hot and fast from her eyes. "I should have never yelled at you or said the things that I did."

"Shhh," Orion soothed and put a hand on the back of her head. "I should never have started the fight; you didn't deserve it."

Terra sobbed into his shirt, blubbering for gods knew how long until the tears finally began to slow. Orion never said a word and held her close to his chest. Once the tears began to slow, she became painfully aware that they were curled up together on the filthy dungeon floor and she was embarrassed by their proximity.

"I'm sorry I ruined your shirt," she sniffled and pulled away from him.

"It's okay Terra," he replied and got to his feet. She felt his hand take hers in the dark and he pulled her to her own feet, not letting go of her hand. "The last thing I am worried about right now, is my shirt." His voice was weary, the exhaustion hanging over him like a cloud.

"What was that place?" she whispered. She was almost afraid to discuss it as if merely mentioning that place would draw out whatever terrifying creatures and secrets it was hiding.

Orion was quiet for a long moment. "We have a lot of talking to do. Let's get a cup of tea and we'll find a quiet place."

As if the whole castle wasn't a quiet place, Terra nearly said, but the words caught in her raw throat. She had so many questions, so many thoughts rattling around in her head that she didn't even know where to start. With his hand still in hers, he led her out of the dark and towards the light.

Terra sipped at the hot tea gratefully and relished in the mundane action that provided a small sense of normalcy in the wicked chaos that was happening. When they had left the dungeon, they had found the dogs waiting patiently as if nothing abnormal had happened. If Terra second guessed herself any more than she already was, she might even believe that it was entirely a figment of her imagination.

Orion sent them away and led her up the stairs and down a hallway that Terra now recognized. Before he even opened the door to the parlor room that she had discovered the other day, she knew that was where they had been heading.

Orion was unnervingly quiet, his expression unreadable. Terra wished she knew what was going on behind the closed doors of his mind and behind his hard exterior while she watched him. He approached the portraits hanging above the fireplace and looked at them solemnly. Terra was brimming with questions, but she held her tongue and allowed him to gather his thoughts in silence. Even though he has always been closed off with her, she knew that this time was different and that he would speak when he was ready.

"My mother would have like you, I think," Orion said eventually and she could see that his facade had cracked a bit.

Terra could see the pain in his eyes and the longing he felt for his mother without him having to say. "You are a lot like her. Very kind, thoughtful, and passionate about your family."

"What about your father?" Terra asked and stepped beside him to gaze at the portrait of the late King.

Orion's expression hardened at the question. "He wouldn't have been here ever to pass judgement. He was a wicked and cruel man, but at least he was absent most of my life. That was the only good thing he ever did for us."

"You and your mother?"

"And my siblings."

Terra's interest piqued. "I never knew you had siblings."

"I might as well not have any now," Orion laughed bitterly. "I have three older sisters that were off and married before I could even walk so it was just my two younger brothers and I."

"Where are they now?" Terra dared to ask.

Orion shrugged. "Only the gods know, it's rather irrelevant if I am being honest. My brothers most likely would kill me on sight if they ever saw me again."

"And what would you do if you saw them?"

The corner of Orion's mouth quirked up, the edge of a grin lying there. "I would probably do the same."

"I'm not sure if I'm supposed to believe you or not," Terra joked and sipped at her tea. They both fell silent again, Terra waiting for him to speak more and Orion lost in his thoughts. *Perhaps about killing his little brothers,* Terra thought and shuddered a bit. She wondered what had happened that their relationship fell apart so terribly. She could never imagine being so estranged from her sisters that they would wish to kill each other. It was a bitter thought that she pushed harshly from her mind as quickly as it had appeared.

"You should not have been able to go through that door," Orion stated abruptly and shook his head in astonishment. "It's supposed to be impossible for you to go through that door, but somehow you did. And even better yet, you survived."

Terra took another drink of the tea in her hand before speaking. "Orion, what was that place?"

His jaw twitched and she saw a flash of raw emotion flitter across his face before he turned aloof once more. Over and over he was trying to hide his emotions, but she wished that he would stop trying so hard to hide himself. She wanted to see the real him, the one who has fears and desires. She wanted to hear it all and she wanted to wash his pain away.

"That was the Underworld," he answered simply. "And I'm its King."

The metal cup that was in Terra's hands clattered against the floor and the tea emptied into a pool around her feet. Orion looked at her sharply and his eyes went to the cup on the ground. "I- I'm sorry," Terra stuttered and reached down to pick it back up with a quivering hand. "I—uh—thought I heard you say that we had been in the Underworld. It caught me by surprise."

"Terra," Orion said in a low voice and bowed his head to level his gaze with hers. His eyes were weary, drained of emotion and luster. Dark bags sat heavy underneath his eyes and he almost looked older and more worn out as if he had aged overnight. "We *were* in the Underworld."

Terra opened her mouth to reply, but closed it, repeating this multiple times as she struggled to make sense of what he just told her. Thoughts overwhelmed her and all she could hear was the roar of her own mind trying to process what it couldn't. She crossed her arms over her chest with the cup still in hand and brushed past Orion to open the curtains of the window. Outside, the sun was beginning to set and she peered over the landscape, focusing on calm and steady breaths.

"Terra, please, say something." Orion approached her and put a soft hand on her arm.

Terra took a deep shuddering breath and chuckled. The chuckle increased to a small laugh and grew and grew until tears streamed down her cheeks and the laughs nearly made her double over. Orion watched her with an almost horrified look on his face until she finally stopped to rub the happy tears from her eyes. "This explains everything." She let out a relieved breath. "This. Explains. Everything."

"What do you mean?"

"You!" Terra exclaimed and ran her hands over her head. "This explains everything about you. About this castle, your lifestyle, and just *you* in general. You've been harboring this dark secret this whole time and while I thought you just *hated* me, you were scared."

Orion scoffed, but she was relieved to see the hint of a smile on his mouth. "I was not *scared*."

"Don't even try to tell me you weren't." Terra touched his arm hesitantly. "It all makes sense now. Well, not everything, but you know what I mean." Orion looked at her funny and a blush crept up her cheeks. "What? Why're you looking at me like that?"

"You're extraordinary," he mumbled in amazement. "You find out something that should be completely earth shattering to your very existence and instead of panicking or running away, you just *laugh*."

"I'm panicking on the inside a bit," Terra admitted. "But I'm closer to understanding you now and that's very relieving to me."

Orion looked a bit relieved himself. Terra knew that this had to be weighing him down and to what extent, she didn't know yet, but it clearly did some damage to his psyche. "I'm sorry you ever thought that. That was never the case," Orion said. "I guess... I guess I was..."

"Scared?" Terra supplied with a smile.

Orion rolled his eyes. "Sure, I guess I was scared."

"What were you scared of? Me finding out?"

"That, and of your life being at risk. There is a lot of danger that comes with this information, Terra. This isn't something to regard lightly and you don't even know the half of it."

"Then why don't you tell me?" Terra stepped closer to him and slid her hand into his. "After all, I am your Queen. Doesn't that make me Queen of the Underworld?"

Orion gave her a small smile and rubbed a thumb over the jade ring on her finger. "I suppose in a sense that does, but that isn't quite how it works."

"Then why don't you tell me?"

Orion smiled halfheartedly before he began his tale. "There once was a Prince who lived in a beautiful land full of happy people. There was prosperity and the people thrived, holding festivals and celebrations at every chance that they could get. They lived in peace for many years until the King got sick. They did everything that they could, but the King passed away, leaving the Prince to rule in his place. The people though that the new King would rule peacefully and compassionately like his father had before him, but that wasn't the case. Instead, he ruled with an iron fist, using fear and intimidation to weed out those he deemed as unloyal. The kingdom that had once been prosperous had turned into one of ruins and poverty. But still, the King wasn't satisfied.

"At this point, he had taken a Queen to rule beside him and who bore him many children. His family didn't prevent him from ruling so cruelly, though, not at all. The King, they said, had grown paranoid. He was paranoid to the extent that he sought out so-claimed oracles and fortunetellers to tell him what was waiting for him in the future. Most of them were thieves and liars that spun tales of good fortune and escapades in order to earn a few meager coins from the King. But one woman...she was no thief. She spoke of the harsh future that awaited the King and from then on, he was never the same. She told him that his end lay at the hands of one of his own children and that one of his children would be the one to steal away the power he had worked so hard to gain.

"So begun his journey to avoid his fated downfall. He did everything that he could to try to outrun what was waiting for him. He sought out witches, shamans, spell casters, and any other possible lead to someone that could do something, anything, to undo what was prophesied. But this time, she found him. She was a powerful enchantress that claimed that she could change his future, but there would be consequences to doing so. He didn't care, though, if there would be retribution for the deal and without hesitation, he accepted.

"What he didn't know, was that his acceptance would curse his family and his entire lineage. His children and their children and their children's children would suffer under this curse forever. They were forced to live out their days in a frozen state, never growing older even as the world around them continued to age and die. It wasn't until the Queen, the only one in the family who avoided the curse, for she didn't share the King's blood, gave her life to make her own deal with the Enchantress. It was a deal for him to be overthrown.

"So, in the King's desperate attempt to escape his fate, he ran right into fate's grasp. He lost his power and his life at the hand of his youngest child, ending the vicious cycle of his rule. The children saw their mother fade away with a smile on her face, glad to have done the one final good deed before she passed. The children went their own way, each ruling in a different part of the world and building their own lives. Their curse remains though and affects the continuing bloodline unless one day a solution may be found."

Orion trailed off and Terra was left with a strange feeling. He was quiet and analyzed her as he waited for her reaction. Terra chose her words carefully. "This... King... where was he from?"

"I think you know."

Terra looked again at the portraits hanging above the fireplace, the King looking cruel and the Queen looking loving and kind. "They were your parents, weren't they?"

"Yes," Orion replied, his voice barely more than a whisper.

"So..." Terra drawled and racked her brain. "That means that you're cursed? Cursed to live forever and... rule the Underworld?"

"Every one of us was impacted differently. I was given control over the shadows and the areas just out of sight, the Underworld included. This is what happened to me and I live with it every single day—"

"Forever and ever," Terra finished and shook her head. "That makes you sound like a god, is that what you are?" Orion barked out a laugh that caught Terra by surprise. It was a genuine laugh, one that was infectious and one that she didn't hear very often, especially from him. "What's so funny?"

"Oh, how my brothers would have loved to hear those words. I'm not a god," he wheezed. "Emphasis on *like* a god. Definitely not a god, I am a King."

Terra threw her hands up. "I'm trying to wrap my head around all of this okay? There's no need to make fun of me."

"I'm sorry," he took her hands in his, a grin still on his face. "I appreciate you being understanding and this is not easy for me either, I just - the comparison is really ridiculous and you would see that if you were in my shoes."

"Whatever," Terra grumbled and her vivid thoughts made her pause. "Forever is a long time. I feel like that would get quite lonely."

Orion nodded. "I would be a liar if I told you that it wasn't a lonely existence to deal with."

"I don't think I would ever want to live forever," she admitted. "I wouldn't want to see my family and loved ones grow old and pass while I still lived."

Orion lifted both of her hands and kissed the top of them tenderly, causing her to cast away her pondering thoughts. "Good thing you will never have to."

"Tell me more about the Underworld and how that works."

"There is much that you don't need to know and it would risk your safety if you would know. There are things there that would be more than excited to cause you harm to simply get to me. Never, *ever* step foot in there again. You may hear them now calling to you, begging for you to open the door and come back to them, but you can't, got it? Promise me. Promise me you won't go back there."

"I - I promise," Terra choked out. "Why would they hurt you to get to me? I thought you hated me, after all."

"Oh, it's far from that." Orion took a step closer, his emotions finally raw on his face. "I care for you, I truly do. I had to protect you and I didn't want to believe that you were someone that I could be honest with. I didn't know how you would react to the monster that I am and I'm really, really not good at this sort of thing as you have already clearly seen. This truly changes everything, Terra, and I can see that now. You are what I never knew I needed, or ever thought I deserved." He reached his hands for her face and held it gently in his hands. "You are the beauty and kindness that this world needs, that *I* need."

Orion drew her close and pressed his lips to hers, the shock electrifying every nerve in her body. A fire that Terra had just begun to notice flickered deep in her belly and grew to a roaring flame. She put her hands over the top of his as he kissed her, relishing in the crisp scent of snow and forest that he always seemed to be covered in. She wanted to touch his arms, his chest. She wanted to run her fingers through his hair until she was gasping for air, but he pulled away far too soon. She felt the blush rush up her cheeks and they both were breathing heavy, their eyes raking over each other.

It was in that moment that Terra realized that he was her counterpart that she didn't even know that she had been looking for.

Chapter Sixteen
Orion

Orion never had been much of a dreamer. Most likely because he never slept much to begin with, but the last few weeks dreams plagued what little sleep he did have.

Orion's dream-self found himself in Terra's bedchamber overlooking her sprawled among the sheets grinning at him. She was wearing nothing except a thin chemise that hugged her natural curves in a way that made his body ache. Against his control, his legs carried him forward until he stood over her close enough where her soft hands could then run along the planes of his stomach and to the hem of his pants.

Terra pouted when Orion regained control and took a step back. "Don't you want me, my King?" She turned onto her stomach and rested her cheek on the palm of her hand.

"Not like this," he choked out.

The features on her face flickered so he momentarily saw a glimpse of someone that wasn't her before it once again was Terra's face. "Don't shy away from me. I know you want me, your deepest desires tell me so." She sat back up and slid off the edge of the bed so that the act caught the hem of her chemise. The fabric rode up on her slender thighs for him to catch a glimpse of the tan skin.

"I know what you think about in the dead of the night. I know that you fantasize about me, my King. Why do you act like you don't?" With every step she took towards him, Orion took another backwards. Her face began to flicker again until it was nothing but indistinct shadows.

Orion tripped over the edge of the rug so that he was sprawled on the bedroom floor. Terra's form blurred until she was the shadow figure whispering into his mind. *I know your darkest desires, my King.*

Then he awoke with a start. The dream still clung to him heavily and his heart still raced. Panic suffocated him and he threw his sheets aside so he could throw his window open to breathe in the cool air. Dawn was just beginning to break and he knew that there was no way he could fall back asleep, not after that.

A few weeks had passed since the incident happened, which is now how both him and Terra referred to the events that day. Although the incident had forced Orion far from his comfort zone, it was a blessing he had begun to realize, even if the dreams-turned-nightmares were a consequence.

After Terra and him departed each other that day, he had immediately raced to Edith to tell her everything and to seek solace in her wise advice. He was shocked, really, by what happened and he hadn't realized how much he was until he went to talk to her. He had tried to find the words to tell her what happened and how he may have screwed everything up, but instead the words never came. He had rendered himself speechless the one time he desperately needed to speak, which was ironic in itself and even Edith had gotten a kick out of it.

Once Edith finally managed to get the story out of him, she simply laughed in his face. Orion had been incredibly embarrassed and surprised by her reaction. "Maybe you'll finally stop being such a jerk to her," Edith had told him. "It's about time you play nice with her. Don't waste this opportunity, Orion. You may not get another." With that, she chased him out of the kitchen with a wooden spoon and that was the end of it.

Since then, Orion had mulled her words over and over more times than he could count. He was scared, truly. Scared that he would cause Terra harm and scared that he would fail her. It was a weird thing for him, he had to admit, but he had decided that very night that he would do everything in his power to do things right between them. He wanted to make her happy and he wanted to protect her now that the doorway to the dark had been opened to her.

Their relationship had also grown stronger. Their breakfasts together had been less intense and overall they had been more at ease with each other. She would ask him questions periodically about everything he had told her, but otherwise they didn't discuss it too much. They especially hadn't discussed the fact that he had kissed her. Even though every fiber of his being wanted to kiss her until he felt drunk with euphoria, Orion promised himself that he would do right by her even if that meant keeping his distance physically.

Orion had barely made it outside of the castle before Darren found him. Still cranky and irritable, Orion continued to walk towards an area of the grounds that he had recently been spending a lot of time in. "What do you want, Captain?"

Darren kept pace with him as they trudged through the snow and shielded his eyes from the blinding sunrise. "We just got a report from late last night that a patrol came across another family murder."

Orion faltered and stopped. "Was it recent?"

"Quite recent, couldn't have been more than two or three days ago."

"So the three men that were executed either weren't guilty, or they weren't the only ones. Do we have any more clues?"

"Not this time," Darren admitted. "I think there were more accomplices than what we had thought originally. I have my men working on it and scouring the realm, but so far there's been nothing."

"Keep working on it and keep me posted."

"Yes, Your Highness." The Captain's gaze turned towards the structure that lay ahead of them. "New project?"

"I think our Queen deserves a place where she can run off and hide, don't you think?"

"I'm sure she will love it. Again, I'll keep you posted."

Once alone again, Orion dove into the greenhouse that once had been dirty and empty, and now was beginning to glow from all the work that Orion and Laurent had been putting into it. Yesterday the two of them finally finished it up and it was ready to present to Terra.

He busied himself with finishing final preparations until the sun rose high enough in the sky for him to convince Terra to venture outside with him. "Think she'll like it?" he asked his dogs who gazed forlornly at the piles of dirt that he had yelled at them for digging up in the days prior.

Orion found Terra in the kitchen with her coffee and looking quite drowsy still. It took him a while to convince her, but once he said the word "surprise," she finally agreed to come with him.

Terra looked at him crossly as they walked through the path through the snow and Orion swore that she was fighting the urge to stamp her foot like a young child throwing a tantrum. "Why must you be like this?"

"I told you, it wouldn't be a surprise if I told you, now would it?"

"Again, why do you have to be so aggravating?" Terra huffed but let him continue to lead her. "This better be worth it." They rounded a corner of the castle exterior and before them was a glass structure that was now cleared of snow and cleaned until it shined beneath the sunlight.

"Is that..?" Terra asked. Her mouth was open in surprise.

"Yes," Orion smiled. "It's a greenhouse. Come." He took her hand in his and led her inside. It was massive with rows of planters full of fresh soil ready to be used. The warmth inside was intense and Orion took off his winter cloak almost immediately. "This is all yours to do with as you see fit. It needed some work done, but I think now it should do perfectly for whatever you choose to do with it."

Terra's eyes were misty and her face was frozen in shock. "You did this for me?"

"I thought that this might help give you a hobby to keep you busy. I know we haven't talked about it much, but Edith told me that you loved to garden and grow plants when you were at home. I wanted to give you that here as well. I want to help make this place your home. And, maybe, this will help convince you to grant me forgiveness for my many past transgressions." Orion gave her a rueful smile.

"Thank you," Terra said softly and squeezed his hand once before pulling away to walk down the row of planters. She stopped at one and plunged her hand into the soft soil, a wide smile breaking out on her face. "Oh, how I missed this. I thought winter would never end and that I would never get to feel the earth in my hands again."

"Everything is ready for planting," Orion explained and walked towards her. "All you need is seeds which Edith can get in the village." Orion paused and watched the slight disappointment flash across Terra's face, just as he expected. "You'll have to go with her of course, to choose what seeds you would like to get. I hope that isn't too much of a hassle." He gave her a wink. "Edith also mentioned how much that you have been wanting to go."

Terra gasped and flung herself into his chest. "Thank you, thank you, thank you!" she squealed and nearly jumped up and down in excitement. "Today might as well be my birthday!" She pulled away, breathless and grinning. "Thank you, Orion, truly. It means a lot."

"I'm glad I could make you happy," he replied genuinely and couldn't help but return her grin. "It'll be a cold ride, but it shouldn't be too long of one. It's still quite early. I'm sure if you ask Edith she would be more than happy to go with you today."

Terra took one last look around the greenhouse before sliding her hand in the crook of his elbow and allowed him to lead her back to the castle in search of Edith.

Before long, both women were mounting two horses that Laurent had been so kind as to saddle and ready for them at the small stables. With a final wave goodbye, Terra and Edith rode off towards the village.

"Hold down the fort for me?" Orion asked Laurent as soon as the two were out of sight.

"Of course, Your Highness."

Taking advantage of the fact that Terra was soon to be far from the castle or its grounds, Orion hurried back inside. One sharp whistle in the foyer had his dogs running from one of the upper corridors and at his side. Since the incident, he had avoided going through the door in the dungeon at all costs and he was beginning to feel the effects of it. He hadn't dared though, lest he release any dangers and put Terra at even more risk. But now, after the dreams, there was no evading it. He couldn't risk having the darkness leave their realm to haunt the living.

With his dogs at his side and a lantern he had taken off one of the corridor walls, he plunged down into the depths of the dungeon.

The walls and floor vibrated in excitement as if it was a living and breathing thing that had been expecting him. Orion had barely touched a palm to the door and it was already shining bright, brighter than it usually did. The door swung open and he slipped through it. His dogs trailed behind him with their teeth bared and fur standing on end. The door slammed shut behind him and the moving darkness was kept just far enough at bay due to the lantern burning brightly in his hand. "Come and get me," he growled into the nothingness before strutting ahead.

Orion didn't hesitate, even as his nerves were screaming at him to turn around and run away from what was ahead. Dark thoughts and fears flicked through his mind as he shoved his way through the tree branches and closer to the wide-open field. Already they were in his head. He usually wasn't a frightened person, he truly wasn't, but now that he had Terra to watch out for, he was. He could deny it until he was blue in the face and gasping for air, but she truly had changed everything for him and as much as it scared him, he was thrilled by it. She was his newfound purpose in his lonely existence.

Orion burst through the tree line and waiting for him was a black shadow in the faint outline of a man that could only be seen when Orion looked at it straight on. If he so much as turned, the shadow would ripple away into nothing. There were no discernible features. No nose, no mouth, no jawline or eyes, only the basic outline of a head, a torso, and legs. Even before Orion could seek out the figure, it was waiting for him.

"To what do I owe the pleasure?" Orion asked. His body was tense and his dogs on high alert on either side of him.

Your Highness, the voice whispered in his head. *We missed you. You haven't visited us in weeks. We were beginning to get lonely.*

"What do you want?"

Simply to make polite conversation, of course, the shadow said. *You are looking quite worn down, have you been getting enough rest?*

"I'm not here to play your games," Orion deadpanned. "Spit it out, what do you want?"

Have your dreams not plagued you? I thought that facing the deep recesses of one's own mind might make rest a bit more difficult.

"Your attempts to sway my mind will not work. So what do you want?"

I bring a message from your father.

"I am not interested in hearing what my father has to say. He is banished from here and if you continue to push me, I will find a way to banish you from here as well. Don't tempt me, I know the depths would love to have you. Or even better yet, I'll give you a physical body finally and let my dogs here tear you to shreds." As if on cue, the dogs growled nastily and Silas even took a step forward to snap ferociously. The shadow's faint outline merely shuddered tauntingly in response but wasn't bothered at all.

I merely bring a message from him, Your Highness. Would you banish your gatekeeper? Your one and only companion here? He wanted me to let you know that he likes this girl. He said that this one has fire in her at least, unlike the others. It was quite risky of you if I do say so myself to bring another girl here as your Queen.

"Don't you dare speak of the girl," Orion said in a dangerously quiet voice. He could feel the anger quivering in his bones, threatening to lash out.

The shadow moved closer to him, spinning around him once with a small breeze of air to taunt him. *I quite like this girl myself,* the figure purred. *What a mystery, she is. No mortal enters the Underworld unscathed and makes their way back out. How did she do it, I wonder? It must be fated. She can hear me, you know, out there. She doesn't think she can, but she does. Maybe I should visit her in her dreams and show her what you truly think of her.*

"Stop. You do not speak of the girl and you will leave her alone or I *will* banish you from existence, you hear me? I will not be trifled with." Orion knew that if the figure could smile, then it would at this moment.

And he hated every second of it.

As you say, Your Highness. You came here for something, did you not? Please, ask for the information that you seek.

"There have been more murders, and those I executed were not the only ones behind this. You have access to see beyond your plane of existence. Tell me, have you seen who is masterminding these attacks?"

Perhaps. But what do I get if I tell you?

Orion rubbed the bridge of his nose with a forefinger and thumb. "I swear to the gods that I will cast you out for all eternity if you don't tell me what you have seen. You and my father would make the best of friends."

There are a few men, where they are from, I do not know but what horrors they have been implementing on the village and on the kingdom… well… there are few things in the mortal world that would be worse than what they have been doing. You had slain the others, but there are definitely more. There will always be more.

Orion furrowed his brows. "What do they want? Are they doing it for fun, for sick enjoyment?"

That I am not sure of, potentially for the enjoyment of it I'm sure, but I don't think that is wholly the reason why. They are looking for information that it seems they have yet to find.

"What information are they searching for? I'm not playing these games, *out with it!*"

They are searching for information about you. They are under the impression that the glorious King holds some sort of immortal power.

Orion was taken aback. He was careful. Only those who have worked for him would suspect anything, but they have taken a vow of silence that would bind them from sharing anything odd they may see. Where did these men come from and who sent them?

I apologize, but I do not know what they are seeking specifically, only that they have not found out what they want yet. But I would proceed with caution, they have managed to leave us enough souls to keep me company for quite a long time.

"Thank you for the information." Orion frowned. His mind was still racing and confusion still racked his brain. Were they searching for a way to steal his throne, to steal his kingdom or his power? It didn't quite make sense, why wouldn't they have tried to march to the castle themselves? "If you find out anything else, let me know at once." Orion turned on his heel to head back into the trees and back to normalcy, but the shadow's next words stopped him dead in his tracks.

You know where your fate lies, don't allow yourself for one moment to think that she will be different than the others, Your Highness.

Orion turned around slowly. "You know nothing of my fate." He ducked back into the woods and the shadow figure dissipated into nothing.

The sun was beginning to set by the time Orion found Laurent in the kitchen. He had lost all sense of time while he was down below. Laurent was just about to bite into a buttered roll when Orion entered in a flurry. "We have a problem," Orion told him breathlessly. "I have to leave, sooner rather than later."

Laurent paused mid bite to glance at Orion before setting the roll back down onto his plate. "What is going on, Your Highness?"

"There was another murder last night. The three executions weren't the only guilty parties and I have to find out what is happening. As soon as Edith and Terra return, I will tell them as well, but I need to leave first thing in the morning. I need you to keep an eye on them."

"I understand," Laurent said solemnly. "And I'm sure your Queen will understand as well."

"I hope so." He would need to find Darren and have him strengthen his patrols while he was gone.

A pang of guilt sang through Orion's body at the thought of abandoning Terra here for an unknown amount of time. It was cruel of him to leave her now that they have just begun to come to an understanding with each other but liquidating this threat to his kingdom had to be more of a priority. *You are not like your father*, he reminded himself, but couldn't quite believe it. *You are not abandoning her, Terra will understand.*

Chapter Seventeen
Terra

The air was crisp from the winter cold but Terra's excited heart pumped blood rapidly through her veins to fend against the chill. Her hands were snug inside of her fur-lined mittens and her cloak was pulled tight around her. The horse's hooves crunched the snow below as Edith and her made their way on the so-called "hidden path" to the village. Much to her surprise, the path was actually *less* treacherous than Wolf's Pass and, according to Edith, took less time.

To pass the time, Edith spun stories regarding the shops and secretive booths that could be found throughout the village if only one knew where to look. The village had seemed overly quiet for the most part the first time Terra had passed through, but Edith made sure, with a glint in her eye, to let her know that was definitely not the case.

"The villagers aren't a fan of outsiders," Edith explained. "So they stay hidden for the most part. There are plenty of hole in the wall type places that if you know enough to know they exist, they will open their doors to you."

Not too much later, the two of them reached what appeared to be a wall of pine trees standing tall and with their luscious branches interlocking. Edith quickly dismounted, telling Terra to wait there and she raised a branch to reveal just enough space for them to lead the horses through. Once Edith told her the coast was clear, both of them led the horses through quickly. Terra found that they were on the normal road once again and were barely more than ten minutes outside of the village. "I wish I knew about this the first time," she grumbled. They mounted once again and continued on.

The village was quiet just like it was the first time she had visited. Very few citizens roamed the streets and they passed only two or three carriages. "Why don't we start with lunch?" Edith suggested. "There is a wonderful inn here that serves a spread that even rivals mine. The innkeeper and I go way back, as well."

"That sounds splendid to me," Terra replied and her stomach growled right on time.

Edith led them down a few cobblestone roads and Terra was pleasantly surprised to find that Edith had been referring to the inn that her and Cassi had spent the night in while they were traveling to the castle. *And where we snuck out of,* Terra thought to herself and a wistful smile crossed her features at the happy memory. Even though she had known it would be one of the last nights she had with Cassi, it still hadn't seemed real. Instead, it had felt like any other mischievous adventure of theirs despite the clock ticking down. *Gods I miss her.*

So much has changed since then. Terra was no longer a young girl, but a young woman. She no longer spent her time frivolously finding trouble (well, for the most part) and the thought almost saddened her. Even though she always had known she would one day have to grow up, she never once thought it would have happened this quickly. Maybe she had been foolish for thinking otherwise, maybe this was the harsh reality of life and of growing up. One day you are racing around the palace with an angry Ms. Astrid hot on your heels for some silly prank you had pulled, and the next day you are a married Queen in a kingdom so unlike your own. It was difficult to wrap her mind around it, really. Even when she considered the change in her relationship with Orion, she couldn't quite believe it.

Terra remembered how derisive he had been the first moment that they had met. He had been wicked and insulting and for weeks he had pushed her aside. But now everything was different. Orion felt like that first gulp of ocean air after being trapped under the surface, lungs burning from holding her breath far too long and the currents pulling her in every direction. She found herself desperately breathing him in. That night he kissed her, she felt a warmth flow through her that she had never felt before and she couldn't stop obsessing over it.

Orion had been fire and heat, burning her skin in the places he had touched and leaving behind unseen marks that she could not scrub off.

Terra shook herself from her thoughts and snapped back to the present. Edith had already dismounted and was leading her horse around the inn to where there was a thick wooden pole to tie the horses to. Terra followed suite and the horses began greedily sucking down the unfrozen water in the trough in front of them.

Terra followed Edith through the front door of the inn and relished in the warmth that was spreading from the crackling fire. The inn was just as busy as the first time that she had been there with persons of different ages, ethnicities, and background bustling about each other on their way to do gods knew what. She spotted the innkeeper at the front desk arguing with a burly man who, apparently, was not too pleased with the noisy neighbors he had in the room next to him judging by the snippets of conversation that Terra could hear over the bustling crowd.

"Frankly, it is not my problem," the innkeeper snapped. "Every room is currently booked and if you have a problem, then you can sleep out back with the horses. It doesn't affect me what you do, but you barging in here, being disrespectful in *my* inn, will not be tolerated."

Terra couldn't see the man's face, but she imagined he had been rendered speechless by the older woman. She stood tall, her hands on her hips almost if she was daring him to complain even one more time, just so she could throw him out.

"Well?" the innkeeper said. "What is it going to be? Sleep with the horses, or shut your mouth and deal with it?"

The man grumbled something unintelligible and lumbered away to make his way back upstairs to his room. The innkeeper let out a weary sigh, rubbing the bridge of her nose with a thumb until she happened to meet Edith's gaze through the crowd. "Finally! Some good company!"

"It's nice to see you Margaret." Edith and the innkeeper, Margaret, hugged like long lost friends would.

"I swear I might throw one of these men through a door if they keep *complaining* like this." Margaret's eyes turned to Terra. "It's nice to see you again as well. Do tell, how is your King?"

Terra was caught off guard. "How—"

Margaret waved her hand through the air. "Pah, I know everything. It wasn't hard to figure it out. After all, the villagers cling to rumors like flies cling to shit. I hear all in my inn." Margaret grimaced. "Even the things I would rather not." She saw Terra's slightly terrified expression and leaned in close to say, "I know all, darling, get used to it. How was your late-night stroll to the tavern? I do hope it met your expectations, they do have great dancing music."

Terra's ears turned hot and she looked down, acutely aware of the embarrassment flashing like a bright torch across her features.

"I'm just playing with you darling!" Margaret guffawed and wrapped a comforting arm around Terra's shoulders.

"Let's get you something to eat, you two look positively starving."

Soon, Terra was seated at a discreet table with Edith and Margaret towards the back of the dining hall and with a heaping plate of pork, slices of bread, a rich gravy, and a pile of fresh green vegetables. Without hesitation, Terra dug in and instantly remembered how fantastic Margaret's food truly was. Edith was an amazing cook herself, but Margaret somehow managed to surpass even her.

Terra zoned out while she ate and was only slightly aware of the idle conversation happening between Margaret and Edith. They spoke about the weather, how business had been, even about Margaret's grown children and their own children. When the conversation turned, however, Terra immediately perked up. "What did you say?" she asked.

Margaret looked over her cup of steaming coffee and grimaced. "I said that there have been attacks happening recently and no one can figure out who is doing it… or why. There are people that will be found beaten to death in their homes or some have been abandoned off the beaten path where they may have never been found. Even after the three suspects were arrested, one still happened again last night."

Terra herself also had thought that the culprits were caught. She saw Orion execute one herself after all. But they were still happening? A chill shot through Terra as she pictured it — families being attacked and slaughtered, defenseless women weeping and their bloodied bodies being discarded like an animal carcass for some poor soul to discover.

The thought made her feel sick.

Edith frowned. "I'll have to talk to Orion about this," she said quietly. "Are there any rumors about who may be doing this? Outsiders? Villagers?"

"No one seems to know anything." Margaret shook her head. "There are no witnesses and no survivors. It's as if some spirit slaughters them and then takes off again into the night, never to be seen again."

"I'll see if Orion knows anything about this, he'll be able to do something at least to get to the bottom of it." Edith took a thoughtful drink from her own cup of coffee. Her eyebrows were furrowed and she seemed older and more burdened. It worried her a bit and she wasn't quite sure why, but she had a bad feeling eating away in the pit of her stomach.

A few loud voices intermingled and drew Margaret's attention to what appeared to be an argument between two men over something frivolous. "Really?!" Margaret shouted and groaned dramatically. "Don't make me come over there!" She got to her feet and shouted over her shoulder, "It was nice to see you two! Stop by again soon!"

"Does this happen often?" Terra asked Edith.

Edith gathered their dishes to put in the designated wash bin and chuckled. "Oh, yes. Winter always makes men feel a bit cooped up around here. They get brash and always want to start a fight over the silliest things. Margaret is a full-time nanny most days around here."

With a final wave goodbye to Margaret, the two of them stepped back outside into the brisk air and Terra shivered. She yearned for the bright sun of Solaris and the taste of salt in the air. This winter seemed never-ending and bleak. Edith instructed her to leave the horses where they were and they took off on foot, aiming for what Edith claimed was the "most magical market that ever existed." Terra highly doubted that any market could be more magical than the one in Solaris, but she still followed her without any hesitation.

They wove through alleyways and side streets until Terra was thoroughly turned around with no idea where they were.

The buildings appeared to press together tighter here and they were far from the main road. Just when she thought that they would be lost forever in this twisting maze, Edith led her around a corner and before them rested a sprawling market full of people that took her breath away.

Lanterns towered high above everyone's heads and small rings of fire were placed strategically throughout the open space where one could stop and warm up for a bit before proceeding on their way. Grey smoke curled up in the sky but the buildings surrounding the square courtyard entirely hid any trace of the market from the main road or elsewhere. Wagons and stalls were crowded together to show off foodstuff, textiles, barrels of ale, trinkets, jewelry, and anything else one might want or need. The splash of color against the desolate landscape was intoxicating and Terra couldn't help but drink in the sight. The market of Solaris was one of the best, no doubt, but this hidden gem was tough competition for her homeland's market.

"This place is incredible," Terra said to Edith in disbelief. It was almost sensory overload after having been on her own with little to no socialization for the last few months. Her mind fought to take it all in and to memorize every detail, but there was too much for her to focus on. It was intimidating.

"It sure is," Edith replied as chipper as ever. "Stay close, no one would be very happy with me if I managed to lose you in the crowd."

Glancing around rapidly, Terra didn't even realize she was not paying attention to where she was going until she bumped into a warm body and two hard grabbed her arms to steady her. "Oh!" she gasped. "I'm so sorry I—"

"Terra?"

Terra blinked at the man before her, his face looking vaguely familiar, but she couldn't quite place him.

"We met a couple of months ago in the tavern, you were with your friend—"

"Cassi!" Terra finished and finally it clicked. It was the man she had met that wild night Cassi and she had snuck to the tavern. "I remember you. Caius, right? The one with all the secrets about Valerian."

Caius grinned. "That's right." He realized he was still holding onto her arms. He blushed and took a step back while lowering his hands back to his side, spotting Edith standing a little way away watching their exchange. "I'm sorry to interrupt, I saw you and I just had to come say hi. I'll let you be on your way—"

Caius took a step to leave, but Terra stopped him.

If anyone would know who was still behind the attacks or any leads, it would be the one who claimed to know everything around the village. If she could talk to him and question him, she might be able to get information to give to Orion.

"Oh no, it's perfectly fine." She turned to Edith. "Why don't you get everything else you were needing and we can catch back up to you?"

Edith frowned and didn't make any move to leave. "We still need to find the seeds that you desire and you are not sure where you need to go."

"Do you mean Ms. Lillian's seeds?" Caius asked.

Edith turned to him in surprise. "Why yes, that was where we were going."

"Her and my mother go way back, I can certainly escort Terra there to get what she needs."

"Sure." Terra smiled. "Edith, we won't be too long."

Edith looked at her long and hard, her expression clouded by a feeling that Terra couldn't pinpoint. "It's okay, Edith,"

Terra repeated. "We can finish up quicker this way and head home."

"Alright," Edith finally relented. "I will meet you at the northern end in half an hour, okay? No longer than half an hour."

"Certainly."

Edith watched as Caius led her away deeper into the market.

"I see that you have gotten married," Caius said to her once they were a ways away and he gestured to the ring that she had forgotten that she even had. The bright amethyst was eye catching against the glittering black band that it was set against.

"Yes, I had. Are you married?"

Caius let out a small laugh. "No, no I'm not. I'm sure my parents would love if I found a nice girl to settle down with, but it just hasn't happened yet…" he trailed off and left an awkward air of silence lingering between them. "So, tell me, are you still looking for deep and dark secrets about Valerian?"

Terra let out a laugh and it drew a grin from Caius. "I'm always open to hearing gossip about the kingdom. What dirty secrets do you have for me?"

"Hmmm," Caius tapped a finger against his lips. "You see that young maiden over there talking to that man?"

Terra nonchalantly glanced in that direction and saw a beautiful redheaded girl with a small smile who was talking to a dashing older gentleman before her. "Yes, what about her?"

"Well," Caius grinned. "She is a rich merchant's daughter and she is engaged to that gentleman that she's talking to, but notice that ragged boy over *there*?" Terra looked and saw a dirtied boy struggling to take barrels of ale off of a wagon and place them upright on the cobblestone. He was watching the girl intently in the most obvious of ways, but it was clear that he was trying to be discreet. "Well, he's absolutely head over heels for her and her for him. Of course, their union would never be acceptable to her father for he is a poor man."

"You really know the darkest secrets."

"I make it my business to know what goes on around here."

"I must admit, I did want to ask you about something," Terra dropped her voice low. "If you know everything that goes on around here, what is going on with the attacks?"

Caius paused and looked at her in surprise. "You are asking a very difficult question Terra, one that should not be answered where others may hear. Let's get your seeds then we'll go to a quieter part of the market."

Adrenaline spiked through her at his words, she was right to assume that he would have answers. Caius let her to a stall and introduced her to Ms. Lillian. Not too long later, she was leaving with the seeds carefully wrapped and placed into the folds of her dress. She was able to get seeds for plants she had never heard or have only heard in passing at Solaris's port such as cornflower and chamomile. She was excited to be able to get seeds for hyacinths, lavender, and a few other plants that grew native in Solaris that, with enough love and care, she hoped would flourish in the greenhouse.

"Where are we going?" she asked Caius. He had led her away from the depth of the market and down an alleyway that was vacant and dark with a cold breeze cutting through it.

"A private place where we can talk about the attacks," he answered. "We don't want anyone eavesdropping on us." He stopped and turned to face her, his eyes suddenly very serious. "What do you know of the attacks?"

"Not much," Terra admitted. "I do know that three suspects were caught and punished, but now more have been found dead so there has to be more to it all."

Caius nodded gravely. "Indeed, everyone thought that the arrests would put an end to them, but clearly that wasn't the case." He was quiet for a moment as if he was lost in thought.

"Caius?" Terra asked hesitantly.

"What does your Keeper of Souls think of the attacks?" Caius questioned, his voice low and husky all of a sudden. He took a step to the side and waited for her answer.

Terra reeled and stepped in the opposite direction to keep him in front of her. "My Keeper of Souls? What are you talking about?" Her voice shook as she said it and even before the words left her mouth, she knew he saw right through her lie.

"I know everything around here Terra, there isn't a point to lie to me about it. I suspected it that first night in the tavern and it didn't take very long for my sources to confirm. So tell me Terra, what secrets do you hold?" He reached into his pocket and the dagger that he withdrew glinted, her eyes darting to it immediately.

Terra swallowed hard and internally begged her heart to stop beating so damn fast. Without her even realizing it, he had cornered her against the wall and twirled the dagger flippantly in his hand. "I don't have any secrets."

Caius laughed except this time it was not full of humor. "Don't lie to me Terra, they don't call him the Keeper of Souls for nothing." He cocked his head to the side and appraised her. "Or should I call you, my lady?"

"What do you want with me?" Terra's hands found the solid wall behind her and she splayed her shaking fingers upon it.

"What I want are answers to my questions, my lady. It had to be fate when you basically fell into my lap that night at the tavern. I knew you could be the answer that I have been searching for. None of the others had answers, for they were under codes of silence, so they had to be dealt with. But you," he pointed the tip of the knife towards her. "You will give me everything that I have been searching for."

"The King will find you, you know, and will make you pay," Terra growled. Sudden bravery coursed through her and was controlling her tongue. "And it's *Your Highness*." In one sudden movement, she jabbed a knee sharply at the area between his thighs and he released the knife to clatter on the cobblestone. Terra immediately dashed away but a firm hand wrapped around her ankle. She plunged to the ground with a cry and flipped over just in time to find Caius straddling her. His sheer body weight held her in place and he threw a hand around her throat.

Gasping for air, Terra tried to throw him off her, but he was too big, too heavy in comparison to her. Spots started to dance across her vision and everything grew fuzzy as the air began to leak from her lungs.

"I would love to see your King try," Caius purred and squeezed harder. "Are you going to be a good girl and answer my questions about your King?"

Terra flailed, reaching and scratching to get a hold of any surface, any sliver of skin that she may be able to claw to shreds. Her hand brushed a sharp edge along the ground. *The dagger.* She clutched it tightly and swung it at him with all her might. She felt his weight lessen and heard him roar in anger. Throwing her hips sideways, Terra managed to upend him and finally sucked in deep gulps of air while hacking from the damage to her throat. Caius was bleeding profusely from a gouge down his cheek and his hands were already covered in the bright red blood from the wound she gave him.

Letting the knife clatter to the ground, Terra rushed to her feet and ran as fast as she could back towards the market. She faintly could hear him shouting after her, but she refused to stop.

People stared as she hurried through the maze, unsure of where she was going and trying her best not to trip or stumble into anyone. Tears fell from her eyes even though the adrenaline still pumped through her. Just when she thought she would be lost forever, she finally spotted Edith waiting patiently right where she said she would be. Edith saw Terra only a split second before she barreled into her. She hugged her tightly as she sobbed into the fabric of the dress.

Edith, bless her heart, didn't ask what happened but instead first rushed to get them out of the market and away from prying eyes. Once they were safe in an empty alley, Edith held her out in front of her to take in the damage. "What *happened?*" she hissed when she saw the bruises already forming over her throat from where she had been choked. Terra gave her a tearful account of what had transpired and begged her not to tell Orion.

"Of *course* I'm going to tell Orion!" Edith nearly shouted. "This is not a secret that we are going to keep from him. We will be telling him everything, Terra."

But Terra didn't even want to think about telling him what happened. "Please," Terra hiccupped. "Please let's just go home."

Dread filled Terra as her and Edith left the stables and made their way back to the castle. She couldn't kick the horrible feeling in the pit of her stomach that was a mixture of fear, embarrassment, and most of all anger at herself for letting herself be in that situation. "I'm going to bed," Terra mumbled to Edith once they were inside in the hopeful chance that she could avoid Orion entirely. She didn't want to be there when Edith told him what had happened.

Terra had just reached the middle of the staircase when she heard his voice. Her head snapped up and there he was at the top of the stairs. His wide smile immediately disappeared when he looked at her and was instead replaced with intense anger. "*What happened?*"

Drawing her cloak tighter around herself, Terra could feel that she was beginning to shrink in on herself and she looked down at the stone beneath her boots. Before she could protest, he was right there in front of her, so close that she could hear the angry rise and fall of his chest.

"I said," he growled and looked at Edith down below. "*What. Happened.*" Tears threatened to spill over once again as he took her face gently in his hands to look at the damage. His cloudy grey eyes were suddenly clear and she could see every ounce of anger burning inside him with a hint of pain.

She couldn't stand it.

Terra pulled out of his grasp and brushed by him to hurry to her room. She could hear him shouting at Edith as she went, his booming voice saying, "You left her *alone?* I will find the man who did this and he will never again see the light of day." She ran the rest of the way to her room and slammed the door shut quickly behind her, a sob choking out from deep in her throat. Barely managing to get the dirty cloak and her boots off in time, she plunged deep into her bed and buried herself deep under the covers.

There she sat, the sobs ripping out of her for what felt like ages before she heard a gentle knock at her door. "Go away," she blubbered.

"I'm not leaving," Orion called from the other side of the door. "Not until you talk to me."

"Go away," Terra repeated and sunk deeper into the abyss of her blankets.

Orion sighed from his side of the door. "Terra, darling, I'm not leaving until I can make sure you're okay. Please."

Terra sniffled but poked her head up from the blanket. "Fine," she sighed and disappeared back to her cocoon before the door opened softly. Orion closed it behind him and she heard his footsteps approach the bed but then stopped. After a few shuddering breaths, she finally dared to peek her eyes out to look at him. His mouth was twisted into a frown, but his eyes were filled with worry.

"Terra," he said softly and put his hands in his pockets. "Why don't you come out of bed, darling, and talk to me."

Terra shook her head and dove back under her covers. "I would rather not," she squeaked.

Orion sighed and she imagined him rubbing his temples in frustration, but his voice remained calm and sweet. "And why is that darling?"

"Because I'm scared you're going to yell at me."

A soft chuckle floated to her ears. "I'm not going to yell at you, I promise. I just want to make sure you're okay. You gave me quite a scare."

Terra thought for a brief moment before she poked her eyes back out to look at him. She swept aside one of the sides of the blanket as an invitation. Orion looked at the open spot beside her and back at her, his hesitation clear. When Terra didn't lower the blanket, he carefully took his boots off and sat on the edge of the bed. Terra shook the blanket insistingly and he sighed again before finally obliging and laying underneath the covers with her, so close yet so far away.

"Do you know how sick it makes me feel to know that you and Edith were in danger? That you were hurt?"

Terra rolled to her side to look at him and was quiet for a moment before answering. "I'm sorry."

"Darling, there's nothing to be sorry for." Orion rolled onto his side to face her. "I should have known better than to let you go alone, to think that you wouldn't be in any danger because of me. I was wrong and I - I might have been the reason why you never see your family again." He swallowed hard. "That thought *guts me.*"

"I was trying to get information," Terra said so quietly that she was surprised he even heard her. "For you, about the attacks. Margaret had said that there was another one last night. That's why I went to talk to him. I wanted to do something to help."

Orion saddened. He reached out a tender hand to her cheek and tilted her jaw so that he could see the injury that Terra hadn't even wanted to see. He sucked in a sharp breath at the sight and she thought she could almost see his eyes watering. "I'm so, so sorry." He leaned forward and gave her a soft kiss on her forehead. "Will you ever forgive me?" he murmured against her hot skin.

As if he had broken a spell that was placed between them, Terra was overcome by a strong urge to touch him, to let him hold her and erase the stains that Caius had left upon her. Every mean word or action that had ever happened between them didn't matter anymore. All that mattered was what was said right here, right now. The past can be forgotten and she realized that she already had forgiven him weeks ago.

Leaning forward, Terra pressed her lips against his and she felt him tense in surprise. "There is nothing to be forgiven," she whispered against his lips. A small groan escaped from his chest and his hands cradled her face to pull her in closer.

The fire that had been burning deep in her belly flickered and grew, trailing its way upwards to her chest as he intertwined his hands in her hair. She savored the taste of him, the smell of him, the feel of him. Every last sense of hers was on fire. She gripped his shirt and pulled him closer.

Orion became undone at the gesture. In one fluid motion, Terra found herself on her back with him between her legs, one hand underneath her head cradling her and the other on her cheek. He kissed her along the edge of her jaw and his one hand moved from her arm and down to her waist. She tensed at the unfamiliarity of the touch and he noticed immediately, pulling away.

"I've never done this before," Terra admitted shyly, suddenly embarrassed by the statement.

Realization and guilt flashed across Orion's eyes and he sat back on his heels. "I'm sorry, we can sto—"

Before he could even finish his sentence, Terra sat up and met his mouth with hers. She pulled away, the fire burning red hot in his eyes. "I don't want to," she whispered. That was all he needed to hear.

Orion cupped her face and kissed her deeply in a passionate way that made her head positively spin with joy. He kissed her in a way that allowed her to feel his emotions. She could feel his concern for her, his worry and his guilt for blaming himself. Most of all, she could feel his affection for her. There it was, hidden deep within and heavily protected, but it was blooming now and demanded to be noticed.

Terra gasped as Orion dared to run a hand up her smooth leg and pushed aside her heavy skirt so that she could feel the trail of fire in every place that he touched. It was un*bearable*. She reached for his shirt to unbutton it with shaky hands. Orion understood and quickly slid it off his shoulders to toss onto the floor. She drank him in, taking in the hard lines of his muscles and the inches of skin she had never had the pleasure of gazing upon before. She ran her hands over his sturdy chest before pulling him back in, shortly realizing that even though his shirt was easy to deal with, her dress was not.

"Orion?" she asked quietly. He pulled away again in alarm, his face searching hers for any indication of what was wrong. "I need help...with my dress."

Orion chuckled low and deep, sending a hot flash through Terra from her thighs and up to her chest. "I would be more than happy to oblige, darling."

Quivering, Terra stood next to the bed to stand with her back facing him. She felt him stand behind her and begin to undo the buttons with slow and deft fingers, pausing to plant a kiss along the bare skin of her back every few buttons. She let the dress fall to the floor with her undergarments until she was standing before him, naked and vulnerable.

Orion sucked in a sharp breath through his teeth as his eyes raked her up and down. "Gods, you are absolutely beautiful, darling. Come here."

Terra obeyed, stepping forward to take his outstretched hand. He pulled her closer and ran a tentative hand down her bare back and to her bottom. Terra moaned and he put her back down on the bed, kissing her bare thighs and the apex of her thighs while she quivered beneath his touch

"Please," Terra panted when she rested her eyes on him. "I want you."

There was only a few moments of pain and an odd tugging sensation but then there was nothing except pure pleasure. Orion whispered sweet nothings in her ear, running his hands across her smooth skin and feeling every part of her. Every nerve was on fire and she thought that she would never grow tired of this, of *him*. She raised her hand up his neck and twisted her fingers tightly into his hair as if she was hanging on for dear life.

"I love you Terra," he murmured against her lips. "I've always loved you." The world shattered around Terra, sending her spiraling into a galaxy of stars where nothing else existed except her and Orion.

Chapter Eighteen
Orion

The last remnants of dusk illuminated Terra lying in his arms, breathing softly as she dozed. Orion didn't want to disturb her or wake her, or at least not quite yet. The feel of her warm against his chest relaxed him in a way he hadn't been in a very long time. For once, the outside world didn't matter. Anything that he had to do, or any expectations placed upon him, dissipated. This is all he needed, him and her warm in her bed and her safe in his arms.

But Orion had to leave. He meant to do so hours ago.

Terra stirred in her sleep and he froze, hoping that he didn't wake her. Her neck came into view and he swallowed hard at the sight of the handprint shaped bruises flourishing over her skin. His temper flared and his mouth suddenly went dry. Edith had told him everything she knew, which wasn't much, but he vowed to himself that he would find the man who did this to her and he would make him pay. Very painfully, and very, very slowly.

Terra's sleepy eyes fluttered opened and she smiled softly when she saw him before letting her eyes shut again. "Hi," she murmured and sank deeper into his chest. He grazed her bare back with his fingertips and enjoyed the softness of her skin.

"Hi," he answered.

"Why do you look so sad?"

Orion didn't answer her. He didn't want to tell her he was leaving her, abandoning her like his father had done to his mother so many times. He didn't want to choke out the words that he had never planned on saying during his lifetime.

"Orion?" Terra was suddenly awake now. She sat up to look at him with a worried expression. Her voice was raspy yet, whether from the sleep or the attack he wasn't sure and the thought pained him suddenly. He wanted to know her in every aspect. He wanted to know how it felt to sleep beside her every night, to wake up next to her, to spend eternity together. "What's wrong?"

"I have to go darling," he said softly and pressed a kiss against her forehead.

Terra frowned. "Go where?"

"I have to find out who is behind the attacks. There are more men out there who need to face justice. I'll only be gone a few days though, I promise."

"Why do you have to go? Why can't you stay? Can't you send the patrols to take care of it instead?" She rested her head back onto his chest and held him tight.

"Because darling, I have to do something to protect my people and my men haven't been able to track anyone down."

"When are you leaving?"

Orion hesitated and glanced out the window to see the sun almost completely shrouded as the night grew closer. "I meant to leave a few hours ago, when you came home. I should leave before it gets too late. I'll leave Ash here though just in case, okay?"

Terra only frowned and pulled the blanket closer to her body. "Okay," she finally said softly.

"If there was any way I could stay here, I would."

Terra nuzzled in closer to him. "Are you sure there is no way I can convince you to stay? If you don't leave, I promise we won't have to leave bed for another entire day. Don't make me beg."

"Mm if you convinced me to stay, then you wouldn't be just begging for me to stay." He nipped her ear playfully and the small giggles she let out warmed his heart.

"I understand that you have to go." Terra looked up at him with sadness in her eyes despite her valiant effort to convince him otherwise and it cut right through him.

Orion ran his fingers through her hair. "Please don't be sad." The locks were long and wild, yet still silky to the touch. He thought about how nice it felt to run his fingers through it and he bit the inside of his cheek. He had to go before his lustful thoughts got him in trouble and convinced him to stay.

Terra watched him as he finally rolled out of bed. Her eyes followed his every move while he put on his previously discarded clothes lying on the ground. She continued to watch him even as he laced his boots back up and tried to smooth down his own hair that had been mussed.

Orion buttoned up his shirt and Terra, still lying in her same spot, let out a small sigh. "Will you please at least be safe?"

He slid the last button through and leaned down to give her a final farewell kiss. "Yes, I will be safe." She sighed again when he pressed his lips to hers, awakening something deep within him that made it even more difficult to pull away from her. With one final glance, he left her room and left her still lying naked among her wrinkled sheets. When he returned, he would have to hold her to her gracious offer to stay in bed all day.

Everything Orion had packed was already stacked in a neat pile in the foyer and he discovered that Edith had added more, mainly dried jerky and cheese wrapped tightly in cloth. *As if I would forget to eat,* he thought. Just as he was about to go in search of Edith to say goodbye, his dogs bounded from the direction of the kitchen and a frazzled Edith wasn't too far behind them.

"Don't you dare leave before saying goodbye," Edith quipped and pointed an accusatory finger at him. "Otherwise I may just lock you out of your own castle."

Orion chuckled. "I wasn't going to leave without saying goodbye." She wrapped him in a hug and squeezed him tight.

"You better be safe," Edith said. "Be careful and come back to us."

"I will." Orion pulled away. "Please, keep an eye on her and keep her safe. Ash will stay with you and make sure Laurent is nearby. If you need anything, go find Captain Darren."

Edith nodded, looking pale and worried. "Laurent is in the stables, readying your horse."

"Thank you." Orion hauled his supplies over his shoulder and his back before giving Edith one final hug.

Outside, the skies were a cloudy grey mixed with the last tinge of sunlight from the day. It was going to snow. Orion could smell it in the air. He let out a sharp whistle and in no time, his two dogs trotted after him while he commanded Ash to remain where she was. Silas and Milo both followed him to the stables where Laurent already had his horse waiting for him.

Laurent helped Orion get his packs settled on the saddle and made sure everything was secured before giving him a tight hug goodbye as well. "Safe travels, Your Highness," Laurent said and handed the horse's reins to him.

Orion nodded to him before leading Theos outside. He mounted the horse and glanced back at the castle. High in a window, he saw the shape of Terra watching him go. He waved a hand and she waved back before placing her palm against the windowpane. Without another look back, Orion set off with Milo and Silas running beside him.

The night got very cold very fast. Even with his multiple layers of clothing and his thick fur cloak, the cold nipped at Orion and managed to chill him to the bone. But yet, they pressed on. He headed northwest so that he plunged into the darkest parts of the forest where even his soldiers wouldn't go. Here, the forest was unbelievably thick and the terrain grew even more mountainous until the only path that Orion could travel was a rocky trail leading past sharp cliff edges and deadly ravines. Anyone else would have been called mad to even attempt this path during the day, but he took it to a whole different level by traveling in the dark.

The full moon that hung heavy in the night sky lit the way and threw shadows dramatically against the tree trunks and the land. Snowflakes begun to fall and coated the ground with a slick layer. The rocky precipice made him wary, but he knew that he couldn't stop now when he was so close to where he needed to be.

What seemed like hours later, Orion and the dogs finally reached a plateau on the ground that led into a large clearing in the forest. The snow was coming down quicker now, the wet flakes clinging to his cloak and his boots. Theos was breathing hard and seemed relieved when Orion dropped to the ground as did Milo and Silas. Without hesitating he let go of his horse's reins for him to wander and instead strode to the middle of the clearing with his dogs close at hand.

There, Orion waited. The world around him was muffled by the snow and allowed him to focus on any sound that didn't belong. Minutes turned into hours and yet he still waited. Silas paced impatiently and Milo dug out a patch of the snow aside to comfortably lay and rest. Finally, when the moon was about at its highest point in the sky, something around him changed. It began with a breeze picking up. It ruffled his cloak and his hair while also catching the top layer of snow on the ground. His dogs were quickly alert and stood with their fur pressed into his legs growling.

"I know you're here," Orion called into the void. "There's no need to pretend that you're not. Come out, we need to talk."

A slim figure surrounded in a thick fur cloak hiding her face appeared behind a tree and slunk towards him. She stopped before Orion and waited in silence for him to speak. He could see the quiver of arrows slung across her back and a small glimpse of the smooth wooden bow hiding beneath the folds of the fur.

"Celeste." Orion's tongue suddenly felt swollen and dry. "It's nice to see you again. How long has it been?"

A small chuckle came from the depth of the hood. "Too long, I would say." Slowly, the figure reached for the hood and threw it back to reveal her silver white hair and slender features. She had a gold circlet around the top of her head with matching gold cuffs in her ears that stood out from her fur-lined layers of clothing and boots made from a wolf pelt to fend against the snow. Instead of the flakes dusting her face and hair, they seemed to avoid her entirely and instead found their place on the ground like the rest. Her pale skin glowed in the moonlight and her eyes presented a mix of emotion, mainly confusion at his presence but also fear. Why she was frightened, he wasn't sure. "Hello, Uncle, what brings you to my forest?"

"I come in search of information."

Celeste cocked her head. "What makes you think I would have the information that you seek? It has been decades since we have last spoken."

"I'm not a fool Celeste," Orion said, his voice growing cold. "I know you stalk the grounds around my castle, around my entire realm. I know that I am being watched when I'm in my own land. I'm aware of your comings and goings when it directly affects me. If anything, I should be asking why you haven't dropped in to say hi sooner."

"What do you want?" Celeste hissed. "Have you come to apologize for your men for slaughtering more of my wildlife?"

"We hunt in my own realm. Maybe you and your hunters should reside elsewhere." Orion peered around Celeste when he said this, knowing that the shadows shifting among the trees meant that he was right in assuming she had not appeared here alone.

Celeste's eyes flashed bright silver. "Have you come to insult me Uncle, or to gain information?"

Orion's lips twitched and threatened to break into a smile. It was so easy to get under her skin. She forgot that he had been around a lot longer than what she had and that he was immensely more powerful than she was.

"Or, perhaps, you have come to find me for a way out of your newest marriage. Tell me Uncle, are you sick of your Queen already? Do you wish for me to teach her how to be a true Huntress?"

Orion's blood turned to ice, but he kept his face expressionless as he let the anger simmer deep in his belly. Instead, he kept the shadows at bay and kept himself composed. "I am very happily married, Celeste, but thank you for your concern."

Her eyes turned to the dogs at his side. "I see you are taking care of your presents, but one appears to be missing. Left with your wife, I presume? Funny how the Queen of such an apparently powerful man needs such protection. The rumors say she is young, far too young for the likes of you."

Celeste shrugged. "But I suppose she can't be as bad as the last one and it makes sense that you would need some whore to keep you busy during your lonely existence."

In one quick movement, Orion flicked his fingers at his side and shadows morphed out of the trees to warp and stretch around Celeste. With another swipe of his hand, an impenetrable wall of shadows surrounded them and stretched high above their heads until they were entirely enclosed and cut off from Celeste's hunters. Celeste squirmed and tried to break her bonds of darkness to no avail. A shadow climbed over her mouth, effectively gagging her while her eyes cut right through him.

"You forget your place," Orion growled and stalked around her. "You forget that I am older, more powerful. You forget that you are in *my* realm and you are only here because I *allow* you to be." He stopped behind her and leaned in close. "You do best to remember that next time you think to insult my Queen." Orion snapped his fingers and the shadow covering her mouth disappeared. Celeste gasped in a few breaths and he could feel her anger rolling off of her in waves.

"What information do you seek?" she hissed through gritted teeth.

"I'm sure you are well aware of the violence happening in my kingdom, since we both know how much you enjoy watching mortal women."

Ignoring the jab, Celeste nodded stiffly. "The murders? Yes, my hunters have heard reports. What about them?"

"I need to know who is behind them so that they can be stopped," Orion said simply. "I have already executed three guilty parties, but there's more. I myself don't appreciate the unnecessary slaughtering of the innocent, unlike your father. So, tell me Celeste, who is behind the attacks?"

Celeste was quiet for a moment, her eyes grazing over his face until a sharp laugh bursted from deep within her chest. "You can't be serious, you don't know?"

Orion strode forward and grabbed the front of her cloak, pulling her roughly towards him. "What is that supposed to mean?"

She grinned, the smile starting small and creeping wider and bigger. "I suggest that you start looking at the highest peak, Heaven's Gate, and maybe you'll figure it all out on your way. Goodbye, Uncle." Celeste closed her eyes and she dissolved into a bright silver light that cut through the shadows binding her.

Orion ducked and covered his eyes, opening them again to only find himself alone once again in the falling snow. "Celeste!" he roared, but he knew she was already long gone. Growling in frustration, Orion stomped back to the other edge of the clearing where Theos was calmly resting. "Why does my family have to be so frustrating," he complained to Theos, but mostly himself. "Is this how Terra feels about me? Just constantly *aggravated* to no end?" Theos nickered in what Orion convinced himself was an agreement with him.

"Heaven's Gate," he mused and turned to Milo and Silas who were still alert but resting tiredly among the snow. "We'll set up camp here for the night and set out in the morning." Digging through the packs, Orion dug out a canvas tent, fur blankets, a bedroll, and food and water for himself, the dogs, and Theos. By the time he turned in for the night, the dawn was just beginning to peek above the horizon. Both Silas and Milo curled up on either side of him and quickly fell asleep whereas Orion was left tossing and turning from a sense of impatience to get along with his journey.

"Heaven's Gate," Orion muttered to himself again when he finally began dozing off. "What could be waiting there?"

Mere hours later, Orion was already packed and on his way once more despite the lack of sleep plaguing his body. He had slept fitfully, his dreams filled with glimpses of Terra that only made his heart ache. He still felt terrible that he left her alone and his entire being was fueled with the intense desire to get back home to her as soon as possible.

More snow had fallen, but now it was finally done with. Orion, astride Theos and with Silas and Milo following closely, led their miniature caravan back the way they had come. They had to head west if they were going to make it to Heaven's gate before nightfall. Luckily, the mountain peak was even closer to home than Celeste's clearing was which eased his mind a bit more.

Orion frowned at the thought of Celeste. She had gotten under his skin, much to his amazement. Usually it wasn't an issue for him to remain calm, cool, and collected in front of his family, but her mention of Terra brought out a fury he hadn't even thought he possessed anymore.

They still managed to find a way to be a pain in his ass.

The landscape blurred as the time passed, Orion focused on nothing and instead allowed himself to get lost in his own head to help the time fly by. Hours later, they finally reached the foothills of Heaven's Gate. The peak was intimidating and carved a jagged outline against the faint blue sky above. Steeling himself, they began the journey upwards. It was precarious, even more precarious than the path they had followed last night. This brought them even sharper upwards until they reached a point where Orion knew he had to continue on foot. He found a safe area where there were still trees for shelter and set up camp to make sure everything was set for the animals in his absence.

If he hadn't brought Milo and Silas with, a part of Orion would have been worried about folks stumbling across his camp, but instead he knew that the dogs would rip any thief to shreds and this made him smile. He bundled up and tucked a knife in his belt before grabbing his bow and saying goodbye. Milo whined as he walked away, but Orion didn't look back. He shouldn't be gone too long. Looking upwards, he could see the path he needed to take to reach the top.

The path had him panting and sweating profusely but he pressed on. The wind grew stronger and the air grew colder as he climbed. An hour later, Orion finally crested the incline and in front of him spread a wide area where the wind whipped violently.

What was he supposed to be looking for? Spinning around, Orion cursed. There was nothing here. He was at the top of a dangerous peak in the middle of winter with nothing except wind, snow, and "-*rocks*," he muttered to himself. Down a small hill on the other side was a pile of rocks and boulders that almost looked like a cave of sorts that he knew that he should check out, or at least rest by before starting the slow climb back down.

Just as Orion reached the top of the small hill and was about to go down, a voice called his name from behind him. He whirled around and chuckled. "Are all my nieces and nephews seeking me out after all of these years?"

Chapter Nineteen
Terra

Terra felt Orion's absence like a sharp knife in her chest. It grazed against her heart every time she moved too abruptly, took too deep of a breath, or anything else really. It put her in a foul mood and she never left her bed until the next morning.

Feeling confined and trapped within the castle walls, she spent the next morning instead planting the seeds in the greenhouse with Ash by her side. It was tough work but Terra was grateful for the distraction. Over and over she dug her hands deep in the dirt and dropping in the seeds, making sure they were watered and well-tended so that they could begin to bloom quickly while surrounded by the heat.

While she worked, Terra thought. Her mind was brimming with chaotic thoughts darting amongst each other to the point where she was almost dizzy. Her mind went to a deep memory of her childhood, one where her mother and father had taken her and Calli, the only two sisters who were born at the time, to the market in Solaris. Even when she was that young, Terra was a curious child. Her parents constantly had to stop and redirect her away from snatching some shiny object off one of the tables. One of the times though, Terra had noticed a bejeweled lamp glittering in the sunlight. She had reached out for it and stopped in her tracks to take in the beautiful fixture. As soon as she remembered that she was with her family, however, she looked up and found that her family was gone.

Terra still remembers the panic that had struck her hard in the chest at the realization that they were gone and it almost felt like she did right now.

Tears had begun to stream down her face and she darted among the stalls while crying out for her parents. Her sandal had caught on something and she plunged hard to the rough pavement. Her knees were busted up and bleeding from her fall which only had made her cry harder, of course. Just when she thought she would be lost forever, her father's face appeared in front of her own as he crouched down.

"Terra sweetie, why are you crying?" he asked. Terra could still hear the low timber of his voice and could smell the scent of the sea clinging to him.

"I- I lost you," she blubbered. "And then I f-fell."

Her father had given her a reassuring smile and took her legs carefully in his hands to kiss right above the raw scrapes. "There's no need to cry, it'll be okay and we'll get you cleaned up. Do you know why we feel pain Terra?"

She sniffled and wiped her runny nose before shaking her head no.

"So that we know the good when we have it. Always remember that, sweetheart. We have to go through the bad and the pain and sadness to get to the good." Her father picked her up in his arms and went to find the others to cheer her up.

Terra's heart hurt at the memory of her late father. She missed his laugh, his smile, his easygoing personality, the silly jokes he would pull on the girls, and even her mother. She missed her family so much that she thought the retched feeling would never cease.

Terra stopped what she was doing and instead sat back with her butt on the ground. Ash groaned and padded over to plop down in her lap. Ignoring all the fur that she was shedding over her dress, Terra scratched her lovingly and doted on her which Ash immediately ate up. Her tail thumped the ground hard and Terra couldn't help but smile at the memory of her once fearing the dogs. In her defense, she hadn't understood that they were members of the family as well.

She froze in realization. Even though her family was far away and she was no longer with them, that didn't mean that her family was gone. Instead, she was here, starting a new family and the thought brought a semblance of comfort.

"I suppose we should get dinner since we skipped lunch," Terra said to Ash and they both got to their feet. Terra dusted herself off and put all the tools neatly away before drowning herself in her cloak for the walk back to the castle. When they were almost to the doors, she stopped. Something wasn't right, she realized, and she couldn't quite put her finger on it. Even the silence around her caused the hair on her arms to stand up. As if Ash was just realizing the same thing, her hackles began to raise and she started to growl.

With nothing to use as a weapon, Terra approached the front entrance cautiously and when she came to it, she found that it was open just a sliver. Frowning, she inspected the door and pushed it open slightly so that a loud creak sounded. She knew that she closed the door tightly, she always did. Maybe it was just a patrol or some of the soldiers that had come without fully closing the door. But still…

A strike of fear cut through her as her mind imagined Caius waiting inside to finish what he started. A hand went to her throat where the bruises still blotched darkly across the fair skin. Taking a deep breath, Terra pushed the door open fully.

Half expecting to find someone waiting for her on the other side in the foyer, she was surprised to find no one. "Maybe I'm just overreacting," she muttered to herself before turning to Ash. "Am I just crazy? Am I overreacting?"

Ash's jet-black eyes gave her no answer. Her fur was still on end, but she was no longer growling which Terra assumed meant that she had been just feeding off of Terra's fear in the first place. *Nothing is wrong,* she told herself. *You just left the door open and gave yourself a scare, that's all. One of the guards may have stopped by or something, too.*

Shaking off the nervous feeling, Terra undid her cloak and her and Ash headed for the kitchen. Expecting to find Edith there, Terra was surprised to find her absent. "I wonder where she is," Terra said to Ash and Ash wandered away to sniff at the nooks and crannies she usually wasn't allowed to be around in Edith's presence.

Terra began to fix herself a plate and went to grab a bowl of water for Ash when she noticed that the dog was nowhere to be found. Calling for her, she began to look around and even poked her head in the hallway with no luck. "What the hell?" Suddenly, she heard a faint whine and followed it deeper into the kitchen. She noticed that a pantry door was cracked so she swung it open to find Ash nuzzling an unconscious Edith who was tied up and bleeding from a nasty wound on her head.

Terra gasped and heard a noise behind her. She turned around to see a stranger blocking the exit from the kitchen. Taking a step back, she put a hand on the wall behind her to steady herself. "Who are you? What do you want?" she asked in a shaky voice.

The man smiled and played with the wicked dagger he had in his hands. He was unfamiliar to her, immensely tall with solid muscle on him and he had long black hair that fell loose to his shoulders. He had tanned skin that was unfamiliar in the land of Valerian and was more like her own which made her think that he was from Solaris. Maybe this was all a mistake and maybe he wasn't here to hurt her or Edith, but to protect them.

"Are you from Solaris?" Terra stumbled over the words. "Did my mother send you?"

The man only laughed. "No, Your Highness, your mother in fact did not send me. Although," his eyes narrowed dangerously. "I think you will wish that she had."

In the blink of an eye, the man let the dagger fly and Terra managed to duck just in time. The blade impaled itself deep into the wooden door of the pantry directly where her head had been moments before. Terra yelped and saw him reaching into his pocket for another knife. Ash followed her as she ran around the center counters and ducked again to avoid the next throw. Ash took advantage of his momentary weakness and struck, digging her teeth through his pants leg and deep into his flesh. The man roared and Terra scrambled onto her feet to dash out of the kitchen with Ash hot on her heels before the man could react to them fleeing.

Panting, Terra stopped in the foyer, not sure what to do or where to go. She whirled around to try to find anything to use as a weapon, but there was nothing. She wasn't even sure where anything would be kept and she was out of time, the man was still coming for her. How had he gotten here and through the patrols without being caught?

Terra ran down the hallway with Ash following her and she darted into the first room she could. It was a parlor room that her and Edith would use at times to have afternoon tea together, which wasn't the best option in terms of barricading. Terra immediately thew the door closed and went for the heavy couch, grunting and pushing will all of her might until she managed to bar the door with it. She was just in time it would seem, for the man pounded a heavy fist on the other side and Terra jumped back with a choked noise that caught in her throat. She snatched a heavy candelabra off of a side table and held it at the ready. Backing towards the far wall, Ash stood in front of her with her teeth gnashing.

The man swung again, and again, and again until the door began to give away and splinter. Adrenaline pumped through her body, but her mind couldn't focus. She was out of options and there was nothing she could do.

Terra was trapped.

The stranger delivered one final blow and managed to shove the couch far enough back so he could crack open the door. "Don't try to run, Your Highness, it'll only make this worse," the man growled and tried to squeeze himself through the door.

"You underestimate me," Terra hissed back and chucked the candelabra with all her might. Her aim was true and she struck him right in the middle of the head and, hopefully, knocked him unconscious when she watched him slide limply to the floor. Terra stepped closer to look at the man slumped to the ground and found him clearly dazed, but still moving. Before he could get back to his feet, Terra tried to slip through the door and just when she thought she escaped, she felt a strong hand wrap around her ankle.

Terra fell to the ground and immediately kicked out with all her strength. She slammed the heel of her boot into his nose and a burst of blood caused him to let go to cover his face. Ash again attacked and shredded his shirt and the skin of his shoulder with her teeth. The man cried out in pain and flung Ash into the hallway wall. She slumped to the floor with a yelp and Terra paused when she saw that she wasn't moving.

"I'll kill you!" the attacker yelled and tried to stumble to his feet. "You little bitch, I swear to the gods I will slit your throat!"

Terra turned and ran. She fled down the hall with her skirts in her hand and sweat dripping down her face and her back.

She made it back to the foyer and choked back a sob that was threatening to break loose. She was all alone. Orion was gone, Edith was unconscious, and they probably did something absolutely horrible to Laurent as well. Thorn Hall was too far and she would never make it there before he caught up to her. Besides, she had no clue how to even get there and she would probably become lost in the process. There was nowhere she could hide where the man wouldn't find her. Unless…

"I'm coming for you," the man called from deeper into the castle, his voice echoing and carrying through the corridors.

She would have to take a chance.

Going to the door leading down to the dungeon, Terra plunged into the dark and closed the door behind her. Her exasperated breaths seemed to echo louder in the dark and she suddenly regretted her decision to trap herself down here in the dark. The door was waiting for her at the end of the dungeon as if it was expecting her. The stone was dark and it was firmly closed yet. Orion's words vibrated through her head, but she pushed them away. *"Never go down here, it's not safe."*

"Please work, please work, please work," Terra whispered and put a shaky hand on the door. Part of her expected the inscriptions to glow black and light up to her touch like it did with Orion, but she remained drenched in the darkness. Her lip quivered and a few tears escaped. "Please, help me," she begged and slid down to her knees. In the distance, she could hear the door that led to the dungeon creak open and the man curse when he saw the darkness before him.

"Please," Terra whispered again and let her tears fall openly onto the floor. Her fingers remained pressed on the cold stone of the door. "Help me."

Terra felt a small breeze blow through her hair and it made her shiver against the chill. The energy of the room changed and she felt the static in the air. She was no longer alone.

You are not our Master, a voice whispered in her head. *Why should we help you?*

"I am the Queen of the Underworld." Terra's lips quivered. The words were odd and bulky on her tongue but rang true as soon as she said them. "And I need your help."

And what, Queen of the Underworld, do you think we can do?

"I don't know, and I don't care, but that man is going to kill me unless you help me. Can you do that or not?"

Hmmm, the voice mused. Terra felt a hand brush back a wild strand of hair and the cold seeped deeper into her bones. *I suppose I may be able to assist, but with a price.*

"Name your price. I don't have much time." Just as Terra said it, she saw the faint glow of light from where the stairs would be. The man came back and this time with a lantern to guide him through the unknown darkness.

A favor, that is all I ask. When the time comes, you will do me favor.

"Deal, now help me!"

Your salvation rests in the forest, Your Highness, get there and you will be saved.

Fear clutched at Terra's throat. "That's it? That's all you can do to help me? All you can do is just *tell me to get to the forest?*" The man now was at the bottom of the stairs and heading for her, the lantern held out in front of him to cast light upon the walls.

I can buy you time, the voice explained in annoyance. *But yes, you need to get to the forest. I look forward to seeing you again to hold up your end of the deal, Queen of Iron.*

Before Terra could react or ponder the odd title, the shadow flew forward with such a velocity that it knocked the man back and extinguished his lantern all at once. Terra scrambled back to her feet and raced past him in the dark to find her way back to the stairs. She shot back to the foyer and threw the doors wide open before running outside in the now growing darkness.

Assuming that she had to get to Thorn Hall, Terra guessed which direction she would have to go and plunged into the night. The cold bit at her bare skin and clawed at her warmth, but she didn't stop. Even when she could hear the man chasing after her in her reckless race to the trees, she didn't slow down.

Branches tore at her arms and face and the snow dragged at her boots which allowed him to quickly gain on her. She went to jump over a log, but her foot caught and sent her tumbling down into the snow. He was on her in an instant. He ripped her hair with a hand and held a dagger to her throat with the other. "You're a tough one to catch, you know that? You're going to pay for it though, I promise you."

Terra cried out and he wrenched her hair tighter. There was no more fight left in her. She couldn't keep running. Instead, she closed her eyes and waited for the lash of pain.

She heard the rustle of clothing and a male grunt before the weight of him disappeared. Opening her eyes, she found him sprawled in the snow unmoving. Blood seeped from an open wound in his throat and it stained the white snow around him a dark red. Terra looked around her but there was no one in sight. Creeping forward, she moved his head to the side and found his eyes to be wide open, paralyzed in fear and very, very dead.

Her stomach churning, Terra crawled away from the man's body and wretched into the snow. It was only when she finally emptied everything in her stomach that a figure appeared from behind a tree, causing her to crawl away in fear.

"Wait," the figure said. "I'm here to help, I promise."

Terra stood on shaky legs and took in the new stranger. She was young and not too much older than Terra was. She had long silver white hair done in a loose braid along one shoulder and a bloodied dagger in her belt along with a bow slung across her back. "Who are you?" Terra whispered.

"My name is Celeste, I protect these forests and the women in them," the woman said. "You needed my help, so I was there."

A sudden memory came forward in Terra's mind. Orion had warned her that the woods were not safe and they were not safe for her to be alone in. Was this strange woman the reason why? Was he trying to protect her against Celeste? Terra took a frightened step backwards. "Thank you."

Celeste was looking at her oddly now, her head cocked in curiosity. "You aren't like the others, you know. The Queens before you. There's something different about you."

Terra froze as her words sunk in. "What Queens?"

"The wives that he had before you. Surely you must know." A sly smile tugged at the corner of Celeste's mouth.

Other wives? Terra felt suddenly dizzy and was worried that she would faint. But she couldn't think about it now, not when she didn't know if Edith or Laurent was okay. *Or Ash.* The bile began to rise again in her throat, but she bit it back down.

Celeste turned to leave. "Tell Orion that he owes me one."

In the blink of an eye, the mysterious woman was gone, leaving Terra shaking and traumatized with the dead carcass of her attacker lying in a heap before her.

Chapter Twenty
Orion

"Ah, you must have already spoken to my sister," the man sitting on a rock in front of Orion said.

"You say that as if you didn't already know that that was the case, Aren. I thought you were away in the Dry Lands the last time I checked."

Aren laughed and hauled himself to his feet. He was taller than Orion and his body was lanky and agile. His brown skin matched his mischievous eyes and his hair was shorter than it had been the last time Orion had seen his nephew. The oddest part of his appearance was the lack of clothing Aren wore. Instead of being bundled up in furs and thick material to fight the cold, he was dressed casually in a shirt and pants with the top buttons undone on his shirt to allow a small glimpse of a dark tattoo he had there. Orion knew that the ink pictured two snakes with their bodies twisting around one another.

And yet, Aren didn't seem to be impacted by the cold at all. Even though Orion knew exactly why, it still caught him off guard. Why would he need to bundle up when the messenger was always jumping from place to place in the blink of an eye?

"You are absolutely right, Uncle." Aren grinned and pulled Orion in for a tight hug, one where Orion was clapped hard on the back and he didn't even mind it.

"You seem to be a lot happier than your sister was to see me. I also didn't think she was sending me to see you."

"She wasn't," Aren admitted and rubbed the back of his neck with a hand. "She sent you here to find what is in that cave, but I also took the opportunity to pay you a visit."

"To pay me a visit, or to give me a message?"

Aren chuckled and wagged a finger at Orion. "Straight to the point like always. Maybe I just wanted to visit with my long-lost Uncle and, you know, talk about the weather." Aren snapped his fingers as if an idea had just popped into his mind. "Oh, I know. We can talk about the fact that you *got married* and I *wasn't invited*."

"Oh, Aren you know that wasn't the case."

"I thought I was your favorite nephew." Aren gave him a fake sniffle. "I used to spend every weekend with you until—"

"Until your father decided to be himself," Orion finished in a dry tone. "You know that there was nothing else I could do."

Aren sighed, sitting back on the boulder and he was suddenly serious again. "I know, I know. It just sucks sometimes. But that's a sob story for another time. Yes, I came here to give you a message and you might not like it."

"No more dramatics. What is it? I don't have very much patience left, Aren."

"You'll want to hear this," he insisted and took a deep breath. "I can't say too much, for— for reasons, but I have to do something to help. Orion, this violence in Valerian is a lot bigger than what you think it is."

"What are you trying to say?" Orion had a bad feeling in the pit of his stomach. He should have known something was going on when after decades he saw not one, but two of his blood relatives. He would never have been able to find them if they hadn't wanted to be found.

Aren opened his mouth to speak but seemed to physically choke on the words just as the prisoners that Orion interrogated had. A hand went to his throat briefly, but he swallowed hard and let it drop back to his side. "I cannot say exactly," he said through gritted teeth. A sheen of sweat began to build on his forehead despite the cold from the straining effort. "But what I can say is that you need to tread carefully. There is more going on that you cannot see. And keep Terra safe, she will play a role that neither of you expect."

Orion opened his mouth to ask what the hell he meant, but he was gone as if he was never there in the first place. He shook his head and couldn't believe that Aren dropped a bomb on him and then immediately disappeared. "My family is crazy," he muttered angrily. He could almost hear Aren's offended voice saying "I heard that" in his head, or maybe he did hear it. The messenger always like to play those types of pranks.

Tossing around Aren's words in his head, Orion steeled himself before finally continuing to the cave. Even Aren had said that Celeste had sent him here to find whatever was in this cave so he had to be prepared. Pulling out a dagger from his belt, Orion willed the shadows in the entrance of the cave to converge around him and essentially make him invisible. The cave offered a respite from the harsh wind which Orion was grateful for since the skin on his face had already begun to burn from the exposure to the elements.

Worried that he wouldn't be able to see anything through the darkness, Orion was surprised to find a faint glow coming from deep within the cave. Curious, he padded forward until he reached a point where the path curved sharply to the right. Here he stopped and listened to the echo of voices coming from farther in.

"It's too damn cold outside," one of the voices, a man with a distinguished accent, complained. "I wouldn't be caught dead outside in this weather."

"You act as if you have a choice," another responded. The companion sounded as if he hailed from Valerian whereas the first man came from far away, but Orion couldn't quite place where his accent was from. "You have orders to follow and I highly recommend not defying a direct command."

"Fine," the first man grumbled. "But I'll wait on word from Finn first, to make sure he has taken care of the girl. I would really rather not be there when you-know-who returns to find that mess."

The other man laughed humorlessly. "That would be mighty unfortunate, would that not? Very well. We will wait until we hear from Finn then."

The two men fell into a comfortable silence and listened to the fire crackle. Orion crept closer and hugged the wall of the cave as close as he could. He grew closer until he could go no farther lest he be seen, but he could now clearly see the two men in front of him. The first man was crouched low in front of the fire and was clutching his furs closer around him as he shivered. He had deep brown skin and a foreign tattoo that crept up the sides of his neck and over his jaw to his ear. He had long locs tied back with a band of leather and Orion realized that the accent placed the man from the Dust Lands to the far south, similar to where Aren had been born.

The other man was clearly a local. The dirtied gentleman leaned back in his spot far from the fire and was busy sharpening a dagger against a sharp stone between his feet. His furs were tossed to the side and a sheen of sweat covered his face and arms while he worked. The man was clearly used to the bitter cold that even sank deep into Orion's being.

"I think your knife is sharp enough," the first man claimed and lifted his hands to his mouth in order to warm them with his breath.

The other man twirled the knife deftly in his fingers before holding the sharp edge against one of his own fingers. "I had to make sure it was plenty sharp. That mother and her children the other night really took a toll on it. We don't want to not be prepared when we meet our match, now do we? Ha!" The man pretended to plunge the knife into an invisible enemy standing in front of him.

That's when Orion attacked.

The shadows around him dissipated and he strode forward towards the man with the knife. In one fluid motion, Orion disarmed him and sent a boot hard into his chest, making the man slide against the floor and into the cave wall. Orion whirled and blocked a blow from the other man with his forearm before swinging the hilt of the knife into his jaw. The man crumpled beneath him, groaning pitifully. Before the one who was sharpening the knife could scramble back to his feet, Orion put the heel of his boot on his chest and held him firmly on the ground.

"Tsk, tsk," Orion chided darkly and flipped the knife playfully in his hand. He watched it glint under the glow of the fire and it threw rays of lights against the rock walls. "You call yourselves prepared? *Pathetic.*" The man beneath him grunted and attempted to dislodge him, but Orion only pressed down harder. "I wouldn't try that, if I were you," Orion warned. The other man was creeping closer and Orion pointed the tip of the dagger at him while summoning the shadows to push him backwards until he was held firmly against the far wall.

"*You!*" The man beneath him spat and tried to say more, but Orion's boot only crushed his ribcage harder. "The Keeper of Souls."

"Yes, *me*," Orion said wickedly. "I see that you two have been the ones attacking innocent women and children in my realm. Your confession said as much."

"No! No! Please - pl—" the man beneath him stuttered.

"Tell me why I shouldn't tear you apart limb by limb," Orion growled and held the point of the knife to where the man's Adam's apple bobbed nervously. "Why'd you do it? Does it bring you some sort of sick and twisted happiness to slaughter women and children?" He pressed the tip of the blade down into his skin until droplets of blood welled to the surface and caused the man to whimper. "What's in it for you?"

The terrified man beneath him opened his mouth to speak, but only stuttered incoherently at the sight of the blood trickling down the side of his neck to the cavern floor.

"We did it because we were ordered to," the other man groaned and Orion turned to face him without moving the blade from the neck of the man beneath him. He was struggling to his feet and clutched the bloody wound at the back of his head from smashing against the wall. "Our boss had very specific instructions for us."

"Shut *up!*" the man who had the knife to his neck hissed.

"Who gave you the order? What were you sent here to do?" Orion demanded.

The panting man against the far wall leaned against the wall for support. "We were to get information about you, and to get rid of the gi— "

"Don't tell him!" the other barked to his companion. "You know what will happen. Keep your damn mouth shut!" Orion caught him across the jaw with the hilt again with a sharp *crack!* His cheek split open and more blood began to pool on the ground. The man laughed despite the blow and the harsh sound of it echoed through the cave. "It's too late you know, Finn already took care of the girl and should be here soon." He turned and spat blood on the ground beside him. "You're already too late."

Anger flared deep within Orion and he whirled to fling the knife end over end until it landed precisely in the one man's chest who then slumped down the cavern wall with a low gasp of air. He took the man below him by the front of his shirt and hauled him to his feet, slamming him hard against the wall until they were nose to nose.

"What the hell did he do to her?" Shadows flickered around him as Orion began to lose control to the anger pulsating through him. Aren's words came back to him. *Keep Terra safe, she will play a role that neither of you expect.* "What did you do to Terra?" He roared.

The man spluttered. His face was already starting to bruise in deep shades of purple. "What are you going to do to me, kill me?"

Orion grinned and the shadows danced around him. "I'm going to do much, much worse."

The man's eyes grew wide and Orion closed his. He probed for the power deep within him that usually would be dormant but was now bucking and fighting to be let free. The air surrounding them grew cold and when Orion opened his eyes once more, they were no longer in the cave. Still clutching the man's shirt, both of them were now standing in a field with muted colors as if all life had been sucked out of the place entirely.

"Where the hell are we?"

Orion glanced over his shoulder and the other man was standing a few feet away. The knife was no longer stuck in his chest, but the blood still stained his shirt. "Welcome to Hell," Orion said. Within seconds, the shadow figures whistled through the air and surrounded the two men at his silent request. The men fell to their knees and sobbed for his forgiveness. They begged Orion to let them go, promising that they would disappear and to never be seen in his realm again, but there was no reasoning with Orion at this point.

Your Highness, a voice hissed in his mind. *To what do I owe the pleasure?* The shadow figure materialized before him until the dark outline became clear.

"I've brought you two presents," Orion said and gestured to the terrified men. "These two deserve a fate worse than death for their crimes, don't you think?"

The figured spun around the men as if it was looking deep into their minds to see the horrible things that they have done, the lives that they had stolen long before their time, and the fear that they had caused in innocent people. *Yes,* the figure purred. *I do quite agree, Your Highness. What is their sentence?*

Orion met their gazes, taking in the wide pupils and the tears drenching their bloodied faces. "Destroy their souls," he said quietly.

With pleasure.

Orion merely watched as the figure approached the men who were now terror stricken and had gone completely silent. He has had so much blood on his hands in his lifetime that watching what was about to happen didn't affect him at all.

The men lifted gently off the ground until they were both floating, suspended above the ground in a paralyzed position. Their faces twisted in pain and darkness surrounded them as the shadows twisted around them violently and to stir the long grass around them. A glowing white orb appeared from their chests as the shadows sucked the white souls from deep within their beings. Their faces started to crack and they started to wither until they collapsed in piles of dust that the wind immediately swept away. Almost as soon as it had started, it was over.

Orion breathed heavily as he tried to calm himself against the rising tide of anger. "Is Terra okay?" he asked the figure at his side.

The figure was quiet for a long moment which caused fear to spike in his heart. *I would recommend returning as soon as possible,* the figure finally said. *The whispers say that there was a horrible attack in your absence, but they couldn't say if your Queen was okay.*

"Then find out!" Orion growled. "Or you will be the one to pay." Without waiting for an answer, Orion closed his eyes and opened them to find himself back in the cavern with two lifeless bodies.

Someone was targeting him and he had no clue who it was, or why. Aren warned him that this was bigger than what he thought and that these men were working for someone, but who? Orion couldn't wait to find out though, for he had to get back to Terra.

He only hoped that he wasn't too late.

Chapter Twenty-One
Terra

Terra stumbled through the forest until she found her way back to the castle. She was freezing quivering uncontrollably as she went. She had left the body of her attacker deep in the woods and refused to touch him or move him whatsoever. She was numb. Her brain was working in slow motion and she knew she couldn't just sit there. Instead, she forced herself to get to her feet to make sure that the others were okay.

Now is not the time to give in, she chided herself.

Not knowing where Laurent was, Terra began to wander the grounds and the places he most likely would be. She knew that he would not be in the greenhouse, so she elected to search the stables first. As soon as she stepped inside, she knew something was wrong. The horses were spooked and paced in their stalls, their terrified whinnies echoing sharply. Then the smell hit her: the stench of copper.

Terra peered into the stalls one by one until she found him. Gasping, she reeled back with her fist to her mouth. Laurent was lying on a bed of straw in an empty stall. The horse was still tied up in the aisle and pulling hard at his lead. A pitchfork had been thrust into Laurent's abdomen and his skin was pale where it wasn't covered in dried blood. Terra knew by the size of the puddle around him that there was no saving him, he was long gone. A sob choked out of her and she fell to her knees. Laurent, the sweet soul that had treated her with nothing but kindness and respect, was gone. Orion would be devastated.

Orion.

A strong feeling teased her mind and she couldn't tell if it was worry, or anger. He had left her alone and defenseless. If he had been here, none of this may have happened. Laurent may still be alive and Edith wouldn't be bound in the pantry unconscious. Terra felt guilty thinking it, but the more she dwelled on it, the worst it got. She knew that Orion never meant for this to happen and would never have left if he would have known, but she had to face the facts and the facts were that he could have changed this course of events if he would still be here.

Terra wiped the tears from her face and rose back to her feet. There was nothing she could do for Laurent, not yet anyways. She had to get out of the cold and she had to make sure Edith and Ash were both okay. The sun was high in the sky by the time she got back to the castle and warmed the places where it touched her skin, but still she shook. The castle, which once had felt warm and inviting to her, now felt menacing and cold. Every corner she came upon, she worried that an attacker would leap out and finish her off. Never has she wished more that she had a knife or *something* to reassure her.

A small whimper caught her attention and behind her limped Ash who favored her right front leg, but otherwise looked relatively okay. "Oh, sweet girl," Terra whispered and she began to cry again at the sight of her. "You were so brave." Terra rubbed her face and her ears and Ash gave her a lick. Resigning to carrying the large dog, Terra grunted and lifted her into her arms. She ignored the burning of her muscles and her sore body and the two of them went to Edith.

Terra found her still unconscious right where she had left her. Setting Ash down gently, she went to Edith and tried to wake her. At her touch, Edith stirred and Terra quickly undid her ties. As if she had been electrocuted, Edith's eyes suddenly flew open and her pupils were dilated in fear.

"It's okay," Terra said and touched her hair softly. "It's okay, you're okay."

Edith slowly sat up with her help. "What happened? Are they gone? Where's Laurent?" With a pang in her chest, Terra told her what happened, including finding Laurent and telling her that he was gone. Edith blinked hard, but no tears fell and she spoke quickly and urgently. "We need to be prepared in case others come back. The rest can wait. I need you to go back down to the dungeon. There will be a wooden door to the left and in there you will find anything and everything. Grab everything you can and bring it back here. If there was one... I'm afraid that there might be more and I don't trust that we could get to Captain Darren at Thorn hill safely."

Terra nodded and scrambled back to her feet to hurry off. Instead of heading straight to the dungeon, though, she hesitated in front of the staircases. She had so many unanswered questions and a horrible feeling deep in the pit of her stomach. Celeste had mentioned that Orion had wives before her and if she was right, he had been keeping major secrets from her still when she had thought that she now knew everything. These men came for her because of him, but why? Why was this happening and what was he not telling her? She couldn't stifle the fear that his secrets were the root cause of everything and she couldn't help but feel resentful. If this truly was all his fault, she didn't know if she could ever forgive him for this.

Finally, it struck her. The hidden bedroom that she came across months ago while exploring. She had assumed that it was one of his family member's old rooms that pained him too much to clear, but what if it was an old Queen's instead of a relative's? She headed up the stairs without another moment of hesitation. She had to know now, there was no waiting. If she hurried, she would be able to find what she needed to know, make it to the dungeon, and then back to Edith without letting too much time pass.

When Terra finally opened the door to the bedchamber, it was just as she remembered it. It was still completely untouched with a layer of dust settled over everything. The bed was unmade with the sheets and quilts piled in a haphazard heap. The ballgown was set out as if the occupant of this room planned to put it on but never had the chance to. Terra went to the dirty vanity and saw the hairbrush resting there with noticeable red hair in it. She didn't think that any of his sisters had red hair and she knew that his mother hadn't. Her gut screamed that she was on the right path.

Terra began to dig through the room and looked for any indication of who had once resided in this room. Clothes were folded neatly in the drawers until Terra ransacked through them, but she found nothing except dust. Growing frantic, she took no precaution as she tore through the room but much to her disappointment, she still found absolutely nothing. With her frustration growing, she stopped for a moment and looked around the room with her hands on her hips. There had to be something that she was missing, there was no way that the room had been left undisturbed for what appeared to be years and nothing was left to give her any sort of clue of who the woman had been.

Terra's eyes went to the mattress and an idea sparked in her mind. She went to the bed and lifted the mattress with one hand while she felt around blindly with the other. Her fingertips brushed up against a hard object and, withdrawing it, she saw that it was a leather-bound journal. With her heart pumping furiously, she flipped it open to the first page where she saw one name written in a neat scrawl: Isobel.

She flipped through it and saw what was months' worth of diary entries, maybe even years, but she didn't have time to go through it all so instead she flipped to the last entry. "*September 19th*" she saw written in the top corner and she began to read.

September 19th.

Tonight was the final straw, I can't keep doing this anymore. Orion is keeping secrets from me and he won't give me any answers as to where he disappears to. Even now over two years later, he still evades answering any of my questions. He will make an excuse and say that he is busy handling the day-to-day affairs of the realm, but I know it's a lie. Every day I will seek him out in his study or his chambers, and he won't be there. If I didn't know better, I would almost assume that he is committing adultery but since he holds no royal court in the castle, that cannot possibly be so... can it? He says that he loves me, and I know he does, but I can't help but feel neglected. I can no longer live with the secrets and lies.

So I'm leaving. Tonight. I'm not giving him a choice and I am packing what I can to leave and never look back. I'm fed up with living like this. I'll give up my throne and I'll give up my entire life to run away to another land, to another realm where I can build a happier life for myself. I can no longer be married to a man who won't choose me above all else...even if he loves me.

Terra quickly closed the journal and couldn't believe what she had just read. Here was the evidence right in front of her. He had a wife before her and had made a point *not* to mention it all these months. Whether or not Isobel ever found out the things that Terra knew about Orion, she would never know but she couldn't help but sympathize with the former Queen. She was in the same boat that Terra was but her curiosity had led to her finding answers that it seems that Isobel never had the opportunity of getting.

But he lied. He *lied*.

Orion let her believe that she was special, that she was the only Queen that had, figuratively, taken the throne by his side. All she could see in her mind was a beautiful and vivacious red-headed woman touching him the way that she had, *caring* for him the same way that she had. Isobel had been with him more than double the length that Terra had and even after all that time, Isobel still never got to know the real Orion. Terra had thought that she knew him until she now realized that even Isobel still hadn't after all their time together.

Her stomach did a violent flip and she fought the overcoming urge to get sick right then and there. Terra had given up everything and for what, to be just another wife for him? To be another woman for him to hide himself from and to neglect? Isobel *left* because of him.

And now here she was, shaking and alone while Laurent was dead and Edith was injured. If it wasn't for Edith, Terra would do the same thing that Isobel did and leave. She would go home to Solaris and home to her family. She would forget this ever happened and she would live happily ever after without him. Tears spilled down her face and she quickly wiped them away. The sense of betrayal hurt so badly that she thought she was going to split right open and be torn to shreds. It was his fault that any of this happened and there was no fixing this.

Terra threw the journal against the wall angrily and it fell on the floor in a flutter of paper. There she left it, resigned to be done with it all as soon as Orion returned and as soon as Edith was okay. *Don't think, just move.*

Taking a lantern from the foyer and making sure it was lit, she returned to the dungeon to find weapons for them to defend themselves. Terra shuddered when she looked down the way towards the heavy stone door, for she didn't want to turn her back to it, but she did so anyways. Walking further away from the stone door, she found the wooden door that Edith described and opened it to find an entire armory hiding among the dark and gloom.

Hurrying, she took daggers, a crossbow, and a bow with matching arrows before returning to Edith's side. "Sorry I took so long," she told Edith. "I wasn't sure what to take."

"That's okay," Edith replied and took the crossbow from her. "These work perfect. Help me to your bedroom. We'll camp out there until Orion returns, just in case anyone else decides to show up. Leave everything else here and come back to it, I'll need you to get first aid supplies as well. Ash, stay." Edith took hold of Terra's hand and let her help her onto unsteady feet. With the crossbow in one hand, she wrapped her other arm through Terra's and together they hobbled to her room.

Terra made sure that she was comfortable and resting in her bed, the same bed where just last night she and Orion had been tangled together intimately. She flushed at the thought and instead focused on the task at hand. Leaving Edith holding the crossbow menacingly, she went to find medical supplies, grab Ash, and the rest of the weapons.

Her mind was consumed by the motions she went through and she fought against any thought of Orion or Isobel. She couldn't do it, not now and she feared that it truly would tear her into pieces if she let herself dwell on it any longer than she already had.

Soon after Terra returned to Edith, Edith fell into a light sleep with Ash pressed into her side. Terra kept watch and started a fire while they slept. The sun had begun to fall and Orion still had not returned. Part of her wished he would, but the resenting side of her wished he wouldn't. She dreaded the conversation that she knew she had to have with him and the thought of telling him she was leaving just like Isobel had done made her sick to her stomach, but she also couldn't stomach the thought of staying here with him while knowing he had kept this monumental secret from her.

Is this what heart break feels like?

What was Terra to him, just a means to an end for Orion? Just someone to help him run his realm for him? Terra's chest ached at the thought. How could she have been so foolish and think that she had been special this entire time when she was just another woman in his bed.

Terra's mind wandered to the figure in the dungeon and the promise she made him. The memory made her shiver and the figure gave her a very bad feeling, but she could think of no other way that she could have made it out alive if it wasn't for the deal she had struck with the shadow person. Orion had told her that it wasn't safe for her down there and he would be furious with her when — if — she told him about the deal. *A favor, that is all I ask. When the time comes, you will do me favor.* But if she wasn't here, does that mean she could avoid holding up her end of the bargain?

The figure couldn't possibly find her all the way in Solaris…could it?

Terra sulked in the chair by the fire as the hours passed and her body grew stiff and sore. She was on high alert and listened for any inclination that someone else had infiltrated the castle. The sun set and the moon was already high in the sky by the time she realized that something was off. Ash had raised her head and her ears pricked up almost immediately.

Edith still slept by her side and a low rumble began in Ash's throat.

"Shhh," Terra soothed and got to her feet. Edith's hand rested on her crossbow as she slept so Terra instead took the bow and quiver of arrows with her out into the hallway. Notching an arrow, she made sure to step carefully and quietly while listening for any noise besides the rapid beating of her heart.

"Terra? Edith? Laurent?" a frantic voice carried from down the stairs and from the foyer. Two dogs barked and Terra lowered her arrow. Milo and Silas dashed around the corner and into the hallway with an exhausted Orion close behind them. He skidded to a stop once he saw her and let out a sigh of relief, moving towards her with a hand outstretched. "Terra, are you okay?"

Terra's mind cycled through the many possible ways that she could answer his question. She could tell him that yes, she was indeed okay and so was Edith, or she could tell him that Laurent's corpse was lying cold in the stables and she didn't know what to do with him, or that she was so very scared, or she could even break down into tears now that he was finally home and they were now safe. But no, instead the last thing she ever thought she would say came out of her lips.

"Who is Isobel?"

Chapter Twenty-Two
Orion

Orion was dumfounded. *Why is she asking about her?* He opened his mouth to say something and snapped it back closed again. He must have had a muddled look on his face, for Terra repeated her question.

"I said, who is Isobel?"

"I- I don't understand," Orion said slowly and took a step towards her. His heart stung when she took a step away from him with the bow still in her hand as if she couldn't convince herself to let it go. "Terra, what happened? Where is Edith and Laurent?" *How the hell did she find out about Isobel?*

"Who is she?" she demanded, her voice cracking a bit. "Why didn't you tell me about her?"

Orion licked his lips and let his hands fall to his sides. He had to choose his next words carefully and he could see Terra shaking where she stood. Cuts and gashes lined her face, her neck, and even her hands were dirtied and bloodied. Through the caked dirt and blood, he could see bruises from where she had been attacked. Her long brown hair was ratted and wild just as the expression in her eyes was. She was in shock, that much was clear to him. "Terra," he said softly. "I didn't tell you because that was a very, very long time ago and it is irrelevant to you and I."

Terra fell quiet. Her arms were still rigid and clasping the bow, but she was rocking back and forth as if she was fighting an internal battle. "Did you love her?" she blurted.

Orion hesitated before nodding. He didn't want to hurt her any more than she clearly was, but she would never let it rest until he answered her honestly and truthfully, even if it was against his better judgement. "Yes, at one time I did love her."

This put a crack in Terra's armor. Closing her eyes, she let out a sob and stifled the tears that threatened to break through.

"This was a long time ago, Terra," Orion said so quietly that it was barely a whisper and took a step towards her. She didn't move. "This was before you were even born."

"What happened to her?" Terra opened her eyes and the pain there was evident. Orion swore he could feel his heart being ripped out of his chest just by looking at her.

"She left."

"Did you ever see her again?"

Orion shook his head. "No. She left and I never heard from her again."

"Celeste told me about her," Terra admitted after a long pause of silence. "After she saved my life. She told me that I wasn't like your other wives and that I was different." Terra furrowed her brows at the memory. "I think she knew that you never told me. Who was she Orion? Why was she here in the first place?"

Orion shook his head and took another step towards her, but Terra again put space between them. "It's a long story for another time. We have more pressing matters. I'm worried about you. We need to clean up your wounds, Terra. Please."

"I thought you said no more secrets," she said through gritted teeth and crossed her arms over her chest. "Who is Celeste? Is she the reason why you told me that it wasn't safe to go in the woods by myself? Because she's there?"

Sighing, Orion ran a hand through his hair. "She is my niece. And yes, that is the reason why. She is like me. If Celeste would have seen a beautiful maiden like yourself alone in the forest, I fear she would have kept you for herself to serve her. I didn't want that to happen."

Terra nodded as if it made complete sense and he could tell she was gnawing the inside of her cheek in thought, but he waited patiently, not pushing her any farther until she chose to talk. Finally, she met his gaze and he saw the tears threatening to spill over the brim of her eyes clearly. She bit her lip and silent sobs vibrated in her chest, her fingers finally releasing the bow to clatter to the ground below. You left me. You left me here alone."

"I know," Orion winced. "I should have been here. I should have been here to protect you."

"*Laurent is dead because of you!*" She screeched and the flood gates slammed wide open. She fell to her knees and clutched her arms around her own abdomen as if she was trying to hold herself together while the violent sobs ripped their way out of her.

He rushed to her side and fell to his own knees to try to draw her closer to him, but she pushed him away.

"Was it worth it?" she hissed. "Was leaving me to die worth it?"

"Terra," he pleaded but she cut him off.

"*No!* This is all your fault. They were here for *you*, Orion. We were just caught in the crossfire and Laurent *died* because of you. Keeping yourself hidden from the world on your throne of shadows was so important to you that you never realized how important we were until it was too late. You never realized how much danger you put us in because you could never stop wallowing in your own self-pity. You were too focused on feeling so damn sorry for yourself and the things you've done that I was nearly killed in the process! All I wanted was you, did you know that? I wanted you as you are, but you left me." Terra sucked in a shaky breath and tried to calm herself.

Orion said nothing. He sat back and watched her get back to her feet. She gripped at her messy hair and pulled at it with bloodied fingers.

"He told me he was going to slit my throat, Orion. He nearly killed Ash. When I ran away, I feared that she was dead. I would have been next, but I made a promise that may have cost me everything, who the hell knows." Terra laughed without humor. "But without it, I *would* be dead and lying cold on the dungeon floor."

Dungeon floor? "Terra, what did you do?" Fear began to sneak through him as the revelation dawned on him. *"What did you do?"*

"I made a deal with the shadow person," she said and he hoped, no *prayed*, that she would laugh, to tell him it was a sick joke. But it never came. Her expression remained serious.

"Do you know what you've done?" Orion stood up and gripped her arms hard. "Please tell me you were not that foolish Terra!"

"I did what I had to do," she said in a steely tone and ripped away from him. "Would you have rather found me with my throat slit? They were only here because they wanted *you*."

Guilt flared in Orion's chest. She was right, as much as he hated to admit it. She was absolutely, entirely right. They were using her to try to get to him and the two men he had taken care of had said as much. How did he miss the warning signs? How did he not realize that this was coming? He should have known from the moment Terra was attacked in the village and he should have seen the red flag to act right then and there.

"I'm leaving."

Orion's eyes darted to Terra's. "What?"

"I'm leaving. And I'm taking Edith with me. It's not safe for us here. I'm going back to Solaris before it's too late." With the tears on her face drying, she bent over and picked the bow back up. She turned to walk back to her bedroom and Orion grabbed her by the hand.

"Terra, please," he begged. "Don't leave. I'll fix this. Please, just... just let me try to fix this. I'll do anything you want. Just give me another chance."

Terra looked at him with a hostile look in her eyes that he had never seen her make before. It was one that he didn't even know she was capable of making. "Your second chance died along with Laurent." She tugged her hand out of his and walked away from him.

Orion followed her. The desperation within him grew as he heard her tell Edith that they were leaving. He walked into her room and saw the pitiful scene of Ash laying protectively across Edith's stomach. Terra began tearing apart her wardrobe and her room to collect items in a trunk.

"Edith," Orion said softly and took her hand. "Are you okay?"

"Yes, I'm perfectly fine, just a bit dazed" she said and watched Terra angrily stuff dry winter clothes in the trunk with no sense of organization. Edith lowered her voice. "I heard it all. I think it would be best for us to leave for a while. Let her see her family and let her collect herself. We'll heal up and then I'll see if I can convince her to return. The best thing right now is to get some space."

"But Edith—" Orion's voice broke and he went quiet. He couldn't lose his family, not again. He watched Terra steal away into her washroom and he could hear objects hitting the ground loudly as she tore through that room as well.

"She blames you, but I don't." Edith squeezed his hands tightly in his own. "I may be old, but I am still wise. I need you to trust me on this. Can you do that?"

Orion fought against the lump in his throat. "I'd trust you with my life."

"Then let us go." She patted his hands affectionately just as Terra came back into the room. Orion didn't know if he could, but he would listen to Edith and at least try.

"Edith, let's go," Terra quipped.

Orion stepped forward and took the trunk from Terra even though every ounce of his being was screaming at him to not let her go. He finally realized why there was such a pit in his stomach about her leaving. If she left, he wasn't sure if she would ever come back to him. *Just like Isobel.* Terra shot him a nasty glare but didn't say anything. Instead, she helped Edith to her feet and together they all made their way to the foyer.

Edith convinced Terra to not leave yet and instead had her get more first aid supplies to pack to treat her own wounds that Edith chastised her for. "Orion, help me to the stables. I - I wish to say goodbye."

"Edith I'm not sure you want to see that." Orion himself had yet to see the damage. When he arrived, he had let his horse freely wander the stables and darted to the castle in fear that he had been too late. And so it seems he had been without realizing it.

"Just help me, will you?"

Orion sighed and with the trunk in one arm, he lent the other to Edith. Together, they left the warmth of the castle and plunged into the darkness of the chilly night. Snow had begun to fall again and they hurried across the grounds. Orion's horse was still waiting inside and Orion set down the trunk to switch out the supplies in the saddle bags for Terra and Edith. If they insisted on leaving, he could at least give them the best horse and make sure they would be well supplied for the long journey.

Edith wandered to the back of the stable and was quiet for a long time. Orion gave her space and focused on the task at hand. "I need you to keep them safe," he said softly to his horse. "I need you to take good care of them and make sure they make it to Solaris in one piece. Can you do that for me?" Theos turned his head and chewed on the fabric of his shirt. "Thank you." Orion patted his nose.

Edith returned and was wiping her eyes. "I have made my peace," she said softly. "Would you like to before we go?"

Orion hesitated, but nodded. He had to face it. He had to find out what horrors he had caused. Edith left him alone as he went to Laurent's body. He was horrified at what he saw and he couldn't help but shed tears for the man that had been a strong influence in his life. "I'm so sorry," he whispered and put a hand over his face. He knew that he had to give him a proper burial, to honor him in the way that he deserved. Already his soul would be on the other side experiencing everything that such a wonderful man deserved in the afterlife, and Orion would make sure of it. As difficult as it would be, it had to be done and he would do it as soon as he had the chance to. He owed him at least that much. Laurent was just another life taken by his hands.

When Orion returned, Edith said nothing and took his arm in hers to return to the castle. Terra was waiting for them in the snow at the front door with her arms full of supplies. She walked up to Orion and began packing them away in Theos' saddlebags while bluntly ignoring him. He looked at her, silently asking for her to stop, to at least pause and look at him for just a second, but it never came. Coldness rolled off of her and it took everything in him to not reach out to her to try to stop her. He watched her fingers tighten the straps and remembered how not long ago those same fingers traced patterns on his chest and made waves through his hair. He remembered the sleepy smile she gave him when she awoke and he thought of the feel of her naked body pressed up against his own. It hurt so bad. *Please don't leave me.*

"Orion, can you help me up?" Edith asked and broke the painful silence between Terra and him. Orion nodded distractedly and gave a wobbly Edith a leg up into the saddle. Terra waited a few paces away for him to move, her body language making it clear that she wouldn't accept his help even if he offered it. Instead, he took a step forward and took her face in his hands.

"Let me at least get Captain Darren to give you an escort, please."

"No, I want to travel alone."

"Terra," he murmured and brushed a thumb softly across her cheek. "You were right, it was my fault. I know that doesn't change anything, but I want to make this better. I *will* fix this."

Terra didn't pull away, but she looked away as a few tears slipped out. She bit her trembling lip and remained silent.

Orion pressed a soft kiss to her forehead. "Please come home."

Terra then looked at him with cold and unfeeling green eyes. She took his hands in hers and pulled them away from her face. "This isn't my home. If you love me, you will let me go and you will never look for me." She pulled away from him entirely and mounted Theos in front of Edith. Without a cursory glance back at him, she nudged the horse onwards and they were gone.

Orion stood in the same spot as the snow continued to fall and cover him. He was watching and waiting for them to come back. He waited for Terra to say that leaving was a mistake. She wasn't leaving for good, she couldn't possibly... could she? His breathing grew more rapid as the time passed, but still she didn't come back. He couldn't believe it. She left him.

Orion turned on his heel and made his way back inside the castle as the angry beast began to consume him. With a furious roar, he swept a marble vase off a table in the foyer and watched it hit the floor and shatter into jagged shards. It still didn't simmer the anger and he pulled at his hair, struggling to regain control.

On heavy legs, Orion went to Terra's room and something on the mantle of the hearth caught his eye. He found a piece of jewelry there and when he lifted it, he realized it was her wedding band with the amethyst set in the center. He broke.

Sobs tore through Orion's chest as his wails echoed through the room. He was vaguely aware of his dogs worriedly pacing around him, but he paid them no mind. All he could feel was the burning sensation of his heart being ripped out of his chest.

Hours must have passed by the time his sobs began to cease and he was left feeling drained and exhausted. Orion finally stood on shaky legs and placed the ring on her pillowcase that still smelled of honey and flowers. *It smells like her,* he thought painfully and lifted it to his face.

Even when Isobel left, he had never felt this empty.

Orion caught a glimpse of himself in the mirror and all he could see was the disappointment that he knew that she saw. He was a poor excuse of a man. After all these years of fearing that he would be just like his father, he finally became him. His fist plunged deep into the glass and he hissed at the sting of the cuts on his knuckles. He deserved this hurt, this pain, it was retribution for everything he has done all these years and there was no other explanation for it. This was his fate. He didn't *deserve* Terra and he chased her away when he thought he could be something more, something better for her.

How foolish he was to think that.

Through the pain and the hurt he was feeling, he didn't realize that someone had opened the door until it was too late. His chest exploded in pain and he looked down to realize that an arrow was protruding from his flesh. Blood was already starting to blossom through his shirt and he looked up to see three men in the doorway, one who was already drawing back another arrow to send into him.

Orion roared and summoned the shadows around him but he fell back as another arrow pierced his arm. He gasped for air and the shadows dissipated as his powers drained as quickly as he began to lose blood. His dogs began growling viciously and he suddenly feared the three of them would meet the same end as he would.

"Call them off!" one of the intruders barked. "Or they each get an arrow right through the eyes!"

Orion let out a shrill whistle the best he could. "Back down!" He gasped through the pain. He heard one of the men walk around him and slammed the washroom door shut, effectively locking the dogs away judging by the sound of them throwing their weight against the now shut door.

Orion moaned and clutched the arrow to try to pull it out, but as soon as he gave it a tug, he nearly passed out from the red-hot pain that followed.

He heard a chuckle from one of the men and the attacker leaned forward until his face was in front of Orion's. "Hello, Your Highness. My name is Caius and I'm a friend of you wife. Now tell me, where did your beloved Queen run off to?"

Chapter Twenty-Three
Terra

The cold made Terra grit her teeth, but Edith made no complaints. She was seated tightly behind her with her arms wrapped around her waist and Terra welcomed the extra heat of her body against hers, especially as the snow became thicker and more persistent.

"He means well, you know," Edith said after a long ride in silence. "I know you're hurt and you're scared, but he is, too. He is scared that you will get hurt."

"It's already too late for that," Terra huffed indignantly. "It's far, far too late for that."

Edith was quiet for a while longer and Terra was finally starting to think that the conversation was over with until she spoke again. "He would do anything for you or give you anything if it meant you were happy. "

Terra whipped around in her seat. "Then maybe he shouldn't have left when we needed him the most. Now I would like to enjoy the journey in peace and quiet please while I focus on trying not to freeze, okay?" She faced forward and huffed again. Edith respected her wishes and they continued to trot along in silence through the frozen night.

Terra kept telling herself that she had made the right choice, that she was right to leave and right to never return. But for some reason, she still felt guilty about doing it. Why should she? He made his priorities clear and she and her own safety were not one of them. So why did she feel so badly about it? Terra stretched her neck and rolled her stiff shoulders. Between the cold and the journey ahead of them, she wasn't going to be able to think clearly so she should just stop and instead wait until she made it back to Solaris.

Edith will only make it worse, too, she thought and nearly snorted out loud. She understood where Edith was coming from, but quite frankly she just didn't want to hear it.

The ride to the village took a lot longer than it had the first time Terra had taken the path with Edith. There was next to no visibility in the dark night and through the falling snow. Under normal circumstances, Terra would never have been caught dead traveling in the night through weather like this, but she knew she could never have spent the night in the castle to wait until the sun rose to leave.

Terra was honestly quite surprised that Edith agreed to come with. She almost expected her to have put up a fight and try to talk her into staying. Instead, she had immediately agreed to leave and was almost supportive of her decision to leave. She wondered if it was because Edith had seen Isobel do the same and she may have known it was the only option.

But Orion said Isobel happened long before you were even born, the rational part of herself chided in and Terra frowned. He was forthright when it came to answering her questions, even though they clearly were painful questions to answer. *STOP IT.* She clenched her teeth and willed away all thoughts of Orion. If she continued to replay the conversation in her mind or overanalyze every minute detail there then she knew she would break and return to him immediately. She had to keep going. She had to leave before it was too late for her to do so.

Terra nearly sighed in relief once they reached the final road into the village. Edith was quiet behind her, but Terra knew she was just as cold and miserable as she was. She wished she could urge Orion's horse to go faster, to gallop all the way to the inn for the night, but all she needed was for Edith to take a plummet after she already was shaken up or to nosedive off herself.

Soon, the village appeared before them in the form of vague outlines of houses and buildings. Smoke plumed from the chimneys and it was the only sign of life. The horse's hooves clopped eerily over the cobblestone and was luckily somewhat muffled by the snow. The last thing they needed was for strangers to hear their every move and to draw unwanted attention to themselves.

Terra and Edith finally reached the inn where Terra slid off of the horse and to the ground. Edith slipped off her gloves and took Terra's hand in hers, sliding down herself. She grimaced at the clamminess of Edith's hands, even though they had been gloved the entire ride. "Why don't you get us two rooms for the night? I'll bring up the saddle bags."

Edith headed inside while she led the horse around the back of the inn and out of the cold. The meager stables were almost fully occupied much to her surprise. *Travelers must be opting to pay for a night in the inn versus braving the cold*, she thought. She was glad they chose to do the same. She found an empty stall and led the horse in. With numb fingers, she undid his tack and made sure he was fed and watered for the night before hauling the saddle bags over one shoulder to find Edith.

Margaret was waiting for her inside already and Edith was nowhere to be found. "Hello, dear. I must say, I am indeed surprised to see you two here at this late hour..." She looked her up and down, taking in the blood and the dirt and the messiness of her.

"Everything is fine," Terra replied and forced a smile despite the obvious lie that they both knew she was telling. "We're going to go visit my family and didn't expect the weather to be this way, so we decided to at least stop here for the night."

"A smart choice. Edith is upstairs already. Your room will be the third door on the right and hers is seventh on the left. I'll make a kettle of tea for you dears to warm up with and I'll leave it down here for whenever you're ready." Margaret leaned in close and winked. "I've already also sent for hot water for a bath. It should be arriving for you shortly."

Margaret held out an iron key for her own room and Terra took it from her gratefully. She gave her a soft smile, suddenly feeling exhausted beyond belief. "Thank you, I'm looking forward to it."

"I'll see you ladies for breakfast, good night."

Terra gratefully climbed the stairs with the heavy pack awkwardly slung over her body. She reached the top of the stairs and set it down to try to catch her breath. Her body hurt in ways she never thought imaginable. Every muscle and every fiber burned in agony, but yet she couldn't stop. If she stopped, she feared that she would never get up again so she bent down and picked the pack up again until she made it to her room where she let it once again fall to the floor.

Edith appeared not too long later, no longer wrapped in her wet winter coat. "I can take it," she said softly, the first words she had spoken since Terra snapped at her on the ride there.

Terra shook her head and waved her off before picking up her saddle bag for her. "I have it, which room was yours again?"

Edith reluctantly led her to her own room just as a gentleman had climbed the stairs with two young stable hands, all of them holding buckets of scalding water. Terra directed them to follow them and had them first give Edith a warm bath before fetching more water for herself.

Once Edith was situated, Terra hesitated to leave, not quite wanting to just yet but also knowing she wanted to be alone. "Will they tell anyone that we're here?" she asked Edith. "Seeing as we look like we just returned from battle."

"Margaret knows better than to ask too many questions," Edith replied mysteriously. "And so do those she employs. I wouldn't worry too much about our safety while we're under her roof. However," she leaned into her saddle bag and withdrew a brilliant dagger and sheath. "I will still be sleeping with this under my pillow this evening, and I recommend that you do the same."

"I will." Terra rocked back and forth on her heels, trying to find words. "I'm sorry for earlier," she finally said quietly. "It was unfair to you, and you shouldn't have to deal with that."

"I understand, there is no need to apologize."

"Still, I—"

"Terra," Edith said sternly and put a hand up to hush her. "There is no wrong or right way to handle what you are going through right now. You do not need to plead your case to me. What you need to do is to turn in for the evening and to get a good night's sleep. I talked Margaret into allowing us to stay later tomorrow just so you can rest. We both need it."

Terra nodded slowly. "Okay. Let me know if you need anything else... goodnight." Without looking back, Terra left.

In her own room, she couldn't help but pace the small area. Back and forth, back and forth, back and forth until the gentlemen returned with hot water for her own bath. "Please just leave it," she told them. "I can handle it."

Terra finally could let out a shuddering breath when she closed the door behind them. She slid to the ground with her back against the door and put her head in her hands. Waiting for the tears to come, she stayed just like that as the time passed, but they never came. She was all cried out.

Was Orion feeling the same thing she was feeling? Was he longing for her the way she was longing for him? Digging her nails into her palm, she reminded herself fiercely of the betrayal and the hurt that she felt because of him. It was all because of him.

Her eyes went to the blood caked under her fingernails and she finally rose to her feet to draw herself a bath. The scents and the soaps here were mundane compared to the ones she always had at home, but they would have to do. *Home,* she thought with a cringe. *No, not home. The castle is not my home. Valerian is not my home.*

Terra sank into the tub until her face was entirely covered. She wanted the water to wash away her sadness and her pain. She wished she could stay there forever, just like that, suspended in bliss. If she could never surface and never return to reality, she would. What would it be like, she wondered, to stay in the water and to never feel the earth beneath her? What would it feel like, to never have to worry again about anything at all?

It wasn't until her lungs burned that she finally came up for a gasping breath. Terra coughed at the sensation of water having trickled in through her nose until her chest hurt. Gods, she was a mess, she had to keep it together. She already made it this far and she couldn't fall apart now. So instead, she scrubbed and scrubbed until her skin was clean and rubbed raw from the effort. With every dunk of her head under the water, she imagined washing every thought of Orion away and every painful feeling. By the end, she felt much warmer and much cleaner.

Terra made quick work of toweling herself off and slipped into her nightgown. She braided her hair long down her back before making her way downstairs in search of the tea Margaret had mentioned to her earlier. She was halfway down the stairs when she froze. Voices were drifting from below from unseen sources. It was long past the witching hour and what were the chances that another group of travelers, besides herself and Edith, had checked in this late at night?

What if it's Orion come to stop me from leaving? Terra bit her lip and cast the thought aside. There was no way it was Orion., he wouldn't be so brash as to follow them here. She crept down lower as quietly as she could and tried to peek her head around the corner to see who was speaking. She saw a group of six men, all dressed as if they had been outside and with snow dusting the tops of their shoulders and hair.

They talked in fervent tones that still carried even though they were talking quietly amongst themselves. "We can't wait any longer," one said.

"If we wait, we risk losing our advantage."

"Caius is already on his way. We need to go now otherwise it'll be all for nothing!" The group fell silent as if they all were coming to the conclusion that the last man to speak was right. "We know of the hidden pathway; we don't need to forge through Wolf's Pass anymore. We leave now. By the time morning comes, a new King will sit on the throne."

Terra let out an audible gasp and clamped her hand over her mouth. *Orion. They were talking about Orion.*

"What was that? There's someone there!" One of the men hissed and she heard heavy boots heading towards the staircase.

Terra scrambled to her feet and hauled herself into her room, praying that they didn't catch a glimpse of her or hear her escape before she could lock the door behind her. She dug through her saddle packs until she found her spare dagger in its sheath. Withdrawing it, she waited with it at the ready. Listening closely, she heard the floorboards outside her room creak from the men prowling in search of her. The footsteps paused in front of her door and she saw the knob turn slightly, but the door held fast.

The floorboards creaked again and soon the men were gone. Terra let out a sigh of relief and allowed herself to calm down for a moment for her mind was racing. They mentioned Caius so he had to be behind all of this. And if she heard them right, he was already going after Orion. What were they planning to do to him? Slaughter him so they can rise to power? Stage a coup? She couldn't let that happen, she *wouldn't* let that happen.

Terra knew what had to be done. She tore her nightgown off and dug through the saddle bags, tossing garments left and right until she had a thick woolen dress, a dry cloak, gloves, and her boots. She hastily threw everything on and tucked the dagger safely in the folds of her dress. Pulling the hood up to cover her face, she snuck out into the hallway and downstairs, knowing there was no time to warn Edith of what she was doing. She was just about to go around the corner when she heard galloping hooves. Throwing herself back against a wall to hide in the shadows, six men burst out before her astride their horses at a fast gallop, whipping her hair and her dress as they passed.

Terra ran to the stable and found Theos. He blinked at her sleepily as she threw a halter on him and wrapped the lead rope around his neck. Using a wooden board jutting out in the aisle outside the stalls, she slung herself onto his tall back and kicked him into high gear to tear out into the night.

I'm coming Orion.

Chapter Twenty-Four
Orion

Orion groaned and spat out more blood. Caius stood before him and grinned devishly, shaking his hand from the blow. "That felt *great*," he said and lifted Orion by his shirt. "Seeing you in pain, seeing you *bleed* brings me pleasure, you know that?" He chuckled and let go so Orion fell back painfully. "But do you know what brings me even more pleasure? *Seeing Terra bleed.*"

Orion lunged for him, but Caius used the heel of his boot to push him back down in the pool of his own blood.

"You're pathetic. I never thought that this would be this easy, that you would be so, so easy to take down at the snap of my fingers!" Caius taunted. "You gave my people a hard time, don't get me wrong. There was the unfortunate cave incident and of course Terra kept managing to get away, but in the end, it was still so incredibly easy. Your patrols work like clockwork and leave a ten-minute gap every night while they change shifts. It was effortless to slip through when no one was watching."

Orion's vision faded out. The amount of blood he had lost would have killed a mortal man by now, but he wasn't mortal. His hearing grew fuzzy and everything sounded muffled. He couldn't focus on what Caius was saying and what insults were being thrown his way, nor could he focus on the desperate barking of his dogs still lying trapped in the washroom while their master slowly bled out on the bedchamber floor.

Caius snapped his fingers in front of his face and brought Orion back to reality. When he saw Orion's expression, he put his hands on his knees and laughed some more. "If I didn't know any better," he wagged a finger at him. "I would think that you were going to die on me. But you and I both know that isn't the case, now is it?"

Orion grunted and raised his hand to the arrow in his arm, giving it a tug and letting it slide out with a sickening squelch. He tossed it aside so that the arrowhead clattered on the ground as more blood pooled around him. "I'm afraid I don't know what you're talking about," he spat through gritted teeth. The other arrowhead was still stuck firmly in his chest, unwavering and immovable.

"*Liar!*" Caius roared and grabbed him again roughly. He took a switchblade out of his belt loop and flicked it open before pressing the point into Orion's neck. "Tell me where it is, tell me how you never grow old."

Orion chuckled, the laughter bubbling deep in his chest and straining his wounds, causing him to wheeze. "Is that why you're here? For *immortality?*"

Caius furiously shook him by his shirt. "*Tell me where it is!*"

"Tell you where what is?"

"The thing that made you immortal, the sacred treasure. Tell me where it is and maybe I'll spare your wife of being hunted down and killed like a dog."

Orion swung his elbow, eliciting red hot pain that ripped through his chest and he knocked the switchblade out of his hand. He grabbed Caius by the front of his scruff with two hands and pulled him in close. "You touch a hair on her head, I will make sure you live an eternity in the deepest pain imaginable. You even look in her direction, and I will have you ripped to shreds over and over for as long as the world lives on. I don't have to exist to make sure you suffer for the rest of time."

Caius stumbled backwards and his two companions leapt forward to help him, but he waved them off. He hauled himself back to his feet and picked the blade up off the ground. "So protective of her. You really care for her, don't you? Not that I blame you. She really is a pretty girl. I just think it's a shame you care for her so much and yet, you didn't even exist when she was with me."

Orion internally wavered at his words. Did he really mean that little to her, when she meant everything to him? His mind rushed through every interaction that they've had, every conversation and every touch. Did he have the wrong impression of the depth of her feelings for him this whole time?

"You'd expect her to go on and on about her husband when she was given the chance, especially as a newlywed, but she never mentioned you once. Not one...single...time. Why bother fighting anymore?" Caius leaned down close and whispered in his ear, "You're nothing to her."

Orion stopped trying to move, stopped trying to fight back and he let his pained body go limp. What did he have left to fight for really? Terra had already left him and she made it very clear that she never wanted to see him again. Laurent was dead. Edith was safe with Terra. What else was there left for him to lose? He had already become everything he despised.

Orion had already become his father.

"That's it," Caius crooned and flipped the dagger playfully in his hands as if he was beginning to grow bored of watching Orion struggle on the ground. "Give up, you've already lost, don't you see that? I'm not a fool, Your Highness. Far from it really. Do you really think I would act if I didn't have solid information? You have something, something that gave you eternal life and I want it. So now give it to me, or she is going to be the one to pay for your mistakes."

Orion breathed heavily and closed his eyes against the pain searing through him. A part of him wished that the darkness he saw behind Caius' eyes was Death finally welcoming him home with open arms. It would be easier, he decided, if he was mortal. If he could leave this plane of existence and leave the path of eternity that forged ahead of him, he would. There were so many regrets that weighed heavy on his chest. If Death was able to call upon him and collect him, his dark existence would be erased from the threads of the world in a heartbeat purely from the atrocities and the choices he has made. He would do things differently in his life if he had a second chance, but that's not how that works.

Most importantly, he would have done things differently with Terra. He would have never allowed her to come here. She would never have been exposed to the marring threads of his own existence and she would never have been put in the dangerous situation that being his Queen would involve.

Orion had never truly thought that enemies would arise so quickly and with so much intent on harming what he loved most when he had brought her here. He would be repenting for that choice for the rest of eternity.

But if fate had them intertwined, Terra would have crossed paths with him regardless. If given a second chance, Orion would have treated her differently than he had when she first met him. He would have been kind and compassionate, the type of man he always wished he could be, but now realized that he could never be. Maybe the fates always had him set up for failure. No matter what he would change if he could redo it all, maybe he was always going to fall headlong over the edge.

Orion would never get the chance to redo it or fix it all. He would die here if there was a way. The truth struck him hard and he pondered that thought. *I will die here if they find a way to kill me.* Could he just roll over and let them do it? Was he really resigning to give up fighting and giving up the chance of ever seeing Terra again?

Terra. Orion let out a breath as her name danced on the tip of his tongue. He could see her clearly in his mind's eye. She looked just like she did the day he showed her the greenhouse, with dirt coated hands and the breeze outside the greenhouse catching loose strands of her honey brown hair to pull out of her long braid. Her smile was so wide that the tip of her nose crinkled. He loved to see that smile. Seeing her like this was pure bliss. He longed to see her in summer with the warm sun bronzing her skin and flowers blooming.

With a start, Orion's eyes snapped back open. He couldn't give up. He had to see her one more time, even if it was to say goodbye. He couldn't leave this world with this unfinished. He had to tell her how much he loved her. *I have to see her when the flowers are blooming.*

"You're right," Orion rasped and turned to Caius. His mouth was dry and his tongue felt cracked and heavy. "There is something here that made me immortal and if you find it, it can give you eternal life."

Caius grew giddy when he said this. "What is it? Where is it?"

"I don't know," Orion lied.

Caius didn't like that. He grasped his hand around the arrowhead still protruding from his chest and gave it the slightest twist until Orion roared in pain. "You're lying, you have to know where it is. Where are you hiding it?"

"I said I don't know," Orion gasped. "Terra hid it before she left, I don't know where she hid it. She wanted to keep it safe."

"Then why don't you tell us what it *is* and we can *find it*?" Caius drawled in frustration.

"Fine." Orion searched his brain for something, *anything*, to distract them. "It's a crown, the King's crown to be exact. When the wearer places it upon their head, immortality will be granted to them immediately."

"Simon." Caius pointed at the man holding a bow and had a sheath of arrows just waiting for Caius's signal to shoot another into him. "Stay here and guard him. If he so much as moves, send an arrow straight through his neck. Elias, come with me and we'll start searching for the crown."

Caius and Elias left the room while Simon grabbed an arrow and drew the drawstring back, aiming straight for his neck just like Caius had said. Orion looked around the room the best that he could without drawing too much attention to himself. Simon was staring him down and didn't even throw a glance elsewhere, so Orion would have to work carefully.

Help me, he thought and tossed the thought out into the void. He carefully began summoning the shadows around him while making sure to do it slowly and indistinctly. "You know you don't have to do this," he spoke aloud in hopes to distract his keeper and do anything to throw him off from noticing what he was trying to do.

"Shut up."

That didn't work very well, Your Highness, maybe you should try another tactic, a voice suddenly whispered in his mind.

Orion dared to glance to the farthest corner of the room away from the fireplace casting light across the room. There the figure slowly materialized, its outline stirring in with the writhing shadows around it. He quickly looked away and turned his attention back on his captor. "You know they will probably kill you once they find it. You'd be just one less person to have to share the gift of immortality with."

Simon scoffed as if he didn't believe it, but the way his arms faltered in their position with the bow said otherwise. So Orion kept it up.

"You're a liability, a wrench in their plans so to speak. Caius and — what was his name, Elias? — will finish you off before and then Caius will find a way to finish Elias off." Orion snuck another glance as the shadows converging and morphing into a mass that fed off the light of the fire for strength. He grinned. "Caius is the leader, right? How much do you trust him?"

Simon, now frazzled, tried to hold the bow and arrow steady but failed. "I said shut up!"

"Okay, okay, I just have one more question for you." Orion turned and looked at the mass of shadows waiting for his command. Simon followed his gaze and froze. "Are you afraid of the dark?"

Simon let out a pitiful scream as the shadows rushed him and knocked him flat to the ground. Orion took the opportunity to haul himself to his feet. He reached for the arrow still in his chest and snapped the length of it so only the arrowhead remained impaled within him. He hobbled to the door with a hand trying to staunch his bleeding before going out into the hallway. Breathing hard, he didn't know where he was headed, but all he knew was that he had to get away and find a way back to Terra.

Orion barely made it around a corner when he halted at the sight before him. He could hardly believe his eyes. Elias had his bicep wrapped firmly around Terra's neck with a dagger to her throat and Caius laughed gleefully.

"Don't move another muscle unless you'd like to see how quickly your wife can bleed out with one precise slice to her throat."

Chapter Twenty-Five
Terra

"Terra?" Orion gasped and fell to his knees. Terra pulled against the man holding her but his grip only tightened. Orion looked at her with glazed eyes. "What are you doing here?" He groaned through a wave of pain. "You aren't supposed to be here."

"I couldn't stay away. I couldn't leave you."

Orion's expression was one of a broken man that was trying so desperately to win even when the odds continued to be stacked against him. He was weak and pale, so very pale. Terra's eyes immediately went to the blood leaking around an arrowhead protruding from his chest. "Please, just let her go."

"Why would I do that?" Caius said and he inspected a crown in his hands that Terra recognized as the same one Orion wore on their wedding day and during her coronation.

"You already have what you want, what good would it do?"

"Let's call it collateral," Caius replied airily and let the rubies on the crown catch the light of a lamp just right. "Just in case you were foolish enough to lie to me about the power that the crown holds. And if you did lie..." Caius trailed off and made sure Orion looked him in the eye. "You won't like the consequences."

Terra looked at Orion in alarm. The crown had power? Had Orion known that this is what they were seeking this whole time and he never mentioned that the crown held some sort of power? Not to mention, Orion *gave it* to them.

Caius took a deep breath and held the crown above his head just mere inches from brushing against his hair. "I guess we will find out, won't we?" Caius placed the crown down on his head and Terra held her breath, waiting for something to happen. But nothing did. Nothing at least that she could visibly see. "How do I know if it worked?" Caius demanded, his anger sparking and he turned again on Orion. "I feel nothing. Nothing happened, did it?"

"You can't tell, at least not right away, but it worked," Orion wheezed. He was still on his knees on the floor and unable to get back to his feet. Terra studied his face. She suspected that he was lying, but she didn't understand about what.

"You lie," Caius accused and sent a swift kick into Orion's abdomen. Orion yelped and Terra tried to pull away from where she stood, but the strong arm stopped her again.

Orion laughed and coughed in pain, the action rattling his body. "You can either believe that I am telling the truth, or you can believe that I am lying. You can let me know what you decide when you realize you haven't aged a day."

Immortality? That was what Caius was seeking? Terra frowned and racked her brain to recall what Orion had told her about his own immortality. It wasn't from a crown, or any cursed object. He had told her that it was a curse placed upon his bloodline from the actions of his parents. It was never meant to be a gift, it had been a punishment.

So why did Caius want immortality, and how did he even find out Orion's secret? It was always very closely guarded. Even she didn't find out for months and she lived here, how did he figure it out?

Frustration clouded Caius's face and he began to pace while muttering to himself under his breath. Terra caught small words and strings of phrases as he tried to understand what Orion had said without any luck. Before she could register what was happening, Caius slipped a switchblade out of the loop of his pants and pressed the point into the side of her neck just hard enough to allow blood to trickle down her skin. She didn't dare pull away.

"One last chance," Caius growled and Orion's face twisted in agony, but no words left his mouth. Caius shrugged and wrapped a meaty fist around her throat just as a strangled "no!" left Orion. Caius stopped and Orion shakily got to his feet.

"There's a river," Orion admitted in a husky voice. "If you jump in, and survive, you will be granted immortality."

"Then you will lead us there, or else she dies. If she makes any move to run Elias, take her out. Now *move.*"

Caius shoved Orion roughly with one hand while brandishing his switchblade towards him. Elias pushed Terra in front of them and aimed the crossbow that had been slung over his shoulder between her shoulder blades. Wet and cold, Terra shivered as she followed Caius and Orion from the second floor down to the first. It wasn't until Orion told Caius to grab a lantern to light the way, that she began to piece together where he was leading them.

When Caius refused and told Orion to grab it instead, Orion merely shrugged and didn't move his hand from his bruised rib cage. "I'm not afraid of the dark, I don't need to see where we're heading, but you may want to."

Caius scowled but snatched the lantern off its hook in the wall. Orion led the group to the dungeon door and Terra's heart sank as she realized her fears had been right, they were going down. Orion swung the door open and revealed the dark depths of the staircase. He didn't so much as hesitate as he started to climb down into the dark but Caius didn't go right away.

"If you try anything," Caius called down after him. "I won't so much as *hesitate* to slit her throat. You understand?" He was met with silence as a response so he snarled in frustration and followed him down with Terra and Elias close behind him.

The dungeon felt even more foreboding than usual, as if they weren't alone as they descended seemingly into the depths of hell. Terra was petrified of what may be waiting for them and she feared she would be called upon to fulfill her promise. Already the feeling of being watched unnerved her and she fought the urge to glance over her shoulder.

Orion was already at the stone door pressing his palm firmly against the surface so that the otherworldly light lit up the hollows of his face. The door popped open and he slipped inside before the others even had a chance to catch up to him. Caius plunged through and Terra followed while Elias hung back entirely unsure of himself.

"I have a bad feeling about this," he called to Caius which made him stop. The whites of his eyes were showing and his fingers trembled on the crossbow. The same feeling penetrated through Terra and had since the first time she placed her hand upon the door.

"I don't have time for you to be a coward!" Caius snapped. "Are you going to do your job or do I need to do it for you?"

Elias's eyes flickered between Caius and the vast darkness behind him a few times until he finally shook his head no. Caius strode past Terra while tucking his blade back into his pants. He placed the lantern on the ground and ripped the crossbow from Elias's shaking hands so that he could send an arrow deep into his chest in the time it took Terra to blink. Elias's mouth gaped open and shut over and over as if he was a fish before he finally fell backwards into a still heap in the middle of the dungeon floor. Terra let out a cry and clamped her hand hard over her mouth as Caius whirled around to face her, this time aiming the crossbow at her.

"Get moving," he ordered and jerked the point of the crossbow to emphasize his command. Terra stumbled towards the lantern and picked it up to light their way ahead. The darkness pressed into her chest and made it hard to breath. The ground beneath them slowly turned into hard dirt below them and soon they were among the dead trees towering above them. The blackened branches reached for the nonexistent sky above in a way that made them look like claws scraping against the dark abyss.

Branches grew more closely knit together the further they stumbled along and Orion was still nowhere to be seen. The sharp ends scraped against her skin and pulled at her clothes. Caius swore behind her and jerked the leg of his pants from the low hanging branch that seemed to clutch the cloth firmly in its grasp. Fibers from his pants still hung from the tips even as they continued on.

The further they traveled, the colder the air grew and the stronger the feeling of being watched became until Terra swore she could see figures walking between the trees. Caius must have seen them as well, for he kept swinging the point of the crossbow around them and even behind them towards moving figures that disappeared as soon as you looked at them straight on. Terra kept up her nerve and plunged forward, silently calling for Orion. Had he fallen? Was the journey finally too much for him? Or did he have a plan to get them out of this that she wasn't privy to?

The cold breeze that blew through the trees seemed to carry whispers with it that twirled themselves around and around them until they were impossible to ignore. *You don't belong here,* they seemed to hiss. *Stay with us.*

"Stop it!" Caius suddenly shouted behind her and Terra whirled around in alarm. A sheen of sweat covered his forehead and his upper lip and his gaze zoned in on her when he noticed that she was gawking at him. "Did I say turn around? Keep going!"

The whispers only grew stronger after Caius acknowledged their presence. The figures stopped hiding and instead stood still, watching them as they passed by. She could see small details of them, their hair, their eyes and the curve of their noses. They were people, she realized, and not some supernatural entity preying upon them in the dark. At least, she didn't think they were. The whispers continued and Terra did her best to pretend that they weren't there even when they grated against her ears.

"What are they?" Caius asked and she realized he was talking to her.

"Souls of the lost," she lied, wishing that he would just stop talking about them and stop reacting to them. A part of her thought she was right though, and she couldn't explain it. It was as if they invoked the feeling within her to confirm her suspicions without outright admitting it.

By the time they finally burst through the tree line and into the meadow before them, the whispers invaded Terra's mind and tried their hardest not to leave. As soon as she noticed Orion standing a ways ahead of them though, they released their icy grip and slipped away as if they were frightened of him. Orion had more color in his face, leaving her to suspect that this place lent him strength. He still held himself tall and stiff, however, showing his body still ached from his injuries.

"This way," he said and jerked his head towards a river lying in the distance. "But she stays here out of harm's way."

"No way," Caius sneered. "I won't fall for any more of your tricks. Now keep going. You lead the way and go first."

Caius shot one last glance at the trees behind him and pushed Terra forward so that she was trekking after Orion through the long grass. They left the prairie grass and found themselves along the bank of the river. It was dark, so dark that it seemed to twinkle with stars in its surface. It crept along at a slow pace and filled the air with an almost comforting sound of a trickling brook that one would find deep in the forest.

"Jump in, and everything you seek will be yours," Orion said and waved his hand towards the river. His eyes were blazing, Terra realized, his anger brewing under the surface as strength came back to him. She yearned to reach out to him, to feel his skin beneath her fingers and to reassure herself that he was still here, that they would both be okay.

Caius noticed Orion's returning strength as well. He regarded Orion with a watchful eye and traced every line of his face in the search of a lie. "Her first." Caius gripped Terra's arm hard and yanked her closer to him. Orion took a step forward and Caius brandished the crossbow at him. "I don't think so. She goes first, or she dies."

But I might die if I go, Terra thought fearfully. She gazed at the river and the moving water, trying to see the danger of diving in. Was there a monster that protected it? One that would tear her to shreds as soon as she submersed herself? But she didn't see any other way out of this and, judging by Orion's pained look, neither did he.

"I'll do it," she said softly and Orion looked at her in alarm. "I'll do it and prove it so you can let us go, okay?"

"It's a deal." Caius gleefully pushed her towards the water's edge.

"Terra, please," Orion begged. "Don't do this, you don't want this. This life, an immortal life... it's not worth it. You will never stop regretting it if you do this."

But Terra didn't listen. She crept closer and closer to the edge and steeled herself for what would come next. She kicked off her boots so that her bare feet pressed deep into the soil. *This may be the last time I live to feel this,* she thought forlornly and closed her eyes. Orion was still begging her not to do it, trying to reason with her but he didn't make a move to grab her. She knew without looking that she had a well-trained arrow pointing at her spine courtesy of Caius.

Finally, Terra opened her eyes to allow two single tears to fall. She turned to look at Orion, his frantic expression telling her just how much he didn't want her to do this, how much he didn't want her to make this sacrifice. But she didn't see any other choice.

Terra took another shuddering breath and looked at his stormy grey eyes to memorize every line of his face, every small detail that she never had enough time to take in. "Would an eternal life with you, really be so bad?" She asked him softly.

Just as he opened his mouth to say something in return, she turned and dove headfirst into the surface.

Chapter Twenty-Six
Orion

"No!" The word ripped out of Orion ferociously. He fell to his knees and scrambled towards the edge of the water, not daring to touch it but also searching for a glimpse of her under the surface. The river was quiet with its gentle lapping being the only sound. Caius waited impatiently far from the river and waited to see if she made it out alive or not.

Orion prayed. He prayed to the core of the universe and to anyone who may listen. He prayed that the river returned her to him and he resolved to do everything right this time. He just needed her alive. He needed for her to be okay and to have just one more chance. It became a mantra in his mind and he repeated it over and over.

One more chance.

One more chance.

One more chance.

Too much time had gone by without a sign of her, but he didn't believe that the river had taken her without ever planning to return her to him. He *couldn't* believe it. But yet...

Orion was healing. He could feel his body slowly repairing itself beneath his skin as his internal wounds began to patch themselves up. His shadow realm lent its strength to him, and he gladly had been lapping it up ever since he stepped a foot through the door. He would use his strength to destroy Caius in the worst possible way and he would make him pay for what he had done to Terra.

"Looks like she's not coming back," Caius broke the silence and scoffed. "So, either you had lied, once again, and she paid the price, or you were right and she still ended up paying the price." He lowered his crossbow at Orion. "If you cannot give me immortality, then I will need to destroy you. And trust me, I will find a way."

Orion looked at him sullenly just as he heard something splash in the water. Terra struggled against the gentle current, coughing and choking on the jet-black water that kept pushing its way down her throat and through her airways. "Terra!" he cried and leaned over the water as much as he dared to. He held out his hand to her, urging her on as she pushed herself through the water until he could grasp her arm. He tugged her out hard and helped her crawl up to the safety of the bank while spitting up uncomfortably large amounts of water as she went.

Something about Terra was different, off almost. Orion could feel it rippling off of her in waves and the grass not far from them seemed to reach forward in the breeze to try to graze her outstretched fingers softly. It was power, he realized with a start. He was feeling the power rolling off of her. No longer was she the young woman that had come to him in order to bargain for protection for her family. Instead, she was an immortal Queen having survived the trial and she had come out alive on the other side. This didn't matter to him. She would still always be Terra to him and would always be the girl who loved the earth and the life of the world in all its eternal glory.

Orion whispered soothing words to her and patted her back before he pulled her drenched hair back from her face as she tried to suck in air desperately. She came back to him. *Terra came back.*

"It appears I spoke too soon," Caius stated from his spot far away from the river. "Tell me, my lady, what was it like?"

This caught Terra's attention. She raised her gaze to lock eyes with him and in her expression, Orion could see the darkness of a secret that she would carry with her for the rest of eternity. The river had taken something from her before it had given her back. What it had taken, though, he did not know.

Finally, she spoke. "It will haunt my deepest and darkest nightmares," she rasped through a raw throat.

Caius looked unsettled by this. He glanced towards the river and back at an exhausted Terra lying before him.

"You want immortality?" Orion said in annoyance. "Then go get it you coward."

Caius narrowed his eyes and tossed his crossbow to the ground. He did the same as Terra had done and begun to kick off his socks and boots before standing at the edge of the water. He looked at the slow-moving water daringly before he finally grew the courage to step one foot in. He took another step and another, so that up to his shins was covered. Shivering from the chill of the water, he went to take another step but instead of him touching solid ground, his foot slipped down until his entire body plunged into the depths.

All was quiet as he sank into the depths of the river. Terra continued to hack up water and Orion held her close while he kept one eye trained on the water. Even after Terra's coughs began to slow and she was able to sit up, Caius still hadn't appeared from within. Just when Orion had begun to think that the river claimed him and that it was over, a hand burst through the water followed by a head.

Caius dug his fingers through the water gasping and spluttering, but the water seemed to grow thicker and viscous, slowing him down and holding him within the river's clutches. He kept trying to drag himself slowly through the substance until he was held stock still. "Help me!" he gasped and threw furtive looks at Orion and Terra. *"Help me!"*

Orion and Terra climbed to their feet. Terra was still shaking and looked hollow as her drenched clothes still dripped with water. Orion stepped to the edge of the bank and regarded the struggling Caius with a malicious smirk. His body finally finished knitting itself back together. The arrowhead fell from the now healed wound and landed with a soft thud in the soil beneath him. The only evidence that he had been hurt at all were the drying blood splatters that ruined his shirt, but his skin was smooth and unmarked as if it never happened at all.

Burns began to appear on Caius's face as if the river itself was trying to peel his flesh from his bones. His shouts grew more desperate and more animalistic from the pain that he was feeling. Orion only watched him struggle, feeling satisfaction from watching the thing that Caius had so desperately needed be the thing that tore him apart. He crouched down with his hands clasped together between his bent knees.

Caius wailed again and gave up struggling. He stopped trying to swim for the shoreline and instead floated in place while his skin continued to burn and sear. "What's happening to me?"

"It seems as if you were not fated to be immortal," Orion said simply. The scent of burning flesh reached him and the smell almost made him retch. "This is your punishment for being greedy, for trying to take something that wasn't yours."

Caius whimpered and his body sunk a few inches lower while his limbs became more paralyzed as each second passed by.

"Do you feel that?" Orion asked quietly and leaned in even closer. "Do you feel the river ripping your soul from your flesh in the most painful way possible? Oh no, your death won't be a quick one, nor will it be a quiet one. The river demands payment for all of your sins and all of the horrible things that you have done. You are a special breed, one that they cannot wait to tear apart."

As if on cue, the wind around them began to pick up and rip through the tall grass. Shadows came roaring to life and a high-pitched screaming surrounded them as the shadows danced above Caius, taunting him as he slowly sunk lower and lower. His skin was starting to peel away from the bone and Orion could catch glimpses of the white in his wounds.

"They will enjoy tormenting your soul for the rest of time. You will never stop feeling this pain or this agony and I will make sure of it."

Caius's mouth was now under the liquid and left only his frightened eyes blinking rapidly as a response.

"You will pay for what you did to my family and I will find great pleasure in knowing your punishment has been just."

Caius slipped under the liquid entirely, his physical body no longer existing. The shadows hovering above the water plunged their hands down into the liquid and yanked out a new squirming shadow. They were gone in a blink of an eye, speeding past Orion and Terra until they disappeared in the distance as one last rush of air ripped past them as the only indication that they ever were there in the first place. The river's water turned back to normal and the trickling current picked back up to the usual pace it moved at.

Orion immediately turned back to Terra who was still standing far away from the edge of the river. He strode to her but paused a few paces away, not sure how to interpret the harsh expression on her face. He searched her eyes, studying her and trying to break down what thoughts must be racing through her head in that moment.

After a few sullen moments of looking at each other, she finally spoke, her voice raw and exhausted. "Is it over?"

Orion nodded slowly. "Yes, it's over."

Terra's lip tremored and she began to cry. It was as if a trance had been broken. Orion quickly closed the distance between them and crushed her firmly to his chest. She responded by wrapping her own arms around his waist and dissolving into a blubbering mess of tears. It was a long while before she began to calm down, long enough that Orion was wary of being watched by curiosities wondering who this girl was walking through their realm for so long.

Eventually, Terra did pull back and wiped her nose on her long dress sleeve that had seen better days. Even in her current messy state, Orion had never thought she looked more beautiful. He brushed strands of her hair away from her face gently and cupped her face in his hands. "Please never leave," he whispered before bringing his lips to meet hers.

Terra welcomed him, letting her body mold into his until they fit together perfectly. He was never going to let her go.

Chapter Twenty-Seven
Terra

Terra had never felt so exhausted in her life. Every bit of adrenaline that she had felt when she almost drowned in the river had almost just as quickly dissipated when the time came to return back to the surface. The trek to leave the shadow realm and to reach her wrecked bedroom took more energy out of her than she had ever thought possible. The night had already begun to turn to day and the brilliant colors of the sunrise splashed the sky in hues of purple and pink as if the horrible events had never occurred.

Orion, worried for the dogs still trapped in her bathing room, insisted they first hurry to the second floor to check on them. Edith would have to wait. She was safe and at Margaret's inn, she had reassured him, but she would be pretty upset with Terra tearing off in the night like that. But, in the end, she would get over it when she saw that they were okay.

As soon as Orion threw open the door to Terra's bathing room, the three dogs came barreling out in a flood of gnashing teeth and sleek black fur. It wasn't until Orion called to them that they realized that the danger was no longer here and that their master was indeed safe. They piled around him and jumped on him while trying to lick his arms, his hands, and even his face. Meanwhile, Terra's eyes went to the damage around her.

Pools of blood still rested on the stone floor and coagulated into dark black puddles that reminded her of what they had endured and what they have experienced the last few hours. The pools seemed to suck her in, holding her gaze until she was no longer standing in her chambers, but was once again beneath the surface swallowing in what seemed like buckets of icy cold water. She felt the terror of drowning, of her lungs being shocked into stopping.

Her mind painted the picture perfectly so that she couldn't tell the difference between reality and memory. Bubbles of air escaped her mouth as she screamed, but no one could hear her from the depths. She remembered the icy cold that struck her nervous system and travelled from her toes all the way up her spine to her head. And there, the voices whispered. It wasn't the same whisper that the figure had that she struck a deal with, no, but the whispers were still clear as day as if she was still there stuck beneath the surface.

Trapped.

Princess of Spring, stolen from her home and cast away to the depths of darkness, the voices, all meshed into one, hissed through the depths.

And now, she is the Queen of Iron.

She who walks the realm of death, and lives to see what beauty the next season brings.

She who loves with her soft heart but protects with the strength of a thousand bloodthirsty soldiers.

What do you seek, Queen of Iron?

Through her fight to survive, Terra didn't respond. She was still taking in water at an alarming rate and her body was coursing with adrenaline. But her lack of a response hadn't mattered, for the omnipresent being never needed one.

Ahh, they said. *Selfless, this one. She had not braved the waters of the mighty river for her own gain, no, but as a sacrifice for the one she loves in hope that her act would save him. But foolish girl, a god doesn't need saving from a mortal, now do they?*

Terra began to sink to the bottom of the river now, her body having given up fighting completely. She wholeheartedly believed that this was where she would die. Her vision began to fade and she was approaching blacking out completely. She wished she could shed tears and mourn everything that she would be leaving behind, but not in the depths. Terra thought of her family, of her sisters that she would never get the chance to see again, and of her mother. She thought of Cassi and the adventures that they would never get the chance to go on together. Laurent passed through her mind as well, his death representing all of the good that has been lost in her plight. Even Edith she thought of. Edith, the one who was so kind and wanted nothing more than a family of her own and instead, took her in as if she was her daughter when Terra needed a person the most.

And Orion.

Oh gods, Orion. Terra's mind flickered to him and there it stayed in what she figured would be her final moments. In some far away fantasy, she could see them walking hand in hand on a beach while she showed him all the wonders that Solaris had to offer. She would introduce him to her family and watch her mother and everyone fall in love with him as much as she had. She would show him the gardens and all the flowers and plants that she had helped grow throughout the years. There, Terra would sit him down in front of the fountain that she had jumped in that day so long ago to run from Ms. Astrid. He wouldn't believe that she dared do such a thing, but she would giggle and tell him that there were plenty of more stories about the silly trouble that she would get in.

But none of that would happen, for she was dying.

Yes, Queen of Iron, the voice mused, just as Terra began to fade away. *It is fated for you to find what you seek, for you to find a home for all eternity. You never were meant to stay a Princess of Spring, but instead you were always meant to be the Queen of Hell. Rise, Daughter of the Night, and take your rightful throne beside the Keeper of Souls.*

Electricity struck Terra's core and her eyes had opened in a snap. She watched as her essence had been removed from her chest by a gentle wave of the water. A bright gold shape that looked frighteningly like herself had appeared before her, blinding her with the brilliant light it emitted. Right there in front of her, the two fused together and became one. The combined essence dove back into her and she took a deep gasp instinctively, but water had not rushed in this time.

Rise, the voice commanded again and this time she had obeyed, finding newfound strength flowing through her limbs. Terra had kicked off the bottom of the river and propelled herself upwards until her head bursted through the surface.

"Terra?"

Orion's gentle voice transported Terra back to the present. She was no longer in the river, but in her bedroom with a very concerned Orion regarding her carefully. "Darling, what's wrong?" He asked and took her hand in his.

Terra shook her head and put a fake smile on her face, pushing away the painful memories at the same time. "Nothing is wrong."

Orion hesitated. She could tell he wanted to ask her about it, but he was scared to. He didn't want to push too far, but he still wanted to understand what happened and understand what was going through her mind. Finally, he asked. "Terra, what happened in the river?"

"Nothing important," she lied and waved it off. "All that's important is that I survived." She couldn't help but turn the words over again in her mind. *It is fated for you to find what you seek, for you to find a home for all eternity. You never were meant to stay a Princess of Spring, but instead you were always meant to be the Queen of Hell. Rise, Daughter of the Night, and take your rightful throne beside the Keeper of Souls.* She looked at Orion with a new set of eyes. They were always meant to be if the voice had been telling the truth. There was never any avoiding this fate, even if she had tried to find a way to do so.

Terra was never supposed to live a normal, mortal life.

"I think we should talk about this," Orion pressed. "And what this means for you."

"I'm okay, really. We don't have to talk about it." Terra took a step towards him and placed her palm on her cheek. "Besides, I have you for the rest of eternity, what else do I need?" *One day, I'll tell you all about it,* she thought. *But just not now.*

"I'll be here when you're ready." And she believed him. Terra knew that when the day came when the secrets choked her voice so much that she couldn't breathe, that he would be there waiting to console her and to help her deal with the tragedies that have occurred.

A strong throat clearing took the both of them by surprise and Orion almost immediately threw her behind him as they both faced the new stranger standing in the doorway to her bedchamber. Just when Terra was about to snatch a nearby oil lamp to send rocketing towards the stranger's head, Orion sighed and relaxed his stance.

"Aren, what the hell are you doing here?"

"I'm sorry to interrupt," the man, Aren, said and grimaced when he noticed the dry puddle of blood only a few inches in front of his feet. He took a step back and wiped his hands on his pants as if the mere sight made him dirty. "But I had to make sure you were okay." Aren's dark brown eyes met Terra's and she saw warmth there, as well as something sneaky that made her wary. It was the type of look that didn't make her feel as if she was in mortal danger, but instead like he was going to cheat her out of her money in some sort of scam. He was dressed simply in a shirt and pants, but he had an accent that reminded her of the type of men that travelled through Solaris on their way to some other distant land she didn't know the name of. "This must be Terra."

"Uh, hello," Terra said meekly.

"Well Terra, meet my nephew Aren," Orion said stiffly. "Now what are you doing here?"

"I had to make sure you both were okay after..." he trailed off and gestured at the bloody spot on the ground. "After all of this. I couldn't tell you everything, I was bound under a deal, but I tried to warn you the best that I could."

Orion sighed and ran a hand through his hair, suddenly looking very tired. "It was enough, yes. Thank you. Do you have anything else? Otherwise I would like to enjoy some alone time without men trying to kill me or my wife."

"I told you, this is a lot bigger than you think. Her being included," Aren replied and gestured towards Terra. "Haven't you put the pieces together yet?" Orion looked momentarily perplexed, causing Aren to sigh dramatically. "He is working to take back what he thinks is rightfully his. This is just the beginning, Uncle. The war hasn't even started yet." Aren looked at him pointedly, waiting for what he said to finally click into place.

Orion's expression remained blank at this comment, but he nodded in response. "I understand. Hopefully when I see you again, it will be under better circumstances. Thank you, Aren."

With one final wave, Aren suddenly disappeared and left Terra very puzzled. "How..?" She asked and pointed to where Aren had just been standing.

"He does that," Orion said and begun to pace. The encounter had clearly agitated him, but Terra didn't quite understand why. "Don't worry about that, it's just one of his many gifts."

"What did he mean by that? That 'he will take back what is rightfully his?' Is someone you know orchestrating this?"

Orion grimaced. "Aren is King Theon's messenger and he is bound to serve him. What this means is that my dear brother is after my realm once again, and he will do anything to take it from me. Why now all of a sudden, I'm not sure but it looks like my family hasn't forgotten about me after all."

"So then what should we do?" Terra asked and put a hand on his arm to stop his pacing. "Do we prepare for war?"

Orion shook his head. "No. What we do is we cross that bridge *if* it comes to that. We shouldn't worry about that now though, not until we have to." He sighed and pulled her closer, touching his forehead to hers. "But, until then, I suggest that we spend each and every day in whatever way you wish. I'm yours, Terra, forever and always. I would burn this world down to find you again. I would burn the world down in every life to find you again." He pressed something from his hand into hers and she opened it to reveal her wedding band, the rubies shining brightly as if even they were happy to once again be in her hand. He waited silently and watched her as she turned it over in her fingers. Finally, she slipped it back on her left ring finger where she knew it always had belonged.

"Mine," Terra said softly, tasting each word on her tongue as if they were a magnificent feast.

"Does that suit you?" He trailed a hand up her back until it rested along her neck, tucked under her messy hair.

She smiled. "I would ask for nothing more."

Terra pressed her mouth to his and he wrapped his hand in her hair. Both of them held each other tightly, as if they both feared that if they dared loosened their grips, that they would spiral out of control and never return to reality. Terra pulled away slightly and whispered the words against his lips just one more time.

"Forever and always."

Made in the USA
Monee, IL
06 January 2022